Home Free
(Gifts of the Heart)

by Lea Carter

Chapter 1

The slap of her tennis shoes on the pavement kept Harmony company as she jogged along her route to make her last delivery. The afternoon sun felt good on her shoulders and she was glad to be nearly done. If her car hadn't developed a flat tire a few minutes ago, she'd already be finished.

At the end of the cul-de-sac a group of middle grade kids were trying vainly to get a basketball through the hoop. One of them made a wild throw, sending the ball ricocheting off the rim and toward Harmony.

Deftly, she reached out with one hand to catch it. Dribbled it as she jogged closer.

"Hey, Harmony!" The tallest girl, who knew her from church, waved vigorously. "Shoot a three pointer!"

"Do a layup!" hollered another child.

"Can you play shootout with us?"

"No time for a game right now, guys." As she started into the curve, she threw what she hoped looked like a casual hook shot. It sank with a beautiful swish and accompanying cheers, all of which added sincerity to her tired smile.

"You gotta teach me that shot!"

"Practice your free throws," she laughed. "Practice and more practice!"

It was the same advice that she gave them

every time and, as far as she knew, they still preferred to just chuck the ball at the hoop. At least they weren't out getting into mischief.

"Bye, Harmony!" they chorused.

"Later!" Waving, she rounded the cul-de-sac and headed down the far side. Stopping at her customer's house, she rang the doorbell.

"Harmony." Cara Ansell opened the door to let her in. "You poor thing, you must be frozen!"

"Oh, it's not so bad today." Opening her pack, Harmony set the delivery box of allergen-free items on the table by the door. "Especially not for late October."

"Now that's true." Cara wiped her hands on a towel she wore tucked in her waistband. Delightful scents were coming from the kitchen, where she was preparing the family's evening meal. A woman with three highly allergic children, she spent a significant amount of time making food they could safely eat. "Can I get you anything?"

Harmony shook her head. "Thanks, but this is my last stop today."

"Of course." Cara nodded sympathetically and pulled a check from her purse. "I still can't believe you're able to get these allergen-free items at such amazingly low prices. The soy free items alone…" She trailed off as she ran out of words. "Finding out about your delivery service is the best thing that ever happened to us."

Harmony shrugged as she pocketed the check. "Buying in bulk makes a huge difference." So did owning two of the biggest suppliers of allergen-free products in the USA, but telling people that tended to ruin friendships.

"You're probably eager to get home and relax."

Detecting a note of wistfulness in the other woman's voice, Harmony experienced a twinge of conscience. She'd been lonely, too. She also hoped to someday be a stay-at-home mom. In the meantime, the least she could do was support the dedicated women she knew with a little grown-up conversation.

"Yeah. I've got a mug of hot chocolate with my name on it."

"Hot chocolate?" Cara brightened. "I have some. If you'd like it?"

"That'd be great!" Harmony spent the next twenty minutes slowly sipping hot chocolate while they discussed everything and nothing much.

The hot chocolate finally gave out and Harmony apologetically took her leave. The street was empty by then, the children most likely washing up for supper. It was getting to be that time.

Rolling her aching shoulders, she started back. Squinted at her car, which was parked several houses away. And…spotted someone hunkered down beside it?

"Hey!" She hustled over to see what was happening. "What're you doing?"

The man rose, straightening his slacks as he did so. "I'm examining an impediment."

It hit her like a slap of Ozarkian humidity after two hours in a frigid movie theater. "Oh, yikes." She covered her mouth with her hand. "I'm blocking your driveway, aren't I?"

She looked guiltily at her car. Her first priority on discovering the flat tire had been to get off the road. Knowing that most of the parking on the narrow road belonged to the families, she'd swung into this driveway, assuming the 'For Sale' sign she'd seen for the last six months had either fallen over or been snitched by the less principled teenagers in the area.

"Afraid so. Where's your jack?"

She bristled a little at the way his hazel blue eyes raked over her, assessing and dismissing her. As though she were simply a stone to be shaken out of his shoe. A rather bedraggled stone at the end of its long day. Not that he was completely wrong. Compared with his crisp black slacks and pale blue button-up shirt, she felt rather like a gym sneaker next to a highly polished dress shoe.

She shrugged it off. She didn't know any more about him than he did about her. Could be his family just didn't go in for pleasantries.

"I'll get it." Placing her empty bag in the back of her car, she popped the trunk.

"Excellent." Painfully clean hands reached past her and plucked out the jack. "Allow me."

"Sure." Folding her arms across her chest, Harmony leaned against her car while he set to work loosening the lug nuts. It wasn't hard at all. To watch him, that was.

He was long and lean, without an extra ounce of fat on him. The lug nuts succumbed to astutely applied leverage rather than brute force, yet she had a feeling he could hold his own in a friendly arm-wrestling competition.

Realizing that she was staring, Harmony looked away. Mentally reviewed the process of changing a tire and came to the conclusion that he'd be needing the spare in short order. He must've been thinking along the same lines, because as she moved to retrieve it, he spoke.

"If you'll finish taking these lug nuts off, I'll get the spare out."

"Sure." She nearly rolled her eyes at herself. *Fine conversationalist you are.* "You're new to Cadmia, aren't you?" she asked as she dropped into a loose squat.

"Brand new," he concurred. "This is the most amazing trunk I think I've ever seen."

Startled, she looked up. Found him engrossed in…what?

"I have four sisters and each of them is more disorganized than the next." He shook his head, his short-cropped, sandy-brown hair barely moving. "I shudder to think what would happen to this if one of them ever got ahold of it." He wasn't completely kidding, either.

A charley horse in her left calf brought her sharply to her feet, nearly into his arms—which were already full of spare tire.

"Sorry," she muttered. Her cheeks warmed despite the cool temperatures. "Leg cramp."

"Are you drinking enough water?" He frowned as she limped out of his way.

Amused, she nodded. "Probably short a few electrolytes is all. I missed lunch and wasn't expecting to have to jog the last couple of blocks on my route." Nothing had gone as expected today. Why hadn't she just changed the doggone tire? Cara wouldn't even have noticed she was a little late.

"Hmm." Leaving the spare, he abruptly walked over to his own vehicle, which she now saw was loaded with shopping bags. "Here." Returning, he shoved a bottle and a small, rectangular package into her hands.

He was lifting the spare back out of her trunk before she could even open her mouth to say thanks, so she took a minute to see what he'd given her. A bottle of water and one of those serving-size protein and fruit packages. Interesting. Stock's, the town's one and only grocery store, had only started carrying those packs about a month ago. Just in time, apparently.

"Thanks, Doc."

"What did you call me?"

She blinked at his sharp question. "Um…doc, I think." She popped the protein snack package open. "This is what the doctor ordered, right?"

"Right." He turned his attention back to the tire. The lug nuts were neatly placed and waiting for him on the pavement, reminding him vaguely of the trays of gleaming, silver tools he'd used during operations.

Even more puzzled, she retreated to the curb to think. And gingerly stretch her calf.

"Gotta quit skipping leg days," she muttered around a mouthful of lightly salted almonds and craisins.

"Yoohoo!"

"Oh no." Pasting a smile on her face, Harmony looked over her shoulder. "Mrs. Arnold!" Waved back at the woman, who was struggling to watch the tire-changing process through her passenger window. "How are you today?"

"Wonderful as always!" Mrs. Arnold smiled a little too broadly, as if deliberately displaying each of her perfect teeth.

What does Mrs. Arnold have in common with George Washington? The echo of a child's voice in a sing-song tone ran through Harmony's mind. *They both have wooden smiles!*

Harmony shook her head to clear it of the

schoolyard witticisms she'd overheard the week before. As far as she knew, almost nobody in Cadmia actually liked Mrs. Arnold.

"Sorry to see you're having car trouble, dear."

It wasn't easy, but Harmony kept her own smile in place. "Oh, the car's fine, Mrs. Arnold. It's the tire that needs fixing." *Shoot. Why did I say that?*

Mrs. Arnold's eyes narrowed. "I'm so glad you found someone to help you."

"I found her." The stranger rose, hazel blue eyes fixed with almost comical dismay on his dirty hands.

"Oh, how charming!" Mrs. Arnold pressed one hand to her chest and very nearly fluttered her lashes. "A dashing hero saving a damsel in distress."

The stranger sighed. "Next you'll have us breaking into song." His back still to her, he swung the damaged tire into Harmony's trunk.

Harmony bit her lip to keep from laughing out loud. Should she warn him? Then again, how *could* she warn him about Mrs. Arnold's preeminent status in Cadmia while the woman herself sat staring at them?

"Yeah, well, one good turn deserves another." Harmony crumpled the empty package and tossed it in her trunk. That got his attention, if his frown was any indicator. "I'll get out of your driveway post haste and thank you for your help!"

"Is this your house?" Mrs. Arnold fake-gasped. "The old Palmer residence? Why, what wonderful news!"

She launched into a laundry list of things that were wrong with the house, generously offering her help in contacting the necessary professionals for repairs. And, really, what did a bachelor want with such a big house anyway? Or was his family coming to join him?

"That's right, he's just moved in." Harmony hastily intervened when she saw her benefactor's mouth tighten. "It's brand-new news, too. Why, I just found out myself." That did it. 'News' was Mrs. Arnold's weakness.

"How exciting! Well, I must be off. So glad you're alright!" Mrs. Arnold wiggled the fingers of one hand at them while her other hand rolled up the passenger window.

"Bye." Harmony didn't bother to return the hand wiggle. The 'queen bee' wasn't the type to look back. "Sorry about that."

"Don't be." Forgetting about the dirt on his hands, he scrubbed them over his face. "Every town has at least one busybody." The city he'd left behind had too many to count. Interfering, overbearing snoops who left disaster of one sort or another trailing in their wake. Couldn't Cadmia have been different?

"Yeah." Now why did her voice go all soft like that? Just because he suddenly looked like a weary little boy who needed a cookie for each hand… Clearing her throat, she tugged an antibacterial wipe packet out of her pocket and held it out to him. "For your fingers. And, um, the smudges on your face."

"My face?" He used the rear window of her car as a mirror. Smiled for the first time, making her heart flip. "Thanks."

"Thanks for the rescue." She winked even as she picked the garbage out of her trunk. The faint approval on his face gave her a lift that made absolutely no sense. And even if it did, she couldn't let it.

"How's your leg?" he asked, putting her jack back where he found it and closing her trunk.

"It'll be alright." She smiled. "I've got a heating pad at home." As well as a bottle of pain medication in the car.

"Good." Finished wiping his fingers, he fished keys out of his pocket.

Harmony pulled out her own car keys. "See you around." *I hope*, whispered a little voice in the back of her head that she sternly shushed.

"Inevitably." He groaned inwardly as he noticed his shirtfront. He was never going to get the black rubber stains out.

"Later, Doc." She grimaced back at his scowl. "What? It's not like I know your name or anything."

He wrestled with himself briefly, then grudgingly said, "Grant. Reeves."

He hoped she didn't get any funny ideas. There were several reasons for his not wanting to date right now. First and foremost, he was still figuring out his new life. The repair list Mrs. Arnold so cheerfully recited had been a big part of why he bought the house. To give himself something to do besides watching the second hand crawl around in a circle on his wall clock.

"Hello, Grant-Reeves." She ran his first and last names together to tease him for the way he'd said them. "I'm Harmony…"

"Yes, I heard." He instantly regretted his terse response, but she didn't wait around for a retraction, let alone an apology.

"So you did." Pivoting, Harmony walked to her car. "Welcome to Cadmia, Grant." She didn't know what to make of his obvious reluctance to share his name. In a way, it was eerily reminiscent of her own behavior when she first moved away from home some…ten years ago? Huh. Hard to believe that much time had passed.

Sliding in, Harmony started the engine. Threw it in gear and took off. So. The Palmer house finally sold. Or was he renting? Either way, she wished she'd been aware of that before she parked her car there. She hated making a bad first impression.

Her lips twitched as she thought about his impression on her. Handsome, clean cut, and basically polite, but not friendly. Obviously accustomed to business professional dress, and he wasn't wearing cheap brands, either. New York plates on a mid-range vehicle that, due to its age, she guessed he'd purchased used. None of it matched up. Of course, it could be that he'd recently lost his job.

Well, whatever. He wasn't a mystery she cared to solve. Or so she told herself as she eased up to a stop sign. She was much too busy for that, especially tonight.

She still had a dozen things to do today if she wanted to compete in the drag race tomorrow. Her allergen-free products wouldn't sort themselves. The natural yeast shipment needed to be measured out for her Monday deliveries. Then there were the soy-free items to box up.

Her nose wrinkled as she remembered that the Tabors had changed their order yet again. Someday she was going to get them to settle on exactly how much of what they wanted each month so she could sort it from the get-go instead of having to wait for their unique request each month.

Hmm. If she was busy doing all of that, she wouldn't have time to make supper before going over to her friend's for a movie. Grinning, she reached for her phone. Dialed Blinky's Diner and waited.

"Hey, Harmony!" Susan's voice filled the car.

She grimaced, then was glad Susan couldn't see her. It was just…how sad was it that the local diner knew her number by heart? They for sure didn't have caller ID on the ancient telephone system they used.

"Hey, Susan." A roar of teenage laughter prompted Harmony to hold the phone away from her ear. "Wow, sounds busy tonight!"

"Always busy on Fridays," Susan laughed.

"Too busy to make my usual?" Harmony suppressed a second grimace. How awful would that be? She snickered at herself as she wondered what her former personal nutritionist would think of her eating habits. They'd clashed over 'unnecessary calories' years ago and Harmony hadn't bothered to hire another one, but she didn't have any trouble imagining the disapproving twist on the man's lips if he ever read Blinky's menu.

"Well, now, that depends." Susan covered the mouthpiece and answered a question, then cheerfully continued, "We've got a special deal on our wings tonight."

Harmony sat patiently through the litany of flavors, but jumped in as soon as Susan paused for a breath. "Hey, those all sound delicious." To someone, somewhere, she was certain. "I kind of had my heart set on your spicy chicken sandwich with…"

"With extra pickles and pencil fries?" Harmony pictured Susan shaking her head even as the woman finished, "Sure thing, sugar. We're already boxing it up for you."

"Awesome. I'll be there in a few." There were certain perks to having a routine. They also made her easier to find, but hopefully she was safe from the paparazzi a little longer in Tinytown, USA.

Stepping into Blinky's was kind of like stepping back in time to a black-and-white TV show where soda fountains still existed. An impression eerily reinforced by Blinky's mostly black-and-white décor, right down to the diamond-shaped tiles under her feet.

"There she is." Susan lifted a box out of the warmer. "You sure you don't want anything else? Slice of pie maybe? Or one of our mini-cobblers?"

Harmony shook her head. "No, thanks."

"I admire your won't-power." Susan sighed and took the cash Harmony set on the counter. "If I could resist desserts like you…" She shrugged eloquently and patted her waistline.

"I'm only resisting these so I can have some at movie night tonight. You know how sensitive Noella is about her desserts." Harmony laughed and reached for the box. "Keep the change."

Back in her car, she offered a short prayer before taking a bite of the sandwich. "Mmm. Perfect." Her mouth tingled with the heat of the spices, but as always, it was perfect. And the pickles were so fresh they *crunched*.

Sighing happily, she turned up her music and headed for home—where the first thing she did was to plug in a heating pad and wrap it around her calf. It worked great until she started in on the soy-free packages. Beauty products were on one set of shelves. Baby formula was on another. And so forth.

"Now I know how a dog on a leash feels," she muttered the third time she had to stop and plug the heating pad back in after accidentally walking beyond the reach of the cord. "Maybe it's time to rearrange things by allergy instead of department."

With a little careful planning, she managed to get through the rest of her preparations without tripping and killing herself. She was going to be late for movie night, though.

Chapter 2

"Hello, hello!" Harmony was halfway out of her coat before she made it all the way inside Noella's house. Taking off her hat, she shook her chestnut brown hair free. "Sorry I'm late. Had a flat." She shrugged dismissively, not quite ready to discuss the handsome—if grumpy—man who'd helped her out.

Finding their friend Grace on the other side of the door instead of Noella, Harmony stage-whispered, "What're we watching?"

"*Murder at the Opera*," Grace answered at the same time that Merry chimed in from her seat on the couch.

"With English subtitles?" Harmony looked at Merry over her shoulder as she hung her coat up. Noella had a habit of picking international movies when it was her turn to host, which was fine, but Harmony was too tired to deal with subtitles tonight. Especially the kind that were badly translated, making her accidentally laugh out loud at them.

She'd never forget the time that happened during a tense moment in an old medical drama. Everyone wanted to know what was so funny and she'd had a tough time getting out of it without revealing that she spoke multiple languages. She wouldn't mind telling her friends, except that being multi-lingual didn't exactly fit the 'I'm just one of the girls' stereotype here in Cadmia.

"With English speaking," Noella announced, her finger hovering over the play button. An Acadian transplant from Prince Edward Island, she generally preferred French to English, though she was fluent in Dutch as well.

"English speaking?" Harmony echoed as she stepped out of her shoes. "Wow, tonight must be special!"

"You get the floor," Merry told her as she came around the end of the couch.

"I see that," she laughed. "Oh thanks, Grace." Harmony beamed at her friend, who was offering her a plate with a delicious-looking treat. Some kind of pastry?

Spying the nuts on the other desserts, she discreetly inspected her own and was relieved not to find any. Thankfully, she'd never had worse than a bad rash, but she held firmly to the belief that an ounce of prevention was worth a pound of cure. Plopping down where she could lean against the couch, she bit into her pastry.

"Wow." She gave Noella a thumbs-up. "This is great!" The spices were a little strong for her taste, and she wasn't sure flavored fry-bread was actually better than plain with butter and honey… But if she voiced those thoughts, especially to a friend who owned a menu planning website, it would sound like she was complaining.

Then the movie started and she let herself get lost in it. One thing was certain. The main character, a single woman who lived by herself, had to be making a ton of money. How else could she afford her spacious, split-level home?

Of course, that was kind of a given with these feel-good movies. Comfy lifestyle on a questionable income. Whatever. The male leads were cute, and the dialogue was pretty snappy. Sure, the awesome acting between the female characters made her miss her kid sister. Other than that, though, it was a great way to spend an evening.

When it was over, she kept her place on the floor while the others chatted around her, agreeing that they'd like to see the rest of the series. Then, as if on cue…

"Alright, well," Merry indicated the wall clock, "if I don't get home on time, I'll miss my appointment with the sandman."

"Mmm, the sandman." Harmony grinned, stretched by arching her back like a cat, then bounced to her feet. "Y'know, he's never once gotten my order right!"

"Never?" Noella grinned cheekily. "No dreams about handsome, single billionaires for you?" They all laughed at that.

If they only knew. Harmony never told anyone the truth about herself. Not the whole truth, at any rate. Most people wouldn't understand why a billionaire heiress preferred living and working on the edge of nowhere to staying in one of her family's mansions while the servants fended off camera-wielding boogeymen. Most people didn't understand how lucky they were to just be themselves, either.

Shrugging to herself, Harmony got in line and made sure to give Merry, who was too uptight for her own good, a bear hug. She got a warm hug in return, which only intensified the longing for her younger sister's company.

It was always bad this time of year, so close to the holidays, but this year it was worse. Lydia was turning eighteen this year. They'd be moving somewhere—together—permanently once Lydia graduated from Warrington Academy, the private high school she'd chosen. Not that Harmony knew where they were going yet, but the uncertainty was all part of the fun. Right?

"Text me when you get home, ok?" Grace pointed at her and Merry. "Both of you."

"Will do!" Harmony lived just up and around the corner from Noella, but she appreciated the thought. Particularly from Grace. With her fire-red hair, Grace was the proverbial candle, burning at both ends as she struggled to keep up with most of the county's need for a large animal vet while maintaining a clinic in town.

Leaves crunched under Harmony's feet as she crossed the lawn to her car, where she automatically checked the back seat for uninvited guests before getting in. The odds of being attacked that way in Cadmia were slim, but it was a good habit to have.

She sniffled a little into a napkin as the engine warmed. Having places to be and things to do weren't always enough to satisfy her. Sure, it helped that she was making a difference in the lives of people who couldn't easily afford the allergen-free products she sold for cost—or less. Those people got to have their family close by, though.

The knot in her calf yelped when she moved wrong, bringing her attention hissing back to the present. Pulling into her driveway, she parked and got out. Luckily all she had to carry in was herself, because the cramp was back with a vengeance.

As she closed and locked the front door behind her, she touched the battered baseball cap that she'd hung on it.

Home is where you hang your hat, as the old saying went.

Other people hung pictures or needlework or even puzzles that they'd put together. She'd tried it a few times, but that only made it harder to leave when the paparazzi closed in.

Sighing, she made her way to the kitchen and took another dose of pain killers. Tossed her paper cup in the garbage, which would need to go out soon, and started getting ready for bed.

[Made it.] She sent the promised text to Grace while she brushed her teeth.

Her phone dinged when a smiley emoji came back almost instantly

[Me, too! See you Sunday!]

[See you!]

"Another week gone." She shook her head as she changed into a clean pair of sweatpants and a long-sleeved t-shirt. The comfy knit fabrics were a far cry from the dainty pink nightgowns of her childhood, but a lot more practical in case of a fire or other forced evacuation.

Especially on a cold night like tonight. She shivered as she closed the two doors that led into the living room to prevent drafts and plugged in her space heater.

Producing a fitted sheet and a heavy quilt from the green totes by the wall, she transformed her beige, four-seater couch into a bed for the night. It drove her a little crazy to have to unmake and remake it every day, but she used the bedroom for product storage and had to sleep somewhere.

Her lips twitched at the direction her thoughts were taking. What if she'd opted for the bed, instead? She never had anyone over except for movie nights. The girls were good sports, they'd probably all pile on the bed or the floor.

It would be a lot like when her mom used to bring Lydia in for a bedtime story…

Her smile faded out completely. *Mom and Dad.* Or, more accurately, since her mother had died fifteen years ago, *Dad.* If she cared to call him that, which she didn't. He'd fallen apart like a poorly made tennis shoe after her mother's death, leaving her to raise Lydia with the help of their cook and butler. The courts granted her special guardianship after yet another of his parties ended with the police being called.

The news outlets had loved that—and the fact that her lawyers found a way to evict him based on her grandfather's will. *Billionaire Heiress Disinherits Father.*

Rubbing tired eyes, she shoved the thoughts aside and gingerly stretched her calf. Knelt for prayer.

"Heavenly Father," she whispered, "it's been another long day." Resting her cheek on her folded arms, she quietly reviewed her day in prayer, smiling over most of it. Except… "Thanks for sending someone to help me with that tire." She sighed and pinched the bridge of her nose, wishing that she'd just taken the time to do things right in the first place.

"Please look after Lydia while we're apart for a little while longer." Ending in the name of her Savior, she switched off the lights and crawled under the covers.

The space heater continued making its cheerful racket, almost drowning out the creak of the wind in the tree outside her bedroom. Almost lulling her to sleep. Almost filling the empty spot where her sister's snoring should be.

Only one week until the first of the month. After making deliveries, she could drive out to her storage unit and call her sister. In today's world of high tech spying, she didn't dare keep the burner phone on her person. It would be bad enough to have her name splashed across the headlines again. She'd never forgive herself if they found Lydia.

Punching her pillow, she rolled onto her side so she could stare at the TV instead of the ceiling for a while.

She thought about surprising Lydia with a visit for her eighteenth birthday in December. It was a fun, reckless idea.

Grunting, she leaned over and picked the remote up off the floor. After hunting around for a minute, she found a baking show on one of her internet channels.

"Willkommen zu unserer Kochshow!" A cheery, middle-aged fellow paused in the middle of tying his apron to wave at the camera. "Heute kochen wir…"

Turning the volume down to where it was barely audible over the heater, she watched him start pulling out the ingredients for knödel. If she hadn't been trying to fall asleep, she would've grabbed something to write the recipe down on. Giving up her favorite German restaurant in Portland was the worst thing about leaving.

She'd only gotten two years in Portland. And she'd moved to Cadmia nearly three years ago. It was time and past time to move on before some bored 'freelance journalist' found the golden needle in the haystack.

So…why hadn't she left? Was she getting lazy? Or worse, comfortable? Or perhaps she was just tired of all the running. What would it take for her to live a normal life as herself?

Her drooping eyelids slowly closed, her thoughts whirling on in the form of vivid dreams.

When her alarm went off the next morning, she lunged into a sitting position and nearly fell on the floor.

"Whoa!" Flailing wildly, she regained her balance, then sat there for several seconds until she'd woken up enough to leave most of her dream behind. Smacked her phone to shut it off. "That would make a great kids' book," she muttered, swinging her legs off the couch. "A hiking tour of Arizona in search of a giant, golden knödel."

Shaking her head, she unplugged the space heater and moved it to one corner. Turning, she tumbled to the floor in a forward shoulder roll. Carried the motion through so that she came back up on her feet. Forward and backward she tumbled until her blood was flowing. Sit-ups and pushups came next. Finally, a cold shower and breakfast.

Pulling her hair into a ponytail, she made a fast breakfast of the last of her weekly scrambled eggs and fresh toast. She'd already finished reading the lesson for church, so for scripture study she reviewed one of her favorite general conference talks, taking care to reread each footnote and scripture reference.

"Happiness does not consist of a glut of luxury, the world's idea of a 'good time.' Nor must we search for it in faraway places with strange-sounding names. Happiness is found at home." How she loved that quote from Elder Thomas S. Monson's 1998 general conference talk, "Hallmarks of a Happy Home."

"Already?" Frowning at her phone, she shut off a second alarm.

Well, there was no arguing with the clock. Her stomach fluttered with excitement as she picked up her bag and stepped into her shoes. It would be even colder in the garage, so she zipped up the jacket she was already wearing.

Shivering in anticipation, she opened the door and flipped on the light.

And…just stood there, thrilling at the way her electric blue 1994 Firebird seemed to pulse under the lights like a living, breathing thing. Bolts of lightning streaked back from its nose, lending it an aggressive air.

"I hope you slept well." She patted the hood.

"Because today's a very big day." The first and the last days of the season were always grand events at the Border Wars Raceway in Topaz. Drivers would come from Missouri and Kansas—and maybe Arkansas or Oklahoma— to compete.

Adrenaline coursed through her veins as she settled herself behind the wheel. Pressed the button of the garage door opener and listened to the engine rumble to life.

As she backed out into the gray of the predawn, Harmony basked in the solitude of being the only car on the road that morning. Unlike most of the local racers, she drove a street-strip car that didn't need a trailer. The reds and yellows of sugar maples stood out against the sober green pine trees as she drove, their colors becoming more and more vivid as the sun inched over the horizon.

Traffic slowly increased as she neared the city limits. By the time she reached Topaz, the streets were jammed with early birds like herself. A few showoffs peeled out at the stoplights as if they were already at the track, then hastily braked when a police car came into view.

The chaos became more organized once she reached the track, the spectators going left while the racers went right. Parking at her usual spot in the pits, well away from the stands and the attention-seeking rookies, Harmony got out and stretched.

The last day of the season. Everything looked the same, and yet a little different. A little sad, somehow.

Why was it that the closer she got to something she wanted, the less attainable it seemed?

Oh, great. Now she was psyching herself out.

Looking around, she dragged in a deep breath. The smells of hot grease from the concession stand vied with exhaust for dominance.

Red, yellow, white, blue, black…she was surrounded by cars gleaming in the morning sunlight. Half of them would've fit right in at a classic muscle car show. Racers and their crews bustled around their treasures like ants at a picnic basket.

"Look what the cat dragged in," teased Shot Ballwin from where she lounged against her shocking pink pro stock car. Her hair was dyed to the exact same shade, so they stood out like flamingos in a mismatched flock of parrots. Though she'd only been there long enough to back her car out of the trailer, that didn't stop her from a friendly poke or two.

"Hey." Harmony grinned. She and Sharon, aka 'Shot,' were two of the four female drivers who consistently came. And consistently placed. "Are the others here yet?"

"Haven't seen them." Shot arched professsionally plucked eyebrows in a show of disdain for the cars and trailers forming up haphazardly around them. "Never fails. The first and last races of the season always bring out the weekend warriors."

Even if Harmony had wanted to argue the point, a pair of racers a few slots down chose that precise moment to start a shouting match over who bumped into whom. They were both driving rat rods, or 'piles of junk on wheels,' as she'd heard one older racer disdainfully refer to them. Grimacing, she hoped the drivers calmed themselves down before someone had to call security.

"Is that the twins?" Shot cocked her head to one side. "Or thunder?"

Harmony snickered, glad for the distraction. "Sky's clear." Julie and Jordan weren't really twins, but they both loved loud and fast vehicles.

A screaming-yellow motorcycle pulled into the slot Shot had been saving beside her trailer. Julie's helmet came off, revealing purple and naturally auburn hair that ran long from the left side of her head down over the buzzed right side.

Meanwhile, Jordan waved at them as she drove by, headed to the lanes. Her smoke-gray truck with painted orange flames curling up all around its base was a veteran of nearly a decade of races.

"Fashionably late." Shot smirked at her own

joke. The half-ton trucks were up first today.

"Who's hungry?" Harmony's scrambled egg sandwich had faded into a distant memory. While their traditional soft pretzel breakfast wouldn't satisfy her, she never ate much before a race anyway. Partly to save her stomach the stress and partly for the joy of going out afterward.

"Me!" Julie was always hungry.

The fans nearly blew them out of the concession stands with a wild roar.

"What happened?" Harmony craned her neck in an effort to see the scoreboard, only to find her view blocked by an exceptionally tall man. "Was it Jordan?" Ugh, she couldn't even hear the announcer over the ruckus.

"We're going to sweep today," Julie announced around a mouthful of pretzel. "I can feel it."

"Hey, don't jinx us!" Shot was quick to complain.

"Us? What *us*?" Harmony lifted both hands in an exaggerated motion toward herself. "I'm running last, thank you!" Accepting her pretzel from the vendor, she gave a silent prayer of thanks and bit into it.

They bickered and bantered all the way back to their cars, then settled down to listen to the announcer. Shot handed out bottled water while Julie inspected her bike in preparation for her race.

"Alright!" Julie pumped her fists at the announcement that Jordan had won. "That's what I love about racing, it…"

"Goes so fast!" Harmony and Shot jumped in with the ending of her awful pun.

"You need a new joke," Shot advised, shaking her head.

"I need to get going." Julie polished an imaginary smudge on her helmet. "I can't win from here."

"Yeah, good luck!" Shot jeered.

"If I didn't know you were friends," Harmony laughed as Julie drove off for her event, "I'd be worried about you two."

"Over that?" Shot tossed her pink hair. "You're the weird one, ya know." She paused, something she never did, then seemed to decide that she might as well pour the worms out since she'd opened the can. "You don't cuss or smoke. When we go out to celebrate, you drink water." She gestured loosely at the throngs of people around them. "Never see you with anyone, either."

Harmony rubbed the back of her neck. "True." She didn't often get a chance to talk about the restored gospel and frankly, she was nervous.

"You got some kinda allergy?"

"Nothing like that." The question struck her as doubly hilarious given her business of sourcing allergen-free products.

"But there *is* something?" Shot squinted at her.

"Church." She watched Shot's jaw drop. "Relax, the doc says it's not contagious." *Doc.* Her mind darted back to Grant for some weird reason.

Shot's expression lingered somewhere between unpleasant surprise and amusement. "Church?!" she squeaked.

Harmony did her best not to shrink under the intense gaze.

"I never…" Shot turned in a circle as if looking for help. "I never knew church girls could race!"

The laughter started in Harmony's toes and surged upward, doubling her over. "You…you've got to be kidding me!" she gasped at length. "Wh-why wouldn't a 'church girl' be able to race?"

Shot threw up her hands, half relieved and half irritated by Harmony's reaction to her own reaction. "I dunno."

"Maybe because they ain't fast women," suggested Jordan, who was hanging out her truck window as she parked.

"Yeah, but…" Shot's protest and explanation trailed off into nothing when Jordan ignored her. Grumbling, she turned her attention to her car.

Harmony and Jordan were discussing something or other when the results for Julie's event came over the loudspeakers.

"Oh no." Harmony mock-groaned. "Julie will be impossible to live with after this." Catching sight of Jordan's arched eyebrows, Harmony explained, "She's decided we're going to sweep today."

"Could be." Jordan took a swig of her water. "First I won, now her. Reckon she's half right, at least." She grinned facetiously.

Harmony threw a napkin at her.

Just then a couple of men walked past, snickering. The only word Harmony caught was 'pink.'

"Guess I might as well go home." Shot set her tools aside. White-lipped, she folded her arms across her chest and glared after the men. "Apparently pink is the new green."

Jordan shook her head, her silver-brown hair swishing. "Don't be making fun of that. I know we buck the superstitions routinely, but those crashes were bad." Most of the serious drivers associated green with three particularly nasty smashups and wouldn't go near it. For other, admittedly less intelligent reasons, the male drivers likewise steered clear of pink.

Shot sobered abruptly. "That's a fact," she agreed. Running her fingers through her hair, she sighed. "Guess I'm up." Angling a look at Harmony, she muttered, "See ya. *Sister.*"

Harmony had to bite her lip to keep from laughing at the attempted gibe. And, from the way Shot's eyes narrowed, she could tell. For eighteen months, while on a proselyting mission for the Church of Jesus Christ of Latter-day Saints, 'Sister' had basically been Harmony's first name.

"Something funny I don't know about?" Jordan tossed her trash in a nearby can as casually as she'd asked the question.

"Shot just found out that I go to church." Might as well be the one to tell her.

"Figures." Jordan lifted a pair of mirror shades off her hair and settled them on her nose. "C'mon, let's go get a hot dog. I'm starved."

Chapter 3

"So, what church?" Jordan asked as she lifted a hot dog for a bite.

"The Church of Jesus Christ of Latter-day Saints." Harmony deliberately slowed herself down as she answered. It was such a mouthful—no pun intended—that it was easy to rush through the words without meaning to.

Jordan scooped up some errant onions and popped them into her mouth. "That the same as Mormons?"

Harmony shrugged. "People have been calling us that for some two hundred years, but it's not the church's name."

An excited shriek sounded, telling them Julie had spotted them.

"We're two for two, ladies." She threw her arms around their shoulders. "Shot's turn."

They weren't more than a hundred feet from their spot, but Julie managed to cram a mile's worth of rapid-fire chatter into the walk.

"And then I'm going to use the rest of my prize money to get a new…"

"Whose will are you in, anyway?" Jordan interrupted her good naturedly. None of today's purses exceeded five hundred dollars, and Julie's imagination had her spending well over twelve hundred.

Harmony tasted bile as her memory kicked

into overdrive. *We are here today to read the last will and testament of Moira Barrington Wells.* Wiping her mouth with her hand, Harmony looked around desperately for something to re-ground herself with.

"Or is today some special triple-your-prize-money day?" Jordan snickered, oblivious to Harmony's distress.

Julie pouted. "A girl can dream, can't she?"

Harmony took a deep breath, letting the sights and smells of the track engulf her, forcing her to return fully to the present.

"Shot's pulling into the burnout box." Harmony couldn't see the staging area well, but it was impossible to miss the shocking pink pro stock car as its rear wheels spun, cleaning and heating them for the race. A huge section of fans cheered as she left the cloud of smoke behind her, dramatically overshooting the staging area.

"She's such a showoff," Julie jeered.

"The fans love it," Jordan pointed out pragmatically as she slowed to a halt so she could watch, too. "And there wouldn't be a track without the fans."

"Ready." Harmony watched the two cars back until they were properly staged. "Set." The cars inched forward until their front tires triggered the so-called 'Christmas tree.' Its amber lights would wink on in sequence, counting down to the few seconds they were there for.

"Shot did it! She did it!" Julie sounded like she was about to bust as she repeated the announcer's statement. "That's the best time for her event so far!"

"We heard." Harmony patted her on the shoulder. "The whole place heard." Her drama teacher would've been proud of that calm tone of voice, given the way her insides were jumping around with anticipation. Soon she'd be in her own car, one of dozens of drivers creeping forward in the lanes, impatiently waiting their turn to compete.

With that in mind, she headed back to the pits, where she began swapping her radial tires for racing slicks.

"Did you bring your peanuts?" Jordan asked dryly as she polished off her third hot dog.

Harmony grinned and patted her pocket, making the cellophane crinkle. Most drivers considered peanuts to be bad luck, so she always made sure to be seen eating some right before a race—in her car that had the number 'thirteen' emblazoned proudly on the door panel. Anything to throw the competition off their game.

Shot's pro stock car purred into its place and Shot jumped out to kiss it on its hot pink hood.

"Three for three!" Shot gave Julie a high five.

They both looked at Harmony, who threw

up her hands.

"Like I need the extra pressure!"

"Hey." Jordan grinned at her. "Show 'em how it's done."

"Don't fall asleep at the wheel." Harmony nodded. "Got it."

Her glib response drew more than a few answering grimaces from the drivers and crew members milling around. They all knew how true the statement was. Cheap racing slicks ran about two hundred dollars per tire. Bodywork to add a roll bar or cage didn't get sold for a song either. Tack on the helmet, gas, entry fees, and so forth… All of it wasted if you blinked.

Her ears pricked at an announcement over the loudspeakers.

"My turn." Waving jauntily, she slid into her Firebird. Lowered her windows to let some of the heat out and whispered a fervent prayer for everyone's safety. Starting the engine, she gripped the cushioned wheel cover and crept out of the pits.

The track rules were simple—if you won your head-to-head, you kept racing. Last one standing took home the prize money.

The carbon monoxide levels around her rose as she nosed her way onto the lanes, idling slowly forward, inch by inch. She wiped the sweat from her forehead, but ignored the temptation to turn on her air conditioning. She'd have to turn it off for the race itself and leaving a water puddle on the track only made trouble for the next racer.

"Hey, lady!"

Turning her head to hunt for the source of the slightly squeaky male voice, Harmony stopped cold and searched instead for a semi-familiar face that she thought she'd seen.

Grant! What was he doing here? Or had she imagined it?

"Lady!" The voice, slightly more impatient, bellowed again. "You wanna get me some coffee? Black, no sugar!" The snickering that followed the idiotic question announced how pleased the boy was with himself.

Groaning inwardly, Harmony wasted a glance at the random boy, his second yell allowing her to locate him in a nearby car.

"Ain't you got a kitchen to clean?" was followed with even louder guffaws from him.

"First race?" she called back, ignoring his comments. She couldn't see much of his car's interior, but it looked like he lived in it or something.

"What's it to you?" he retorted, abruptly sullen.

She focused on rolling forward as her line moved, then looked back over at him when his car pulled up alongside hers.

"You can't have anything loose in your cabin. They won't let you race with all that stuff."

His response was liberally laced with expletives and assumptions about her less-than-average intelligence.

"Hey you, shut up!" barked an official. He ran a finger under his collar, silently cursing the unseasonably warm weather—especially after a frosty night like last night—and rapped on the hood of the boy's car. "Pull out."

"What?!" The boy squealed like a startled pig. "I'll lose my place!"

"You'll lose more than that in this death trap," the official snarled. "Go back to your pit and dump all this crap." He gestured generally at the interior. "When you've got nothing in there that isn't bolted down or belted in, you can come back. If we're still open, that is. Now get going!"

A second official stepped between Harmony and the belligerent teen, who seemed to think if he just yelled loudly enough he'd get his way.

"Afternoon, Kelly." She handed her tech card over. "How's the field today?"

"Over sixty cars in this class. Going to be a good purse." Without waiting for a reply, he pointed his pencil at the nose of her car. "Pull up even there and pop your hood."

"Right." She kept her tone casual despite the uptick in her heart rate. More racers meant more heats. More chances to make a mistake.

Kelly and his partner checked the Firebird

from nose to tail, including her safety harness and the condition of the slicks, then gave her a thumbs-up.

Exhaling some of her tension, Harmony drew up behind the racer in front of her and tried to spot Grant again. But he'd vanished. If he'd really been there.

Not that it made sense for her to imagine him.

Nor did she have time to waste on trying to figure it out—either why he was there or why she might've imagined it. The line of cars ahead of her had already begun to curve, which meant the staging area would soon be in sight.

Things had gone smoothly most of the day, thanks to the tech inspections and fair-to-middling driving. The track should be in good condition.

Following the instructions of a track official, she pulled into the burnout box. Choked a little on the cloud of tire smoke the process created, but endured it because it was a small price to pay for the added traction.

The car that pulled up beside her looked like it had gotten lost on its way to the grocery store, which meant absolutely nothing.

Taking a deep breath, she eased into position, triggering the countdown. Amber lights lit up as the other car did the same and…

The force of her acceleration pressed her back against the seat, her breath leaving her in a *huff.* She blinked twice and the quarter mile marker was behind her.

The harness bit into her as she braked and headed for the second turnoff, her competition squarely in her rear-view mirror.

"One down," she muttered.

Like half of the first run's racers, she made her way back to the staging lanes. Waved to the girls as she passed their pit area. After her second run, she saw that some of the eliminated cars were already back on their trailers. That included a few unfortunates who'd broken down, causing delays for track inspection and cleanup.

There were only ten cars left in the third run.

Five in the fourth run.

The fifth car ran solo against the times of the others—and bumped the slowest car out of the race! Oh, the crowd loved that, cheering themselves hoarse at the unexpected upset.

Predictably, the final four were track regulars. Harmony knew them all. Pete Burns, in his '68 Camaro. Walt Hines, driving a 2011 Porsche. Tim Edwards, as picture perfect as his '73 Corvette. Good cars, excellent drivers. Stiff competition.

From the corner of her eye, she saw a red light go off as her car screamed away from the starting line. Fear seized her until she realized it was on Pete's side of the tree.

He'd left the line early, an automatic disqualification.

Ugh. She hated winning on a technicality!

She could've played a song on her wire-taught nerves while she drove around the track to retake her place in the lanes. It didn't help that the adrenaline from the other runs was wearing off. Her arms trembled with fatigue and she rubbed eyes that didn't seem to want to focus.

She had to get it together.

There was still one more run ahead of her. Her last run of the day. *Of the season.*

Back at the starting line, she waited for…Tim Edwards in his sleek Corvette.

Straightening in her seat, she flexed her fingers. Started easing up to the pre-staging line. Almost…almost…

Tim's corvette rolled up, triggering the 'pre-staged' then 'staged' lights in rapid succession on his side of the tree. He looked over and smirked at her. *I'm ready, slowpoke. Why aren't you?*

Inexplicably, she laughed. No doubt he'd hoped the breach of etiquette would rattle her, the same way that she hoped eating peanuts and sporting the number 'thirteen' on her car would get under the skin of her opponents.

Her gumption restored, she triggered the second set of lights on her side. Depressing her gas pedal and brake at the same time, she watched…no, she *felt* the countdown.

Instinctively, she released the brake and her

car leapt forward! Tore down the track toward the finish line. At the last possible moment, she took her foot off the gas and pumped the brakes.

Pete wasn't behind by much, but he was behind, so she headed for the last of the three turnoffs, letting him take his pick of the first two exits. In her rearview mirror she could see him pounding on his steering wheel.

I won!

She nearly dropped her time slip when she stopped at the E.T. shack on her last trip to the pits. It took the rest of the ride around the return road to get herself under control. And still she hesitated when it came time to put her weight on her shaky legs. She stalled an extra few seconds, removing her helmet and setting it on the seat beside her.

"You did it!" Julie hit her like a two-ton train, nearly knocking her over despite her concentrated efforts.

Shot caught them both from the other side, while Jordan made a wild grab for Julie's waist. And so it was that the roaring fans got hundreds—if not thousands—of candid photos of the winners of the four events.

Harmony did her best to laugh it off even as her blood pressure rose. A single professional photo for the track website was bad enough. Her face splashed across countless personal social media pages could be catastrophic! Oh, why had she taken off her helmet?

"C'mon, ladies." Jordan, relieved that Julie's enthusiasm hadn't sent them all into a pile on the ground, linked arms with Harmony. "Let's go smile for our fans."

Harmony ducked her head whenever she could and wished desperately for her baseball cap. Sunglasses. Fake teeth. *Anything* to alter her appearance! How could she have forgotten this part of the day?

If the paparazzi got hold of this story, she could only imagine the headlines they'd come up with. *Hot Billionairess Drives Hot Rod*, or something equally groan-worthy.

Short of bolting for her car and trying for a fast getaway, she was stuck, arms firmly grasped by an oblivious Julie and a mildly concerned Jordan. Which was lucky for the young, local reporter who hounded them after the award ceremony.

"How does it feel to be part of an all-female sweep?"

"I suppose about the same as it does to be part of an all-male group," Shot answered cheekily.

The reporter tried a few more times before giving up, and Harmony wondered if it was her imagination or of he'd homed in on her discomfort. Either way, she had the uneasy feeling that he wasn't done with her.

"You better hurry up and get those tires changed." Shot tossed her keys in the air and caught them. "I'm hungry."

Rolling her eyes, Jordan dropped the tailgate on her truck, revealing Harmony's street-legal tires. "Get over here and give me a hand, then."

Julie and Harmony handled removing the slicks while Jordan and a slightly grumpy Shot put the regular tires back on in record time.

"See you at the Monkey Wrench!" Julie hopped on her bike.

"You comin'?" Shot leaned against Harmony's car, eyebrows raised. The Monkey Wrench was the local bar and grill, and would be jam-packed with semi-inebriated racers and crew by now.

"Try and stop me." Harmony finished off her water bottle and threw it away. "I never pass up a good steak dinner." Besides which, they always ate there after a race. That wasn't going to change just because now someone knew she was a 'church girl.'

Shot grunted and got in her own vehicle.

Despite herself, Harmony kept an eye out for Grant as she made her way to the exits. She didn't see him, but once again Border Wars Raceway's policy of having a separate exit for racers paid off. Ducking out before fans invaded the pits en force was a survival skill she'd perfected.

Unfortunately, she couldn't avoid the congratulatory honks and waves that followed her to the restaurant, so she waved back as cheerfully as she could, but still took an extra turn around the block before parking in the back lot in the hopes of losing them.

Bean Foley, a tall, slender man with prematurely gray hair, led his patrons in a round of applause as they entered. "I hear congratulations are in order!" He beckoned to a hostess and instructed her, "Dinner's on the house for this party."

Harmony and Jordan exchanged amused glances. Shrewd move. He'd do twice as much business tonight by having all four of today's winners eating there.

"Hope y'all are ready to autograph napkins," Jordan muttered as they followed the hostess to a prominently placed table.

"Bring it." Julie wriggled her fingers and giggled.

"Will you have your usuals tonight?" asked Daren, their waiter.

Harmony sat back while the others made mild to moderate upgrades to their dinners, then shook her head when her turn came.

"Same old, same old for me, please."

"Aw, don't be a stick in the mud." Julie pouted. "You could've at least ordered a fancy dessert!"

Harmony chuckled. "Guess so."

"Their chocolate pecan pie is worth the calories," observed Shot mildly. She was coming to accept the fact that Harmony-before and Harmony-after the church 'reveal' were one and the same person.

"Yeah?" That was high praise from Shot, who counted calories like a miser counted pennies. "I'll have to try it." She preferred their gooey, chocolate chip skillet cookie with ice cream, but it was more important to her to stay on good terms with Shot.

"Ooooh, lookie over there." Julie's elbows came to rest on the table, her hand partially covering her mouth as she nodded toward the door. "Who's the man-candy?"

Even as Harmony rolled her eyes, she obligingly flicked a glance in the general direction—and stopped breathing. *Grant*, of all people, was coming into the Monkey Wrench. A very different looking Grant from the button-down and slacks man who'd helped with her tire. This Grant looked…chiseled. His cerulean polo shirt hugged muscles she hadn't noticed before. His perfectly combed hair was now windblown, tempting a woman to reach up and smooth it back down for him.

She swallowed. How did he manage to look so rugged and yet vulnerable at the same time?

Shot leaned forward, a slightly predatory gleam in her eyes. "Where's he been hiding all season?"

"Put your eyes back in your heads," Jordan

groaned. "You're embarrassing me."

"*We're* embarrassing you?" scoffed Shot. "How about them?" She gestured with one elbow toward the bar.

Reluctantly, Harmony forced her attention away from where Grant still stood, politely waiting for someone to seat him, to where Shot had indicated. A group of young women at the bar had also noticed Grant. Young, attractive women in, um, attention-grabbing outfits.

Harmony came to her feet in the same instant that one of them slid off her stool. Her motion attracted the other woman's attention for an instant and she knew she had to act fast.

Striding forward, she arranged her face in a welcoming smile.

"You made it!" Putting her hand on Grant's arm, she came up on her tiptoes and brushed a kiss across his cheek. Was it the contact or his late-evening stubble that left her lips tingling?

What are you doing? she asked herself belatedly. She was so close to him that she felt his breath on her cheek when he spoke.

"Harmony?"

The surprise in his tone did nothing to assuage her sudden second-guessing, but, remembering the vamps at the bar, she shored up her faltering smile. At least he'd remembered her name!

"C'mon." She tugged at his arm. "I want

you to meet my friends.”

“Um…okay.”

She practically dragged him over to the table where her friends were waiting with open mouths. Shot’s ‘deer in the headlights’ would’ve been funny under any other circumstances. Apparently there was a lot she didn’t know ‘church girls’ could—and would—do.

“Everyone, this is Grant.” She bit her tongue to stop herself from launching into an explanation of how she knew him. Of how *little* she knew about him! “Grant, this is Jordan. Shot. And Julie.” The women nodded their heads in turn.

“It’s a pleasure to meet you.” Grant’s wide smile seemed to take them all in.

“Hi.” Julie didn’t move visibly, but the chair nearest him slid out a few inches from the table.

“Oh, he can’t stay,” Harmony hastily inserted.

“I can’t?” He looked down as she looked up and for a slow heartbeat their lips were dangerously close.

“Course, you might prefer a table for two…” Shot’s amused tone snapped her out of it.

“I should’ve said that you don’t have to stay.” Harmony shifted, putting a few extra inches between them.

“Are you here with friends?” Jordan craned

her neck to see around him until he shook his head.

"Flying solo tonight." He flashed a megawatt smile at the group, then shifted his focus to Harmony. "I'd love to join you."

Releasing his arm, Harmony allowed him to pull her chair out for her. Felt his knee brush against hers as he seated himself beside her.

"So, what am I interrupting?" He grinned, his attention evenly divided again.

"A celebration." Shot leaned to one side to let a server place her drink.

Jordan nodded at Grant. "What'll you have?"

"Water, please."

"What?" Julie wrinkled her nose disdainfully. "You can't toast with water!"

"I manage to," Harmony pointed out as her own glass of water was set before her.

"Did you say water?" Daren double-checked. At Grant's nod, he signaled another server to bring a glass over. "Are you ready to order, sir?"

"I, um…" Not finding any menus on the table, Grant shot a look at Harmony, almost as if to remind her that she'd gotten him into this.

"Best steak in the county," she suggested.

"Steak it is." Anticipating the next question, Grant added, "Medium-well, with a vegetable side dish, please."

"You got it."

"About that toast." Jordan raised her glass. "To the four best drivers on the track today."

Though Harmony felt slightly self-conscious with Grant there, she nevertheless tapped her glass against the others. After they'd all sipped, Shot held her glass out for another toast.

"To next season and many more victory dinners."

Harmony's stomach sank as she took her sip. Would she even be there for the next season? She doubted it. Especially if today's picture of her at the track got noticed by a savvy reporter.

Chapter 4

Grant deftly fielded the questions about his life—including the rather blunt 'You married?' from Julie. It wasn't altogether unlike his old job, to be honest. Except that he wasn't trying to worm his way into their wallets, even for charity. In fact, after accidentally crashing their party, he felt obligated to make it up to them.

"I'll take the check," he informed the server who'd come by for the dozenth time to check on them. He had to raise his voice to be heard over the raucous music and clientele, which meant the entire table heard him.

In response to his gallant offer, the server smirked and the women giggled. Harmony edged closer, the scent of her soap and light, flowery perfume a delightful respite from the nose-burning scents of alcohol and body odor.

"Our meals are on the house," she explained.

"Oh." He blinked. "I didn't…"

"That was very thoughtful of you. Thanks." Harmony's hand came to rest lightly on his.

Generous, too. She didn't know many men who could pay for five meals at the Monkey Wrench, plus alcohol, without flinching. Single. Good-looking. Rich, too? She gave herself a hard mental shake. None of that mattered. She wasn't in the market for a boyfriend.

"I guess I'll take my check, then." He put on his best fake smile, the one he'd perfected in front of a mirror.

"No worries, bro." Daren slapped his shoulder lightly. "Bean said to count you in with our celebs tonight." With that, he vanished back into the crowd.

Thoroughly nonplussed, Grant asked no one in particular, "Bean?"

"The man'ger. Y'know, the guy that owns the plashe." Julie shoved a lock of purple-auburn hair out of her eyes. "Tall, shkinny guy."

"You're drunk," muttered Shot.

Julie shrugged. "Little."

"C'mon." Harmony slid her chair back. Shot wasn't that many drinks behind Julie. "Let's get you guys poured into taxis and headed home." She'd been about to leave, anyway. Most of Bean's customers came to eat and talk about cars, but the later it got, the rowdier the crowd became.

"Good idea." Julie nodded and got up. Swayed.

Jordan, who never drank more than a beer per meal, assisted Shot in maneuvering a fairly straight line to the door.

That left Harmony to help Julie, which she didn't mind—and to see Grant slip some bills under the edge of his plate! She ducked her head when he came over to help with Julie, pretending she hadn't noticed.

"You're handshome," Julie giggled.

"Kind of you to say," he smiled.

And that was that. The smart taxi drivers were lined up outside, waiting for fares. Harmony made sure to pick one she knew, then sent Julie home.

"Hey, girl." Jordan, who'd just performed the same service for Shot, came over for a hug. "Reckon you're smart not to drink." She patted her on the back. "Someday maybe I'll give it a try."

"No time like the present," Harmony suggested quickly.

Jordan chuckled. "Next you'll be inviting me to church."

"Any time." Harmony held her breath as their eyes met.

"Yeah." Jordan scrubbed her hand through her short, dark hair. "I'll think about it. We got one of your churches here in Topaz, y'know."

"Great." Harmony stopped short of telling Jordan to call or text, she'd be right over to go to church with her. It hurt to remember that she might have to leave at any time and wouldn't be there for her friend. "See you around."

"Later." Jordan waved at someone behind Harmony and headed for her truck.

"So, Harmony."

The sound of Grant's voice, nearly at her ear, made her jump. She pivoted so she was facing him.

"Um…" He rubbed the back of his neck.

Perplexed, she almost mimicked his gesture. Allowed several seconds to tick by, then gave a mental shrug. "Well. Night." Digging into her pocket for her keys, she started for her car.

"Actually…" He half-reached for her arm, then brought his hand back to his side when she turned to face him. "I, um, have a confession to make." He grimaced. "I didn't drive myself here. I rode with a guy from Cadmia. He said the races would be fun."

"And then bailed on you?" She deduced from his reluctance to make eye contact.

"Basically." He ran his fingers through his hair. "He said he was going to a bar down the street, that he'd pick me up here later, but I texted him just now and—I guess he's not done yet," he finished lamely.

She blew out a breath. "Even if he came back for you, you don't really want to ride with a drunk driver, do you?"

Grant shook his head vehemently.

"I saw you leave a tip." She hadn't meant to accuse him, but who did he think he was kidding? If he wanted to ride with her, fine. This was hardly the smoothest excuse she'd ever heard, though.

"Oh, that." Embarrassed, he shoved his

hands into his pockets. "That was the last of my cash." He lifted his shoulders at her incredulous stare. "I hoped you'd give me a lift. I mean, we do live in the same town." He wilted under her continued scrutiny. "I guess I can go try to get some of it back."

"Seriously?" She pinched the bridge of her nose. "You don't have," she waved broadly, "a credit card?" He shook his head and in desperation she suggested, "No pay-car-ride app on your phone?" She'd never bothered with them herself and couldn't for the life of her think what they were properly called.

"A what now?"

She burst out laughing at his bewildered expression. "Never mind." Defeated, she gestured toward her car. "C'mon, you goof. I'm parked over here."

He couldn't help staring at the car she led him to. "This…is yours?"

Her forehead puckered as she pretended to study her vehicle. "Golly, now that you mention it, I'm not sure. There are so many electric blue cars around that I have to be so careful to get the right one." She cocked her head to one side and peeked at him from under her lashes to see how he'd take the ribbing.

Grant squinted at her in the dim light, then barked a laugh. "Okay, okay. Ask a dumb question and you deserve the answer you get."

His mixing of clichés took her by surprise

and she chuckled. "All aboard."

The radio lit up when she turned on the engine and President Russell M. Nelson's voice flooded the car. "Ooops." She reached for the power button. "Forgot I left that on." She almost always listened to Conference talks or scriptures after drag racing. It helped her relax.

Grant's cool, slim fingers grasped her wrist lightly, stopping her. Her pulse leapt under his touch and he had difficulty recalling what he'd been about to say.

"I love this talk." Their eyes met and, as the interior dome light dimmed, he had the strangest longing to brush his lips across hers.

"Me, too." Hardly sparkling banter, but it was the best she could do with him staring at her like…like she was some kind of Venus de Milo, Queen Esther, and Miss America rolled into one.

Absent-mindedly, he stroked his thumb across her soft inner wrist. "You're a Latter-day Saint?"

Swallowing, she nodded. Extracted her hand and settled it on the steering wheel where it wouldn't tremble. Backed out and started to edge her way out of Topaz.

When she'd gotten control of her voice again she asked, "I take it you are, too?"

"Born and raised." He nodded back. They were on the street now, moving toward Cadmia, the talk still playing quietly in the background.

All thoughts of banter faded into irrelevance as they listened to a prophet of God preaching of Christ and His restored gospel. She didn't shut it off until the choir began to sing.

She warned herself not to read too much into Grant's lengthy perusal. On the other hand, she was having trouble focusing on driving while she had a passenger who gave her goosebumps simply by looking at her.

"It was nice, what you did back there."

She thought that was a weird way to put it, but… "You're welcome."

"Pardon?" He leaned closer, then laughed. "Oh, yes, thanks for the ride. What I meant, though, was the way you took care of your friends when they'd been drinking." It occurred to him that she might have done the same thing with him—popped him into a cab and gone on with her life. He was glad she hadn't.

He couldn't see much of her in the faint glow of the dash lights, but he found he didn't care. More important than his physical attraction to her—and he'd be lying if he claimed he wasn't—was her intriguing personality. On the two occasions of their meeting, she'd been assertive yet gracious. Flirtatious, but not…suggestive. Even as he'd helped with her tire, he'd read competent independence between the lines. In short, she made him wonder if he'd found his ideal woman.

Too bad he was too busy getting the hang of having time to have a life to start dating.

"As you say, they are my friends." She gripped the wheel a little tighter. His cologne had been teasing her all night. It was an alluring mix of cedar and an elusive something that reminded her of spring walks in the park near her childhood home. She'd gotten small whiffs of it throughout the evening whenever a waiter walked past—mixed with whatever the waiter was carrying, so everything from onion rings to spareribs. Being alone with him in an enclosed space with it was an entirely different matter.

She didn't know what it was called, but she certainly had a suggestion. *Distraction.*

"So, where you from, Doc?" She slipped into the local syntax without thinking.

"Why do you keep calling me Doc?"

"Ummm." She lifted her thumbs from the steering wheel in an abbreviated palms-up "I don't know" gesture. "Suits you, I guess."

"Funny." He drummed his fingers against his leg in wordless debate with himself. "I am a doctor." He hadn't decided whether or not to pursue Missouri licensing, but it was an option.

"You are?" She felt as shocked as she sounded. What were the odds? "What kind?"

He chuckled. "I worked in pediatrics for a while. Then spent four years as an E.R. doctor."

Forgetting how dark it had gotten inside the

car, she tried to look at him. To see if he was serious or not.

"You want to know how old I am." He suppressed a sigh. "It's okay. I'm used to it. I turned thirty-one on my last birthday."

Something in his tone of voice made her startled protest die on her lips. It reminded her so much of her own, deeply visceral response to being told she couldn't race because she was a woman. Who was she to tell him he was too young to be a doctor?

"How old were you when you got your degree?" she asked carefully.

"I got my medical degree at nineteen." He waited for her to laugh at him or challenge him in some way. When she didn't, he relaxed even more. Not quite enough to tell her about getting his GED at twelve. "After my residency, I worked in pediatrics because I liked helping the kids. Watching them get better."

He lapsed into a brief silence while he thought back over his patients, some of whom he was still in touch with. "Eventually, I moved to the E.R. because I enjoyed the challenge. There were no quiet days."

"What made you decide to leave it?" Switching on her turn signal, she turned off the highway and onto Cadmia's one main road.

"A bigger challenge." He stared unseeingly at the windshield as he again reflected on his past. "There was a massive pileup one day. I don't even know how many cars were involved, but there were so many victims that the ambulances ran according to need, not hospital affiliation. We were the closest, so we got the patients in the worst condition." He didn't notice his hands closing and opening as he spoke. "I operated for six hours straight, one patient after another. Among the first was a young woman. They hadn't been able to get in touch with her family, but she was wearing a medical bracelet."

Facing her suddenly, he leaned forward. "Her doctor's office didn't just provide blood type and allergies. He used a video call to be present during her surgery."

"Wow, that's…" She couldn't think what to call it. Unheard of?

"I'd never seen anything like it." Nearly throwing himself back against the seat, he blew out a breath. "When they called me to ask if I'd consider working for them, I couldn't believe it."

"How exciting!" Except she could already hear a sort-of-sour note in his voice.

"It was, at first. There were no limits. I could run as many tests as I needed in order to make the correct diagnosis. Their equipment was cutting edge." He paused to gather his thoughts. While he enjoyed not having to sugarcoat everything anymore, he didn't want what he had to say to come out wrong.

"What went wrong?" She signaled to turn

down his road.

"My patients, they…" He shook his head. "They had this symptom or that one and I ran tests, then sent them to our specialists. Chased things around in circles so long I started getting a complex. Until finally our chief of staff called me into his office and explained that…" He hesitated.

"Explained what?" Pulling into his driveway, she shifted into park and turned to look at him, puzzled. Her car's approach triggered a motion-activated light somewhere, so she could barely make out the bitter twist of his lips.

"That the majority of my patients were suffering from a severe case of boredom." He watched her eyes widen as her head jerked back in surprise.

"You're joking." Not that she was amused. Medicine was serious business. Doctors, in her experience, were all too likely to label what they couldn't immediately explain as "imagination." She had her own mother's death as an excellent example of that.

He flinched at her flat tone. Held both hands palms up. "Sadly, no. I mean, some patients had legitimate complaints. I enjoyed working with them to figure things out." He shook his head. "However, unless that area was filled with a statistically improbable number of patients suffering from undiscovered and untreatable conditions…" His voice trailed off. What else could he say?

Or perhaps the question was, why had he said so much? This was the first time in years that he'd spent any kind of time with an attractive woman who was also a member and he'd talked about himself for pretty much the entire drive. *Smooth, Grant. Real smooth.*

"You are single, right?"

She froze, her hand on the gear shift. "What?"

He blinked just as the security light outside switched off, plunging them back into darkness. Ran his hand down his face.

"I said that out loud, didn't I?"

Faintly amused, she shifted into reverse. "Good night, Doc."

"Yeah." Groaning inwardly, he unbuckled his seat belt and opened his door. "See you at church."

He expected her to pull away the second her passenger door closed, but she stayed right there, her car idling softly. Perplexed, he stooped to look into the window. Since the security light had come back on all he could see was his reflection until she rolled the window down.

"Is something wrong?"

"Force of habit." She shrugged. "I never leave until my friends are safely inside."

He nodded once, slowly. "Very wise." Started to straighten, then bent again to ask,

"Would you like to come inside?" Her eyebrows began to lift and he hastily added, "I could make us some hot chocolate? It's the least I can do."

"That's…nice of you to offer." She recognized the desperate note in his voice when she heard it, she just couldn't figure out its cause. "I'm pretty tired, though."

"And it's late." He supplied the next excuse as evenly as he could. Mustered up a smile for her. "Some other time?" In his world, that was synonymous with "tomorrow." As in, it never came, either.

"Great." She didn't put much effort into sounding interested. For all his charisma earlier, she thought he'd fallen awfully flat during prolonged exposure.

She pondered that all the way home from his place. Then lay awake, wondering how a man could be so appealing one minute, then be a smug-but-awkward twit the next. It was almost as bad as taking a bite of a chocolate chip cookie that turned out to be raisin.

Rolling onto her side, she flipped her hair off her face and snuggled into her pillow. Oh well. It was a good thing she didn't really care about Grant. A boyfriend was a complication she absolutely didn't need.

Where should she move the next time she was discovered? Florida? Mmmm, no. She'd had enough humidity for a lifetime. Alaska? Arizona? Ha, maybe she'd go through the states alphabetically tomorrow, skipping the ones she'd already been to. Make a pros and cons list for comparison.

She could always go back to Europe. Lydia could join her after graduation in May. Lydia had never left North America and would get a huge kick out of it.

Rolling onto her other side, she tried getting comfortable. Sure, she left everything behind when she moved, but she also had the adventure of discovering everything all over again. Most people got stuck in their comfortable ruts, only venturing out under such dire circumstances as having their favorite restaurant close for renovations. Or if their dentist retired.

Her? Every couple of years she pulled up stakes and planted herself somewhere brand new. New restaurants. New sights. New people. A new her if she wanted.

Her smile began to fade and she let it. Who was she kidding? Moving used to be fun.

Until it hit her a few moves back.

The faces and street names were different, but that was all. The people in the next town would be eerily familiar. She'd meet someone poor. Someone outgoing. A grudge holder. An apologist. A snob. A busybody. Sort of like meeting the ghosts of all the friends and enemies she'd left behind.

Yeah. Some fun.

Chapter 5

Harmony sat in the back at church the next day. Way back, in the corner. Eyes closed in silent prayer, she didn't remember until too late that this was the domain of young mothers.

"Arthur, sit down!" A beleaguered mother of four hissed at her oldest. Her husband had his hands full with their twins, which left her holding a fussing baby, who'd just been awakened by a curious Arthur.

The bishop hadn't even finished making the announcements, and Harmony could already tell that it was going to be a long Sacrament meeting. Sympathetic toward the young family, Harmony caught Arthur's attention by holding up a hymnal.

"Arthur?" Opening the hymn book, she offered his mother a friendly smile. "Can you help me find the page?" The little boy came over eagerly and she patted the chair beside her. "You'll have to sit down."

He thought it over for a moment, then allowed her to help him up. He was still struggling with the three-digit page number when the organist began playing "I Stand All Amazed," but Harmony knew the hymn by heart.

"I stand all amazed at the love Jesus offers me, confused at the grace that so fully He proffers me." Her eyes were damp as she helped

Arthur hold the book up when he finally found the right page, so he could pretend to sing along.

She felt a slight pang when Arthur slipped his small hand in hers for each of the Sacrament prayers. This was another reason to look forward to her sister's eighteenth birthday. Settling somewhere permanently would mean she could finally start dating in earnest. Hopefully get married and have a family of her own. Assuming she could find someone whose feet didn't turn to clay when they learned how much 'gold' was in her piggybank.

All too soon the meeting ended and Arthur's mother came to collect him.

"Thank you so much." She wagged a finger at her young son. "Somebody has too much energy this morning." She mouthed another 'thank you' as she took Arthur's hand and left.

"Hi."

Jarred out of her wistful reverie, Harmony accidentally glared up at Grant.

"Wow, somebody got up on the wrong side of the bed." He helped himself to the empty seat beside her. There wasn't much time till Sunday school started and he didn't know anyone else. At least, that's the excuse he gave himself for sitting next to the prettiest woman in the room.

He calls me grumpy and sits down next to me anyway. Amused, Harmony couldn't help smiling.

"Hey, that's better." The corners of his own mouth began turning up in response. "Quite nice, in fact."

"Are you flirting with me, Doc?" She couldn't believe she'd asked him that.

His smile vanished. "I'd rather you called me Grant, if you don't mind."

Suitably chastened, she nodded slowly. "Of course, Grant." The creases in his forehead smoothed out and his smile came back.

"Thanks."

Inexplicably, her stomach fluttered. Alarm bells started going off and she reflexively put some space between them. Shifted so her body was facing forward instead of angling toward him.

Luckily, she saw that Sister Phillips, the Sunday school teacher, was making a point of setting a music stand up in the center of the front of the room.

"We better behave," she warned him stiffly.

Following the direction of her gaze, he lifted an eyebrow but obediently turned his attention to the woman he assumed was the teacher. He'd gotten a lot out of his study of 1st and 2nd Thessalonians.

Especially 1st Thessalonians 3:12, which read, "And the Lord make you to increase and abound in love one toward another, and toward all men, even as we do toward you…"

He'd known he needed a change when he realized he'd begun to detach from his patients.

He listened to complaints, processed symptoms, and spit out diagnoses like a machine. No longer finding any similarities between himself as a doctor and the Master Healer, he'd quit and moved.

He hoped to return to medicine. Someday. When he could do it justice.

Odd how Harmony persisted in calling him Doc. Stranger still was the lift it gave him. Like…like a sunbeam had broken through the clouds that hung over his head.

He leaned over to remark on a comment someone had made—and found her chair empty. Startled, he straightened. Looked around, even going so far as standing up a little to get a better view. She was nowhere in sight.

Harmony rubbed the back of her neck as she paced the length of the hallway. Turned right to follow the horseshoe.

"Sister Wells?" Bishop Larsen jerked to a stop in time to keep from running over her.

"B…Bishop," she faltered. He wasn't exactly the last person she wanted to see, yet she suddenly felt like a kid caught cutting class. Probably because she *was* cutting class.

His face softened and he touched her arm gently. "Is everything alright, Sister Wells?"

She didn't answer right away. Outright lying wasn't an option. She couldn't even bring herself to fib to the bishop.

"No." If everything was alright, she'd be in

Sunday school, where she should be.

"Anything I can do to help?" The corners of his eyes crinkled with concern as he searched her face.

Jerkily, she shook her head 'no.' She knew without a doubt that he'd do his best to help. She just couldn't come up with anything for him to do. So for now, she'd have to settle for trying to distract herself from the too-appealing Doctor Grant with...

Just then, she spotted Ken and perked up. Ken wasn't much more interesting than sitting at home talking to herself, but that was exactly what made him her ideal date for the time being.

"Excuse me." She smiled at the bishop and moved to intercept Ken.

"Harmony." Ken grinned at her. "You look great."

She squirmed slightly, the hope in his eyes a little too bright for her comfort. They'd only gone on a few casual dates, and now he was looking at her like he had permanent plans for their relationship.

Sure, she knew how to weaponize her looks and charm when necessary. This, though. She hadn't meant to give him the wrong signals. Changing her mind, she opened her mouth to ask about his sister, whether he had one or not.

"Are you busy on Wednesday?" He beat her to it.

"Um…Halloween?" She tried to laugh.

"Yeah." He leaned closer. "I thought we could try that new place in Fireclay, the Blue Plate Café. They've got karaoke and," he gestured expansively, words seeming to fail him, "everything."

Everything? She forced herself to keep a straight face as she thought back on meals in France, Italy, Africa. Sitting on a sunbaked beach while being served authentic Australian barbecue.

"I'm busy on Wednesday. Out of town, actually." She'd just decided to make her New Orleans' pick up a little early.

"Okay, how about next week?"

Seeing his determination, she gave in. "Sounds too good to pass up." What else could she say? She didn't want to hurt his feelings. Yep, she'd need every minute between now and then to figure out the best way to friend zone' him.

"Great." That must be his favorite word. "What time shall I pick you up?"

"Hmm?" She caught up with the conversation in time to shake her head before he could repeat himself. She might be committed to going out with him, but if things went the way she now hoped it would be an extremely awkward ride back, so… "I'll be making deliveries in that area on Wednesday anyway. Alright if I meet you there?" *Hey, that was a pretty good start.*

She followed up with a "one of the guys" swat on his arm and left without waiting for his response. "See ya."

A bell rang as she walked away, signaling the end of classes. Ducking out the nearest door, she walked halfway around the church building to reach her car, kicking at stray leaves on her way.

Some disciple of Christ she was, getting so distracted by Grant that she couldn't sit through Sunday school. Not that that was the whole story, she amended. To be honest, her current mood had started a few days ago. She missed Lydia. She missed having a life that wasn't half a lie.

"Just a few more months." She muttered that over and over as she drove home, where she stubbornly watched general conference videos for the rest of the day.

She spent the next two days running herself ragged with her business, cramming a week's worth of deliveries into thirty-six hours.

"You're sure this is more convenient for you?" Diane asked, frowning doubtfully as she helped carry boldly labeled boxes from Harmony's car.

Diane was one of a select few of Harmony's clients who acted as distribution hubs for her, saving her hours of travel time by either holding boxes for pickup by her further-flung clients or occasionally going the extra mile themselves. It was the very definition of a win-win situation as far as Harmony was concerned, since she could use their help as an excuse to lower or eliminate what she would've charged them.

"Yeah, you bet. And don't worry, nobody's expecting it right away. Delivery the first week of the month as usual will be just fine."

Harmony set the last box of allergen-free products on top of the stack and took a moment to catch her breath. Her eyes raked over the room, its good natured disarray revealing so much about the income level of this small family. The half-broken chair that had to be sat in 'just so.' The neatly patched clothing on their toddlers. The third- and fourth-hand toys they were playing with.

On the one hand, she'd have happily traded her trust fund for a home exactly like this. The kids and their patched clothes were clean. When the toys broke, they had a special hospital for them where they solemnly assisted while Dad made repairs. And Diane always laughed when she referred to that dumb chair, saying they'd fix it someday. Really.

On the other hand, Harmony was worried about them. She had been from the beginning, which was the root cause of all her "distribution centers," as well as the referral program. Any client could get ten percent off their order per new client family they brought in.

It took a little juggling, but in Diane's case she hadn't charged them more than fifty dollars a month for the last two years. Less when she could convince them she'd found a sale or whatever.

Now that she was getting closer to leaving, guilt rode her shoulders like gum in a toddler's hair. They'd never be able to get these products at these prices anywhere else.

"Harmony?" Concern warmed Diane's eyes as she touched her friend's arm. "Would you like to sit a minute? Warm up over a cup of tea?"

The offer made Harmony smile despite herself. Ever since they'd discussed the word of wisdom last summer, Diane kept a box of tea-plant-free 'tea' on hand just for Harmony.

"Thanks, but I've got another stop to make."

"All this extra effort for a business trip." Diane rubbed her lower back and stretched from side to side. "Must be important for you to do it so sudden-like."

The truth wouldn't have made sense, not even over a lengthy cup of 'tea,' so Harmony just smiled.

"That, and I like a bit of chaos in my life."

Diane hooted at that. "If you like chaos that much, you can borrow the munchkins for a week. Tomorrow's Halloween and after that comes the sugar rush."

Harmony cracked up and tried not to hug her too hard. Noting a certain heaviness in Diane's step, along with the oddly pasty color of her skin, Harmony decided to tuck some prenatal vitamin 'samples' in their next box. Just in case Diane knew anyone who could use them, of course.

At home that night, Harmony threw some shirts and jeans into a duffel bag. She'd only be gone a couple of days. Just long enough to shake the doldrums. See a show. Eat somewhere besides Blinky's. Avoid thinking about Ken. She stopped to massage the bridge of her nose. Pretend like she was a normal, footloose-and-fancy free single female.

She was still convincing herself the next morning when she arrived at Cadmia's tiny airport. Buying her own airplane seemed a little extravagant at first, but she enjoyed flying so much that now she couldn't imagine how she'd lived without it.

"Hey, lady." Bob, the airport's mechanic-handyman, finished shoving the door to her hangar open and paused for a long, leisurely look at her. "Flying my way?"

"Ha, ha." She rolled her eyes. "You've gotta invest in a new pun, Romeo."

He grinned. "That mean you don't need a navigator?" He tried to steal a kiss as she walked past and she pushed her duffel into his arms instead.

"'Fraid not." She'd only gone out with him twice, but he didn't seem to get the message.

Chuckling, he stowed her duffel for her, then found a place to lounge where he could watch her do her preflight checklist.

For her part, she ignored him. She'd learned over the years that men either did or didn't notice her. She'd never gone in for form-fitting outfits or the like, but that didn't seem to matter. Even in her baggiest clothes, she'd had to deal with unsought attentions.

"Okay, good to go."

"Don't get lost."

She stifled the urge to encourage him to do exactly that. Waving, she climbed into the cockpit. In a matter of minutes, she was hundreds of feet up in the air, Cadmia shrinking to a flyspeck behind her.

She drew her first easy breath in days as she banked toward New Orleans. She'd booked a hotel and had tickets to a musical she hadn't seen in far too long, all paid for by savings from her last job. Her business in Cadmia barely broke even.

For the next two days, she did nothing she didn't want to do. She flirted with her waiter at the hotel's fancy restaurant. She spent an entire day being pampered at a five-star spa. Naturally, she ordered room service. Went to bed early and slept late. Rented an exquisite gown in shocking red for the musical.

All eyes followed her as she entered the theater. Thankfully, the headlines were still full from the local Halloween doings the night before and there wasn't a reporter in sight.

"Harmony?" A sleek blond on the edge of a mildly intoxicated group eyed her with interest. "Is that you?"

Ice-cold dread replaced the warm, secure feeling that had accompanied Harmony all the way from the hotel. Fortunately, she'd mentally prepared for just such a nightmare. So she did just as she'd rehearsed—she kept walking.

"Harmony?" The woman persisted, going so far as to clumsily take her by the arm.

Harmony ran through a set of canned responses, starting with surprise, then shifting to mild irritation as she shook her arm free. Addressed none other than Hillary Murray in flawless Greek.

"Whoa!" Hillary reeled like she'd been slapped. "What'd you say?" She planted a fist on a cocked hip, apparently ready to start a fight.

Harmony fixed her former college roommate with a frigid stare. "Who are you?" she asked in heavily accented English. She cringed as she watched the tipsy ex-model wipe her mouth on her sleeve, smearing lipstick across her face.

"Hey, Hillary!" A man lurched in their direction and she turned toward him.

Harmony seized the moment and walked

away, head up, shoulders back but relaxed. Calm, measured steps took her to her seat, where she gave the show her full attention.

In fact, she refused to think about the potential consequences of the sighting. At all. Based on past experience, Hillary wouldn't remember a thing about it. And, Harmony flattered herself that she'd carried off the encounter brilliantly.

Best of all, no matter what Hillary did or didn't do—or who she did or didn't tell—Harmony was done with New Orleans in the morning. Anyway, if someone did happen to spot her picture from the track, having a false sighting way over here might work to her advantage in the long run. Sort of like a magician using redirection in their act.

She was still telling herself that when she checked out of the hotel.

After dropping her rental car off at the local lot, she changed taxis twice on her way to the airport. Arriving promptly at seven a.m., she took delivery of her allergen-free products, and boarded her plane.

As she flew back to Cadmia, the sun rose behind her, dusting the landscape with gold until it looked like she was a landing away from a mythical kingdom. Oh, she loved flying. *Hmm.* Maybe she should keep her plane when she moved. She already had a for sale ad out on her Firebird, but if she flew to her next destination, wherever that was, it would minimize her trail. Something to think about, anyway.

Transferring her gear from the plane to her car, she headed out. Not for home, but for a dingy little storage unit she'd rented when she moved there. Taking an empty box out of her trunk, she carried it under her arm while she walked back to 4J and unlocked it.

Switching the light on revealed an old camping chair, a rickety table, and a single, precious cell phone. Closing the door behind her as she walked in, Harmony set the box down. Her heart soared as she scooped up the phone and battery, fitted them together, and watched it light up.

Dialing the only number programmed into the phone, she held her breath.

"Harmony?" Lydia's voice came through loud and clear. "Good grief, it's about time! I was starting to think you weren't going to call."

"As if." Harmony scoffed to hide the emotions running rampant through her. "It's the first of the month. I'm going to call."

"You didn't…that one time."

Harmony's shoulders tightened. No, she hadn't. Not *that one time* when she'd had a one-in-a-million bad day and bumped into one of the reporters who'd hounded her after her mother's death.

She hadn't even gone back to pack up her apartment that day.

"I'm fine, sweetheart." She pinched the bridge of her nose and tilted her head back in an effort to keep from crying. "How are you? How's school?" The answering groan brought a vivid mental image to mind of Lydia, curled up on her bed and making faces at the phone.

"Ugh, don't mention school to me."

Harmony translated that as, 'I'm fine, too.'

A smile played across Harmony's lips as she listened to Lydia's recitation of everything she'd seen or done or thought of doing since the last time they'd talked on October first.

Chapter 6

"And anyway, I think we should go someplace completely different for my birthday this year." Lydia paused. "Florida or…or a cruise to the Bahamas or something."

"Wow! The Bahamas, huh? Just like that?" Harmony grinned. She'd worked as an entertainer on a cruise ship shortly after high school and wondered if that was what gave Lydia the idea.

"Oh, I know we can't go on a normal cruise or anything." Her small sigh tore at Harmony's heart. "But as soon as I'm old enough to claim my inheritance, I'm buying myself a private yacht and we'll go…"

"Wherever you want," Harmony interrupted. "And that's a promise."

"Thanks." Lydia cleared her throat. "Your turn."

"Um, let's see." Laughing, Harmony tried to think of something to tell her. "I won at the track on Saturday."

"That's awesome! I always knew you were a winner!"

They snickered together.

"Seriously, though, that's pretty much it for me. Life's boring and…"

"That's how you like it." Lydia finished with her. "You're not giving me much hope for old age, sis.”

“Old age? Now wait a minute you young whippersnapper.” She grinned at the sound of Lydia’s giggles. “What do you think being an adult means, huh? It means bills and work and…”

“That’ll be lecture number four hundred and thirty-three, Alex,” Lydia interrupted sweetly.

“Okay, you watch waaay too much Jeopardy.”

“Sister Adams likes it. Says it’s educational.” They sat in silence a moment before Lydia asked, “How come you never talk about boys, Harmony?”

Her heart twisted painfully. “Me talk about boys?” Desperately, she tried making a joke out of it. “I think you do enough of that for both of us.”

“Ha, ha, very funny. I mean it, though. Sister Adams was married at twenty-two.”

Rubbing her forehead, Harmony made a mental note to ask Sister Adams to tell Lydia not to worry about her. In the meantime, she’d just have to be honest.

“I think about men, Lydia. It’s a perfectly normal, healthy thing to do.” Getting to her feet, she paced the small enclosure. “It’s just not the right time for me to do anything about it. I don’t know how long I’ll be anywhere, kiddo.” She swallowed. “I might have another bad day and it wouldn't be fair for me to break a man's heart like that." Or her own, if she was being honest. She'd had a couple of close calls with 'nice guys' who got gold fever when they found out who she was.

"Because of me." Lydia sniffled. "You live like a hermit to protect me."

"Because of Dad," Harmony corrected instantly. The drama worried her. Lydia ran away from her safe house at eight years old because she overheard half of a conversation about their dad's behavior and thought Harmony was in danger. "His…shenanigans keep the family name in the public eye, which we're trying to stay out of. You are not to blame for his bad behavior, do you understand me?"

Lydia sniffled again. "Yes, drill sergeant."

Harmony relaxed. Sarcasm, however weak, was a good sign. She'd worked hard to give Lydia a safe place to grow up and be emotionally healthy. No way was she going to let their dad ruin it for them indirectly.

"And, of course, there's the little matter of making sure you didn't get spoiled rotten," she teased. An alarm sounded on her personal cell phone and she sighed. "Look, it's getting late."

"Don't go."

Thumb screws would've been less painful than her sister's whisper.

"I miss you, too." Harmony was back to pinching the bridge of her nose. "Talk to you soon, okay?"

"You better." Lydia's voice shook a little, but she was trying to sound cheerful.

"Night." Harmony forced the word around the lump in her throat.

"Later."

They never said goodbye. No, that was too permanent. They were just apart for a while.

Harmony shut the phone off and plugged it in. Her thumb stroked the phone thoughtfully. She used to say, 'sweet dreams,' until Sister Adams told her that Lydia couldn't sleep after their phone calls. Something about the dog-eared phrase stressed Lydia out so badly that she wasn't able to get her mind off sleeping long enough to get there.

Rubbing a hand over her face, she set the phone down and checked under the table. Her emergency stash was still there. A little money, a set of clean clothes, and a pair of gaudy old sunglasses that she would hate to have to wear.

Satisfied, she put the phone back the way she'd found it and left, making sure the door was closed behind her.

She swung by Noella's to see if her friend needed a ride to Merry's for movie night, but there was no car in the driveway, so she hurried over to join the others. And was surprised to be the first one there.

Pressing the buzzer to announce her arrival, Harmony blew into her cold hands. When the door clicked open, she hurried across Merry's workshop and up the stairs.

"Brrrr!" Harmony hustled out of her coat, left her shoes on the shoe mat, and scurried over to Merry's pellet stove. The temperature change was the worst part about a trip to somewhere warmer.

"Hello to you, too." Merry grinned from where she was stirring rice krispies into melted marshmallows.

"Heyyyy." Harmony gave one more theatrical shiver, then started washing her hands in case Merry needed help with the dessert. "Is it just us tonight?"

Merry chuckled. "Could be."

It took her a moment to realize that Merry was joking. "Yeah, right." Finished drying her hands, she tossed the towel over her shoulder. "Tell me what to do."

They chatted amiably while Harmony pressed the mix into a greased cookie tray. She got a sugar rush just from thinking about the ingredients, and noticed that Merry didn't snitch any, either.

"Oh hey, they're here." Harmony called to Merry, who was busy rinsing out the dirty pots and hadn't heard the buzzer.

"Would you let them in, please?"

"On it." Harmony hurried over and pressed the button that opened the downstairs door.

Noella rushed in, apologizing profusely for being late, only to have Grace upstage her by arriving via Merry's balcony lift box.

"There she is!" Harmony waved Grace over to the kitchen island where they were all working now. "Thought we were going to have to watch *Mr. Scoutmaster* without you."

Her interest in the old black-and-white movie increased when she realized that none of them had ever seen it. They snickered at the dry humor and munched on rice krispie treats until Harmony was firmly resettled in Cadmia.

The semi-sappy ending hit her kind of hard, though. She agreed with Noella's sentiment that the boy in the movie was better off with his adoptive family than he had been with his aunt, but that didn't change the fact that her thoughts were once again fixed on her separation from her sister.

In an attempt to hide her blues, she laughingly volunteered to take the leftover rice krispies that Merry was eager to get rid of. And let herself be talked into volunteering at the ward wood cutting project in the morning.

Noella linked arms with her on their way out to their cars and eyeballed the plate of desserts. "You are braver than I, my friend."

"It helps that I don't really like them," Harmony laughed.

"What? Then why…?"

"I was just trying to help Merry. Besides, I

know right where to find some kids who'll inhale these." Noticing Noella's puzzled expression, Harmony explained the idiom. Funny that she'd never given the idea of 'inhaling food' a second thought.

"I wish I knew where to find a group of children for the play." Noella sighed.

"Hey, did the committee agree to your play?" Harmony was delighted. Noella had tried repeatedly to get the local community theater committee to take a chance on a new play and Mrs. Arnold—aka the 'queen bee' of Cadmia—kept blocking her. Some people just couldn't stand to see someone else win.

"Yes, sort of." Heaving an even more dramatic sigh, Noella explained that the committee voted for *No Time Like the Present* for the annual Christmas charity play, but refused to lift a finger to help put it on.

"Good grief." Harmony snorted her disgust as Noella unlocked her car. "Listen, if you think of anything I can do, I'll be happy to help, okay?"

"Merci, mon amie."

Harmony carefully balanced the plate while she hugged Noella back, then headed home to try to get some sleep before tomorrow's service project.

Somehow, tomorrow always came earlier when there was manual labor to be done and the next morning found Harmony flexing frozen toes in her sneakers. Looking longingly at Merry's insulated work boots. She'd known it would be cold at the woodcutting project, but she'd grossly underestimated Mother Nature's ability to turn flesh and blood into blocks of ice.

The cheerfulness going on all around her did nothing to improve her mood, either.

Six chainsaws—one of them expertly wielded by Merry—buzzed like an army of bumblebees, reducing tree-sized logs to stove-length chunks.

Glumly, she helped Grace rock the latest chunk of trunk onto its side and roll it over to where a group of maul-wielding men were splitting similar chunks into smaller logs.

Another group further down the line sang as they loaded the smaller logs into wheelbarrows to stack on one side of the Tomlinson's barn. Apparently, wood needed time to 'cure' before being used as firewood.

She shook her head in amazement. The sheer scope of the project had eluded her until now.

"Wow." Grace's back popped audibly as she stretched. "I'm not sure how many more of those I can roll."

"Same." Harmony followed Grace's gaze to the other side of the barn, where a human chain passed cured firewood out from a stack to a waiting pickup truck. Another pickup parked beside the first and laughing— *laughing!*

—teens piled out to join the others.

"Last load!" someone called.

Harmony felt marginally better when the others whooped and cheered at the news. Brightened further when Merry turned off her chainsaw.

"Out of gas?" she asked, not wanting to jump to any conclusions.

"Out of oomph." Merry took out her earplugs, set the chainsaw down, and stretched. "I might help stack for a while, but then I'm done."

Harmony grinned. "Awesome. I'm going to check in with Noella before I head out."

"Good luck at the track!" Grace called after her.

She almost stopped to explain that the track was closed for the season, but decided not to bother. Grace didn't actually care about the track.

The heat of the Tomlinson's house hit her like a blowtorch, melting her nose first and starting it running.

"Delightful," she muttered, snagging a napkin as she squeezed through the packed kitchen.

"Harmony!"

"Hey, Noella." She paused to appreciate the beauty of her friend's tired smile. She'd be grumbling like a bear with a sore tooth if she'd gotten stuck in the kitchen the entire time. It might be warm inside, but it was also crowded with loud people.

"Are you hungry? Have you had lunch yet?"

Harmony held up her hand before Noella could leave the dishes to try to serve her. "I'm good, thanks." Sensing an impending stomach growl, she clenched her muscles against it. "I just came in to check on you. Sure you don't want a ride?"

"There is still much to do." Noella smiled serenely as she declined.

Harmony looked at the pile of pots and bit her lip. "You should at least let someone else have a turn at the sink."

"But who?" Noella laughed as if she could see right through Harmony's ploy. "The others have worked just as hard."

"You mean there isn't one person here," Harmony jerked her head at the room in general, "who didn't arrive late just to talk to everyone else and say they came out today?" In her experience, the odds of that happening were astronomical.

Noella didn't respond beyond frowning.

"Harmony!" A woman bustled over just then. "I didn't realize you were here."

Harmony gave her a quick once-over. She was too clean to have been outside working. Or inside, for that matter.

"Sister Rivers, how nice to see you." Nudging Noella out of the way, Harmony handed over her coat and shooed her along. "I was just wishing for someone to help me finish these dishes."

To her credit, Sister Rivers didn't protest very hard before pitching in. In the meantime, Harmony kept an eye on Noella, who was almost instantly swarmed by the younger kids. Eh, at least she was sitting down while she told them a story. And Noella loved kids.

By the time Harmony handed over the final dish for the rinse water, Noella had already left with the Petersons. Satisfied, Harmony retrieved her coat and carried it over her arm all the way to her car, laughing at how different it felt outside after having been trapped inside for so long.

Trapped. She tossed her coat onto the passenger seat of her car and picked her way through the rapidly dwindling parked vehicles to the road. Footloose and fancy free…and trapped.

Turning the radio on loud, she sang along with popular songs all the way to Blinky's. Struggled into her coat as she shuffled across the parking lot. She should've gone home first and taken a hot bath. But she was *starving.*

"Hon!" Susan dropped what she was doing and came out from behind the counter. "What happened? You look like you got run over by a cement mixer!"

"Thanks." Was it weird that it took Susan's blunt concern to finally make her laugh?

"Oh, you know what I mean." Susan rolled her eyes and bustled Harmony over to the nearest booth, seating her with her back to the door. "You wait right there and I'll be out with your order in a jiff."

"Thanks!" Harmony meant it that time. She was so tired and her back hurt so badly she…well, she might wind up spending the night right there in that booth.

Laying her head against the bench, she muttered, "Van Phillips, if I ever lay eyes on you again…" She didn't bother finishing the sentence. The cocky Australian performer who dropped her during their act five years ago on the cruise ship probably couldn't remember her name by now. Her back would never let her forget him, though.

She never knew what would re-aggravate the old injury, either. Sometimes she could spend an entire day rearranging her storeroom without an issue. Other times, like today, it hurt like it was a brand-new injury.

Ooooh. She shivered when the door opened to admit another customer and a gust of frigid wind wafted over her.

Eyeing the distance between herself and the next booth, she decided she could stagger that far if it meant not feeling like she had a table in the freezer.

One. Two. She braced herself for the back pain. *Three!*

She lunged to her feet. And into the arms of…

"Oh, excuse me." Grant looked down at the woman he was holding in self-defense. "Harmony?"

"Hey…Grant." Maybe she should stay by the door after all. It would take a timeout in the freezer to get her cheeks to cool off. The way she was clinging to him wasn't helping ease her embarrassment, either.

"Going somewhere?"

"Hey, Grant," called Susan. "Don't you let her leave! We're almost done making her sandwich."

"No problem." Amused more than anything, Grant tried to remember the last time he'd enjoyed bumping into someone this much.

Harmony licked her lips, preparing to explain, and a fresh wave of heat swept over her when his eyes dropped to her mouth.

"I, um. I just came in for a late lunch."

"Me, too." Eyes twinkling, he started to release her.

A spasm of pain provoked a whimper from her.

"What's wrong?" His eyes narrowed. "Where are you hurting?"

"Relax." Her smile must not have been very convincing, because he definitely didn't relax. "I just have an acute case of good Samaritan back."

"Uh-huh." Okay, he needed to think of something. Not that he minded holding her, but people were starting to notice. His years of practice kicked in. "Let's see if we can't get you comfortable."

"Not there," she pleaded when he started to seat her at the same booth where she'd started. "As long as I'm already up, can't we go one further in? Away from the door?"

"Sure." Bending, he put one arm behind the backs of her thighs and lifted her as if she were a child.

"Whoa, I can walk," she protested.

"Glad to hear it. Can you sit, too?" he teased.

Grumbling, she held still while he lowered her to the next bench.

"Thanks."

"I'll won't be a minute." He slipped out of his coat and dropped it on the booth's other bench.

She opened her mouth to tell him he didn't have to eat with her, but he was already gone. She watched closely as he spoke to Susan. Wasn't sure what to make of his smile as he returned.

"So." Grant slid onto the bench across from her. "How'd you contract this, this... What did you call it?"

"Good Samaritan back," she supplied a little sheepishly. "I got it at the woodcutting project." She managed to lift one shoulder without it hurting too badly. "Guess I'm in worse shape than I realized."

A small smile played across his face as he considered her shape.

"Hot chocolate with orange flavoring." Susan sang out as she unloaded two mugs onto their table.

"Thanks." Grant slipped two fingers through the mug's handle and started to raise it.

"Hey, be careful," Harmony warned. "She makes hot chocolate with the same boiling water she uses to make the specialty coffees."

His eyebrows rose. "They have specialty coffee here?" Picking up the mug, he blew across its top and took a sip. Then another.

"Yeah." Confused, Harmony pushed her mug away from her. Doubts paraded through her mind, starting with wondering if he kept the word of wisdom. If he did, why was he interested in the coffee options?

"This is pretty good." Puzzled by her rejection of the hot chocolate, he guessed, "Unless you don't like orange?"

"Orange is fine."

The subsequent silence was so loud he couldn't hear the other customers.

"You don't have to worry about burning your mouth," he tried. "I asked her to put an ice cube in each mug."

"That's…that's brilliant." Her jaw dropped

and she peered into her mug. "I wish I'd thought of that a long time ago!" The ice cube must've already melted. More importantly, it seemed he *didn't* care about the coffee options. She brought her mug to her lips, testing the temperature.

He watched her take a sip and smile. Only her smile seemed too big to be just for some tasty hot chocolate. What had he missed?

"Delicious."

"Susan gets the credit." He leaned out of the way to let the server set his plate down. "She thought you'd like the orange flavor."

"She was right." Harmony nodded her thanks to the server, then rested her hands on the table.

"Shall we each say our own prayer?" Grant asked. He wasn't averse to the idea of praying aloud in public, but it made some people uncomfortable.

"Yes, thanks." She didn't know what he'd been up to today, so it made sense for them to say separate prayers. It also made it feel less like a date. Which it wasn't.

"I meant to go to the woodcutting project." He drizzled dressing over his salad after they'd each finished.

"Got tied up fixing your house, I guess?" She pointed at the bruise she'd just noticed on his left hand.

"Something like that," he chuckled. "Also,

I got my days mixed up. I thought today was Friday all day until I tried calling a plumber."

"Sounds familiar." She nodded and took a bite of her sandwich. Wiped her mouth and answered the question in his eyes. "I work for myself. If I didn't set reminders on my phone, I'd think it was Monday all week."

"Ugh, what a terrible thought." He isolated a cucumber with his fork and popped it into his mouth, enjoying the crunchy burst of almost-sweetness.

She wrinkled her nose. "Yeah, you're right."

They shared a quiet chuckle.

"So, what's it like? Working for yourself, I mean." He slid his empty salad plate to one side to make room for the rest of his meal.

"It's about what you'd expect." She couldn't help wondering if Susan had changed the menu. Since when did they offer refried beans, rice, and fried eggs as a single dish here? She also hadn't realized Blinky's served pico de gallo!

"Would you like some?" Grant offered, having noticed her interest.

"What? No." She crammed more sandwich into her mouth for emphasis.

"Okay then." Using his fork to break the yolks, he stirred it all together and poured the pico on top. "More for me."

Oh that looks good. She made a mental note to order what he had the next time she came in and halfheartedly took another bite of her sandwich.

Chapter 7

"I would expect it to be pretty great."

"It what?" Harmony asked blankly.

"Being your own boss." Grant took a gulp of water, wished for a basket of tortilla chips, and continued, "You said it was about what I'd expect."

"Right." She made the connection now to what she'd said earlier. Nodded. "Right. And sometimes it is great. I set my own hours, decide what to sell to whom for how much."

Intrigued by her correct usage of the pronoun 'whom,' he smiled at her.

"But, of course," she stumbled, confused by his smile, "it has its downsides."

"For example?"

She rushed through a handful of instances where being a sole proprietor worked against her, then ate the rest of her sandwich.

"I'm starting to wonder." He set his fork down and finished his water. "If your diet isn't the root cause of your troubles."

"I beg your pardon?"

"Don't jump to any conclusions," he advised with a wry smile. "I absolutely don't think you should go on a diet."

Again his hazel blue eyes flicked over her, appreciatively but without lingering.

"I was referring to the nutrition you are and

aren't getting from your food."

He kept talking, but she wasn't really listening. She already knew he was right. She routinely took on more than she could handle so she could be sure she'd stay too busy to feel very much. And when she was busy, she ate whatever was handy. So yeah, sometimes her health suffered. Simple as that.

What wasn't simple was how she felt when he was looking at her like that. Goosebumps ran the length of both of her arms, making her glad she was still wearing her coat over her short-sleeved shirt. In the back of her mind, she wondered how many of his prior patients had been women. And how many of them went specifically to see *him* rather than to see a doctor.

"If you'd like, I'd be happy to go over a meal plan with you." He didn't think it was very polite of her to keep eating fries while he lectured her on good eating habits. Nor was he particularly impressed with his own behavior. What kind of man wasted a meal with a beautiful woman like he just had?

She blinked. Grinned. "Thanks, but that's not necessary." Good timing, though. She'd nearly gotten lost in his rare, hazel blue eyes.

He clamped his mouth shut before he could resume or rephrase his lecture.

"I see what you're saying, though." She tried her hot chocolate, but it had cooled. "I'll make sure to eat more vegetables from now on."

"Wonderful." He was an idiot. Without a doubt.

"Thanks for the company." Gingerly, she swung her feet out into the walkway. Her back had relaxed while she ate and now it tensed up again in an instant. "Rats and mice and squirrels," she grumbled angrily.

"May I be of assistance?" He couldn't figure her out. One minute she was smiling at him. The next, she was at arm's length.

She squeezed her eyes shut, scrambling to come up with a way around needing help to get up.

"Yes, please." She got out her credit card. "Could you take this up to the counter for me?" By the time he returned, she'd be on her feet—somehow—and could fake feeling well till she reached her car.

"No need. I already paid for us both." Tucking a bill under his plate for the tip, Grant got up and stood in front of her. Crossed his arms at the wrists.

"You did what?!" She couldn't explain the mix of emotions that assailed her at the news.

Ignoring her question, he instructed, "Hold on to my hands. Let me do the lifting."

"I can get up on my own, thank you." And she did manage to get a few inches up off the bench before she lost her momentum.

His hands shot out, catching her by the elbows and lifting her the rest of the way. For the second time in an hour, he more-or-less held her in his arms. He was starting to like it.

"I'm not trying to insult your independence," he told her quietly. "I just want to help."

Unable to back up without planting herself on the bench again, she nodded and pushed against his chest at the same time. Good grief, he was solid!

Together, they made their way out of Blinky's, Susan's eyes boring into them the whole time.

"Nearly there." He opened her car door for her and eased her into the seat.

His face passed much too close to hers when he buckled her in and she fought to rein in her racing heart. Had it really been that long since she'd been kissed?

"I'll follow you home," Grant announced. "I want to make sure you get inside alright."

Again he was gone before she could tell him it wasn't necessary.

On the drive to her home, her thoughts swung wildly from making plans to eat a more balanced diet to noticing hints of his cologne. To remembering his strong arm about her waist.

His SUV pulled up behind her car, and she watched him come up the driveway.

With an effort, she opened her door, but it cost her. Her back had seized up in earnest this time, as if to punish her for not taking it seriously earlier.

"Would you unlock my house, please?" She held out her keys.

Grant hurried to do as she asked and was concerned to find her still sitting in her car when he returned. She'd managed to swing her legs out of the vehicle, but that was all.

"I don't think you're going to like this."

She looked up to find him frowning down at her. She held her breath when he bent down, ducking his head so he wouldn't hit it on her car. Whimpered as his arm slid behind her back, pressed her face against his chest as he gently lifted her out.

"And up we go." He closed her car door with his foot. Carried her into her house and set her on the couch. "It's a little cold in here." He rubbed his hands together. Spotted a pillow and eased it behind her. "Don't you have your heater on?"

"No, I don't like using it." Her eyes were closed, so she didn't see the concern that flashed across his face.

"I see." And then there was what he didn't see. Aside from the couch and the shelves in the room where he finally found the heating pad, the little house had almost no evidence of occupancy. He dared into her bathroom while hunting for pain killers, but that was bare, too. One toothbrush sat in a travel cap on the counter next to a half-used tube of toothpaste. Investigating behind the bathroom mirror, he found an extra container of floss and a new bar of soap.

He eventually located a bottle of medicine by the sink in the kitchen, not far from twin stacks of paper plates and cups. He shuddered to think what he'd find if he opened the rest of the cupboards, let alone the fridge.

"You don't seem to have a bed." He gave her the pain killers and a paper cup of water.

"Who needs a bed?" She patted the couch. "This is much more versatile." Spying the heating pad, she shook her head. "Heat makes it worse. I have some ice packs in the freezer. Um. If you wouldn't mind?"

"No problem." Taking the empty cup, he strode into the kitchen again, where he was relieved to find that her freezer was chuck full of food. Locating the ice packs, he wrapped them in towels and helped reposition her so that she was comfortable with them behind her.

"Now you really will wish you had your heater on," he teased.

Laughing, she directed him to her quilt and sat silently as he tucked her in. At her request, he also plugged in her space heater, which she insisted was all she needed.

Still frowning dubiously, he took her phone from her. "I'm going to put my number in here. Call me if your back gets worse, okay?"

"Deal." She accepted her phone back and when his hand lingered on hers, she didn't withdraw it.

She prayed sitting on the couch that night, taking extra care to consider what she would be fasting for the next day. It probably made her a little odd, but she loved Fast Sunday.

It reminded her of one of her favorite scriptures, found in Isaiah 58:6. "Is not this the fast that I have chosen? to loose the bands of wickedness, to undo the heavy burdens, and to let the oppressed go free, and that ye break every yoke?"

It took Isaiah five verses just to cover the blessings promised for those who fasted, too.

She quoted part of verse eight the next morning as she watched the sunrise, "Then shall thy light break forth as the morning…"

Step by step she got ready for church and eased herself into her car. The ice cold car seat had never felt so good as it did during the short drive. The church was still pretty empty when she got there, so she picked a pew and began trying to get comfortable.

Later, when Grant arrived, he took a seat beside her. Asked quietly, "Got enough hymnals?" He could see that she'd braced two of the books between her upper back and the pew, which told him she must still be hurting. The dress she was wearing had buttons from the waist up and was probably fairly easy to get into. Whatever her reason for choosing it, in his opinion the simple navy blue outfit with whitestripe accents looked great on her.

"I'm okay for now." She rustled up a small smile for him. "Thanks for helping me yesterday."

"My pleasure." He was a little sorry that she was comfortable with just the two hymn books. He would've loved to have an excuse to put an arm around her shoulders for her to lean against.

"I think I can manage today." She gestured at the chapel, which was quieting now that the bishop had risen to start the meeting. "In case you wanted to sit with someone else."

"Would you rather I sat somewhere else?" His eyes narrowed.

"Not…exactly." Of course she would. She was fasting, her back ached, and he smelled good enough to distract her under normal circumstances. Not to mention that in his crisp white shirt, sharp black suit, and blue silk tie that brought out his eyes, he looked like a model from the GQ boy-next-door issue. But telling him that straight out would never do. No, that wasn't how the game was played.

"You're still settling in, aren't you?"

He nodded. They both knew that he was.

"So you've met what, five percent of the ward?" She lifted her eyebrows. "Less?"

"I hardly think Sacrament meeting is the time and place to socialize, Sister Wells." The corners of his mouth quirked up in obvious amusement.

She couldn't argue with that. And she didn't have time to think of anything else before the organist began playing the opening hymn, "Again We Meet Around the Board." Belatedly, she realized that there wasn't a hymnal in reach besides the ones she'd claimed for her backrest. Thankfully, Grant didn't seem to need one.

"Again we meet around the board, of Jesus, our redeeming Lord, with faith in His atoning blood, our only access unto God."

Listening to Grant's rich tenor, Harmony forgot to sing. Then he looked at her, smiling as if to invite her to sing along, and she joined in for the second verse.

"He left his Father's courts on high, with man to live, for man to die. A world to purchase and to save and seal a triumph o'er the grave."

After opening prayer and the announcements, they sang a sacrament hymn, then bowed their heads to listen to the sacrament prayers.

Something shifted in her heart as she prayed and the man sitting next to her ceased to be a distraction from her worship.

Once the sacrament ordinance was concluded, the bishop rose to open the ward fast and testimony meeting by bearing his own testimony of the restoration of the gospel. "And now I turn the time over to you, Brothers and Sisters."

A trio of teenagers went first, each more painfully shy than the last. Their sweet testimonies inspired others to make the long walk up to the stand and soon the allotted time was spent.

All through the closing hymn, Grant counted himself fortunate to have a seat next to the loveliest voice in the room. It was more than that, though. He recognized it as a trained voice. She had to have taken lessons somewhere.

"Still doing alright?" he asked in the brief space between sacrament meeting and Sunday school.

"More or less." Looking into his eyes, she saw genuine concern, just as she had yesterday. "I think I'd be more comfortable with just one book for a while."

He promptly reached around her, supporting her with one arm while he worked a hymnal free, careful not to get his fingers tangled in her loose, sweet-smelling hair. As firmly as he tried to focus on the *why* of the *what* he was doing, he couldn't help noticing how nicely she fit in his arms. He'd thought so yesterday, too.

Which wasn't the point of his actions. At all.

"Is that better?" He looked down at her. She seemed startlingly close. And her eyes— how had he not noticed her eyes? They were the most magnificent green. Not satisfied to be simply green, there were rays of brown shooting out from her irises in a fabulously erratic pattern.

"Much." Harmony tried to ignore the way his proximity set stunt cars to racing around her stomach. They made for an interesting change from the hunger she'd been feeling, but… She put a hand on his chest and pushed lightly.

"Sorry." Straightening away, he spotted a handful of heads whipping hastily around to face forward again. Marvelous. Now when he eventually decided to start dating, everyone would have the preconceived notion that he was already Harmony's.

That wouldn't be so bad, except that she clearly wasn't interested. Judging by her closed posture at the moment, he'd say she was trying to tell him something along the lines of 'forget it.'

He did his best to concentrate on the lesson, yet everything seemed to bring his thoughts around to the woman seated beside him. When the teacher brought up 1st Timothy 2:9-10, reminding them that men as well as women could be vain about their clothing, his mind sprinted back to the last charity event he'd attended before quitting his job.

Tracey Chambers, philanthropist extraordinaire, had shown up dripping in jewelry. The price of one of her diamond bracelets would've provided the amount of hoped-for funds they were trying to raise that night. And she'd still been insecure enough to shriek like a harpy at the hapless waiter who'd dumped half a tray of shrimp and dip on her.

Whereas Harmony, in such extreme pain that she could hardly stand up or sit down on her own, comported herself with quiet dignity.

Harmony tightened her folded arms as Grant leaned forward and rubbed his face like something was bothering him. Like he was thousands of miles away. Then, immediately after the closing prayer, he turned to her.

"May I help you out to your car?"

She tried reaching behind her to catch the remaining hymnal. Exhaled as pain radiated outward from her lower back.

"I could use a hand up." She grasped his strong hand and promptly brought to her feet. "Thanks."

"Sure." Smiling, he continued holding onto her hand as they started toward her car.

A few steps along, she tugged her hand free. "You don't have to worry. The walk will loosen me up. I'll be fine."

"Mhmm." He kept walking.

"Good thing tomorrow's a slow day." She bit her tongue to prevent herself from saying more. She did *not* have to tell him anything.

"Really?" He slid his hands into the pockets of his slacks. "What do you do for a living?"

Okay, she probably should tell him that. Just to be polite.

"I run a small delivery service." That was getting bigger all the time, thanks to referrals.

"I bulk order allergen-free products and redistribute them."

"Ohhh, of course. The boxes in your bedroom."

Caught mid-nod with Ken, who had to have heard Grant's statement, Harmony's cheeks flamed.

"See you, um, Wednesday." Turning on his heel, Ken nearly bowled over an elderly couple in his haste to escape.

"Great." Harmony made a beeline for the nearest door, or tried to. Having Grant sauntering casually alongside her served to underline how slowly she was moving until her frustration and embarrassment came out in a low, angry huff. She took a deep breath of the cold, crisp air when she finally got outside.

"What's wrong?" He'd learned a long time ago not to ask if things were okay.

What kind of a dumb question is that? If everything was alright, would I be acting like this? That's what his middle sister, Gabby, used to say.

She huffed again, though this was closer to a laugh.

"Did you see that guy back there?"

"That…Ken? Yes, I saw him." His brow furrowed as he tried to remember exactly what Ken said and how on earth it might have upset her.

"He heard what you said."

Woops, he was on the wrong track! Grant

mentally reversed direction, the lines in his forehead deepening as he thought back over what *he* had said.

She glanced around to see if anyone was in earshot. "About my bedroom?"

He flinched. "Nothing like overhearing half of a conversation."

"I think he might understandably have some questions even if he'd heard the entire conversation in this case." Sighing, she unlocked her car.

"Is he your boyfriend?" When he saw himself in her car window, his face was flushed.

"Does it matter?" She stopped. Massaged her forehead. "Look. Thank you for your help. Yesterday and today. And don't take this the wrong way, but..." She opened her door and he stepped forward.

"Let me help you in."

"I told you." She frowned fiercely. "I'm fine."

Grant watched her drive away, the cold slowly seeping in through his suit coat and dress slacks.

That evening, when he said a prayer to break his fast before eating supper, he remembered the enigmatic beauty.

Her expressive face haunted his dreams, no matter how hard he worked on house repairs during the day. One moment, she was open and inviting. The next, she shut him down like her life depended on it.

By Wednesday, he gave up and searched the ward directory for her phone number. He needed to find out if she was alright. A hurt back was nothing to mess with.

So…press the button, Grant.

Abruptly, his fingers moved without his permission. The phone dialed.

"Grant, honey! How are you?"

"Hi, Mom." Clipping on his Bluetooth earpiece, he picked up a fresh sheaf of sandpaper and headed upstairs.

"Honey, you sound like you're surrounded by rats or something." Her laugh quickly faded. "Please tell me you're not."

He stifled his guffaws to reassure her, "It's just the stairs, Mom. They're on the list."

"You and your lists," she sighed. "Honestly, the only spontaneous thing you ever did was quit your job and move thousands of miles away from home."

"Yeah." He folded the sandpaper around the hand sanding block. The electric belt sander mocked him from the corner where he'd left it, but he could hardly use it while he was on the phone.

"Was it worth it?"

He paused, picturing her standing in the front room of the home he'd grown up in. If she was looking out the big, bay window, there were three pictures on the wall behind her—

one of the temple where she'd been sealed to her husband; one of the Savior; and one of them as a family. In the lower, right-hand corner of the family picture was a smaller picture of the family as it was now, with her four sons-in-law and five grandchildren gathered around a picnic table in the backyard.

In short, her home reeked of…of *home*. No one could walk into it and wonder if someone lived there. Unlike Harmony's rental.

Chapter 8

"I say, was it worth it? Grant?" His mother's voice called him back to the present.

"Huh?" He shook his head to clear it of the boggling discrepancies between his mother's home and Harmony's. "Well, that remains to be seen. This is the first time I've ever flipped a house, you know."

"Don't be ridiculous," she scoffed at him. "I know you better than that. If you've bought that house and you're going to the effort of fixing it up yourself, you're planning to stay there."

He looked down at his hands with a sigh. "Things don't always go according to plan, Mom."

She waited a sympathetic moment before agreeing, "No, sweetie. No, they don't. I'm so sorry. I know how much your career meant to you."

"Thanks, Mom." On his knees by the closet, he started pushing the hand sanding block back and forth on the hardwood floor.

"Is that why you called? To listen to me tease you about moving?" Her tone was soft, almost wheedling. She knew that wasn't the case.

He chuckled. "Oh, I just called to see how everyone was doing." In his family, his mother was information central. She talked with her daughters each week and often visited his oldest sister Stephanie, who lived the closest *and* had two of the five grandkids.

"Everyone's fine." The amusement in her short answer seemed to say she wasn't going to be distracted that easily.

He flinched at her choice of words, Harmony's voice echoing in his head. *I'm fine.*

"Great. That's uh…that's great."

"Grant, stop sidestepping and tell me why you called."

He swallowed, hard. "Tell me about your house."

"Grant." Exasperation flooded the single word.

"I'm serious. Tell me about how you decided what to put where and how much of it and…all of it. Tell me all of it." She was silent for so long that he reached for his phone to see if the call had dropped.

"We started with just the basics. The kitchen things, of course. A dresser for our bedroom." She laughed softly, warming to her subject. "One of the gifts we got from your father's parents was a very expensive couch. You know, the kind that pulls out into a bed? It was top of the line at the time and they let us know they expected to be invited out to help when the children started arriving."

"No pressure there," he muttered under his breath.

"Oh, they meant well. It was quite sweet of them, really. So many of our friends our age were from broken homes, we were sort of the oddities having just one set of parents apiece, and I think they wanted to support us however they could."

"That does sound like them," he admitted, picturing Grandpa Frank and Grandma Stella. Silver hairs and golden hearts, both of them.

"Well anyway." She continued with her story, sharing the backstory of her favorite pieces. Showing him, without realizing it, that the comfy home he thought of wasn't built by one person or even one family. "I think it was our…yes, our tenth anniversary that the Millers surprised us with that picture of George Washington kneeling in prayer, you know the one that hangs—"

"On the wall of the staircase? Yeah, how could I forget? I get goosebumps just thinking about that picture and all it represents."

"Yes, me, too. Oh! My phone is ringing." She paused. "It's Betty!"

"Better take it." Just thinking of his little sister made him smile. "Love you, and tell her I love her, too."

"I will, sweetheart. I hope you sort out what's bothering you."

He lifted the earpiece out and stared at it. Tucking it into the pocket of his jeans, he pondered. Had he sorted it out?

A better question was why he cared about how Harmony kept her house. It looked clean enough, that much he was sure of. The full freezer proved she wasn't starving. So what business was it of his if she put up pictures? Or had colorful towels in the kitchen? Or…anything.

Still absorbed in convincing himself that he wasn't interested in it, he reached for the belt sander. Switched it on. Choked on the instant cloud of wood dust.

Shutting it off, he evacuated the room and coughed until he cried in the hallway. Stupid, stupid stunt. He knew better than to use a belt sander without a dust mask!

His coughing slowed to a wheeze and he wiped his eyes. That was enough renovating for one day.

Running his fingers through his hair, he got a good grip and held still, thinking.

"I need to get out of this house."

Half an hour and a quick shower later, he shrugged into his coat and locked the door behind him. Bob, the same guy who'd abandoned him after the races in Topaz, had also recommended a restaurant in Fireclay, a town about forty minutes from Cadmia.

Why not? As long as Bob wasn't driving, that was.

Grant whistled his way to his car, programming the Blue Plate Café into his phone as his destination. A night out was just what he needed.

"Uh-oh." He chuckled as he pulled into the parking lot and saw a large, neon sign announcing 'Karaoke Wednesday.' Parking carefully, he headed inside anyway.

Another sign, just inside the restaurant door, invited him to, "Pick a seat!!"

Wisely, he chose an empty table on the far side of the room from the stage. The house lights lowered as he started toward it and he completely missed seeing a table along the wall to his left–or the couple seated at it.

Harmony, who'd bitten the bullet and called Ken to explain Grant's remark on Sunday, sat awkwardly across from him.

"Are you sure you want to do this?" she asked, noting the sweat beading Ken's upper lip. The room was warm, but not that warm. He was scared out of his mind.

"You bet." He grinned and shifted his chair for the third time in five minutes. "It's going to be great."

"Karaoke *is* a lot of fun." Though she still had her doubts that he would survive the experience, it didn't mean she had to deliberately discourage him.

"Oh?" He wiped the back of his hand across his mouth. "You've done it before?"

"Yes, a few times." She probably shouldn't count two years of performing twelve times a week on a cruise ship. Not that she'd sung every time she performed. They saved that routine for the 'sing for your supper' crowd.

"Ladieeees and gentlemen!" A middle-aged man was suddenly visible under three separate spotlights. "Welcome," he stepped back and dramatically gestured at the stage he was standing in the middle of, "to Karaoke Wednesday!"

Ken tugged at the collar of his tee as the other guests cheered, whistled, and clapped.

"I'm Bibber Carmody and I'll be your DJ tonight." He held the mic against his chest, grinning at the second round of applause. "Is everybody ready for our mystery duets?!"

Intrigued, Harmony leaned forward, resting her folded arms on the table. A mystery duet, according to Bibber, involved two lines of singers—one male, one female—separated by a curtain. When a couple reached the head of the line, he'd hand over the microphones. Partway through their song, the curtain would be drawn back, allowing the singers to see each other.

"And if they're lucky, the couple may decide to kiss!"

Harmony snickered. The odds of that weren't very high, at least not while the participants were mostly sober.

"I don't think I've ever heard of mystery karaoke before." Her smile disappeared when she got another look at Ken. She'd seen wax statues that looked healthier.

"Ready?" Ken got to his feet, grinning despite the uniquely green tinge of his skin.

"Absolutely." Harmony got up as well and linked her arm through his in an effort to support him. She hadn't seen anyone this terrified since her last opening night on the cruise ship.

"Great." He swayed slightly, then headed for the stage, gravely determined.

She talked about nothing as they walked, trying to get his mind off…well, whatever he was afraid of. 'Stage fright' sounded so cookie cutter, so one-size-fits-all, which was nothing like the truth. Some people were afraid of other people. Others watched the edge of the stage like it was going to chase them down and make them fall off it onto their faces.

She hoped he wasn't suffering from a fear of other people, because the line-up was small and surprisingly crowded.

"This is gonna be fun."

She nodded and tried to ignore the way his fingers were digging into her arm. Bit her lip when the first couple got started. They were painfully off-key, but if she reacted at all, that would only make it worse for Ken.

"I sing better than that," he scoffed, surprising her.

"Okay." She patted his hand as the line moved forward. "See you in a few minutes."

"Huh?" He stared at her, wild-eyed.

"We're at the curtain." She tugged on the thick, black curtain, smiling brightly.

"Oh." He released her like she was too hot to continue holding onto. "Yeah. See you."

Safely on one side of the curtain, she still practiced keeping a straight face for future use. Most of them were pretty decent singers, but there were those who simply couldn't carry a tune.

Only two women were ahead of her when there was a sudden disturbance on the other side of the curtain. It sounded like someone tripped over something, followed by upset muttering.

"Golly, hope they're okay over there." The woman ahead of Harmony twisted her hands and tittered nervously.

"I'm sure they're fine." Harmony smiled.

"I just...I just wanna get it over with, y'know?" She brushed at her hair, flipping it back over her shoulders. "I'm here with this guy, my mom set us up," she rolled her eyes, "and he got all excited when the DJ said there might be kissing in this crazy karaoke."

"Ugh, sounds creepy." Harmony was honestly sympathetic. She'd gone on far too many first dates in her life not to have had a few regrets.

"You couldn't..." She was back to twisting her hands. "You couldn't swap places with me, could you?"

"That might not work." Harmony frowned as the thought occurred to her. "I mean, how many women are in line compared to how many men? What if we switch places and he's the fourth one back, not the third?"

"Oh, yeah." The woman chewed her lip. "Hadn't thought of that."

Harmony hesitated, then caved. "What you could do, though, is hang back. Just let everyone go ahead of you until your guy has finished singing."

"I could do that!" Then, with a sassy grin, "Just puhlease, don't call him mine!"

Harmony laughed with her. Stepped cautiously past her at her wave. "Sorry, Ken," she muttered. It wouldn't really matter, would it? This was completely luck of the draw, after all. She could no more guarantee that she wouldn't be his partner now than she could've been sure she would be before trading places. Right?

A low murmuring came from the other side of the curtain. It got closer and closer until it stopped as abruptly as it had begun.

"Wish me luck," giggled the girl ahead of Harmony.

"Yeah." Harmony slid her hands into the pockets of her jeans and stretched her jaw. Did her best to yawn in case she got one of the lower-pitched songs.

And found herself with a handful of microphone. The karaoke monitor was scanning down through a never-ending list of songs, so she studied the mic. It wasn't professional quality, she hadn't expected that, but it was better than she anticipated.

The song list slowed. Down to a crawl. Stopped on "Rewrite the Stars."

Her eyes widened as her vocal partner started to sing. Beautifully. That couldn't be Ken—there wasn't a hint of nerves. Yet, the voice was familiar. She cocked her head to one side, trying to remember where she'd heard it before.

Lifting her microphone, she took a breath and came in for her part of the duet. She knew the words by heart, but still kept an eye on the screen in case they were using a different arrangement.

The chatter in the dining area dropped off to occasional whispers. The serving staff moved quietly, or not at all, as the entire room fell under the spell of the song.

A strange feeling came over Harmony as she sang about changing a destiny. The music seemed to swell up and out of her, like a genie breaking free from an uncorked bottle.

Her partner stayed with her as the song soared hopefully —then came crashing down at the end.

Harmony lowered the microphone and her chin, allowing her shoulders to slump ever so slightly to portray the anticipation of defeat that the lyrics depicted.

Grant stared in shock at none other than Harmony Wells. She looked so different, so vulnerable, standing there with her eyes downcast.

Then she straightened and the illusion was broken. Gone was the despondent young woman and in her place was a confident, breathtaking vision of loveliness.

He didn't even register the thundering applause until she dropped a half curtsy.

She nearly dropped her mic when she turned and saw who her partner was.

"Grant?"

"Harmony?"

"Hey, folks, aren't they great?" The DJ's voice cut off any further discussion.

"Encore!!"

"Sing again!!!"

"More!"

"Wowwww, listen to that!" The DJ's grin was only a few watts dimmer than a US Coast Guard searchlight. "How about it, folks? Want to sing another one?"

Grant quickly handed over his microphone. "No, thanks." He waved at the audience.

Harmony set her microphone down as well. "It's been fun!" She made eye contact with Grant and they ducked back behind the curtains by mutual agreement.

"Want to get out of here?" he asked, catching

her by the hand.

"And how! Let me get my coat."

"Oh, right." He peeked out into the dining area, which had settled a little. "Meet me at the front door."

She collected her coat and half a dozen admirers at the same time.

"What's your number?"

"Hey, do you sing professionally?"

She zigged right around a table, left around a waitress, and straight to Grant.

"Oh, wait. Ken!" She tried to stop, but Grant took her hand and pulled her out the door.

"C'mon!"

"I can't leave," she protested. "Ken hasn't sung yet."

"Ken's long gone." Grant swept her up and around the side of an extended cab truck. "Shhhh."

Her hands braced on his biceps, she looked up at him while he watched the night for signs of pursuit. She liked her job better. His clean-shaven jaw was mere inches away and she began toying with the idea of kissing him. What would it be like?

"Where'd they go?" A strange voice called.

A car engine started somewhere in the parking lot.

"Over there!" Sounds of half a dozen or more people rushing off filtered back to them.

"I think we're safe." Grant took a final look

around. "I'm parked over here."

"And," she caught his sleeve, nodded in the other direction, "I'm parked over there."

He blinked. "You didn't ride with Ken?"

She shook her head. "Speaking of Ken…"

"I'll explain about him over supper somewhere." He grinned. "I just remembered I'm hungry."

"How about the Purple Skink?"

"The…what?"

"You'll love it." She sketched out basic directions. "It's only about ten minutes from here."

"See you in ten."

They split up and headed for their cars, then drove the few blocks over.

"So this is the Purple Skink." He took a deep breath, inhaling tantalizing scents. Glancing around, he admired the colorful decorations. "This may be the best smelling restaurant I've ever been to."

"Wait until you taste the food."

"I believe it. Look at this crowd." A harried waitress left the kitchen carrying a heavily loaded serving tray and he whistled. "They're going to need a shoehorn to get us in there."

"Harmony!" The owner's wife bustled over and hugged her, speaking Spanish all the while.

Grant watched, amazed, as Harmony responded in the same language. He smothered a smile behind his hand when the woman, whom Harmony addressed as Inez, described him as attractive.

"Inez, it's a pleasure to meet you." He interrupted in Spanish before Harmony could respond. Somewhere in Connecticut, his mother smiled approvingly at him for not continuing to eavesdrop.

Harmony's heart skipped a beat when she realized he'd heard and understood everything they'd been saying.

"My friend here tells me you make excellent food."

Inez giggled, complimented his accent, and seated them at a corner table Grant had overlooked before. She took their orders, winked at Harmony, and vanished.

"So." He grinned boyishly at her. "Why *has* it been over a month since your last visit?" It might be impolite to listen in, but since he couldn't possibly have avoided it this time, he might as well have fun with it.

Harmony blushed as he echoed Inez's question. "You first. What happened to Ken?"

"I'm not exactly sure." He blew out a breath. "I sat down to study the menu and the bus boy spilled a half empty glass of something on me. On my way to find some paper towels, I saw a guy staggering out of the karaoke line."

She covered her mouth with her hand. "Not Ken!"

He nodded. "Poor guy made it to the restroom just in time." He cleared his throat. "Anyway, he spotted me and begged me to take his place in line." He shrugged. "He told me he had a date with him and would I please go sing with her."

"Just like that?" She was impressed. "How gallant of you."

"I don't know about that." He coughed, embarrassed by her assessment. "I have to ask you something."

"I lost track of time."

Chapter 9

"Beg pardon?" Bewildered, Grant waited for Harmony to explain.

She shrugged. "I lost track of time. I usually come here after picking up a big delivery, but last month I, um, wound up going somewhere else." New Orleans, but he didn't need to know that.

"Makes perfect sense." He leaned to one side to allow Inez to place his food. "What I was going to ask, though, was where you learned to sing."

"Oh." That was almost worse. "Would you believe it was in a private school outside of Mount Airy, Maryland?"

He squinted at her, unsure whether to believe her words or her goofy smile. She bowed her head over her food and he followed suit.

"Where did *you* learn to sing?" She turned the tables on him in an effort to get the attention off herself. He already knew more than she wanted him to.

"Me?" He started loading a tortilla with fajita mix to stall. "I sang with a community performance choir for a few years." He'd needed social interaction and the choir had proven a safe place for it.

"A few years?" She scraped her refried

beans into her chicken taco salad. "Wow, I don't know of many places that even have those anymore."

"Me, neither." He smiled a little wistfully. "Tenby is a pretty unique place."

"Tell me about it."

He tried to keep it short, but she kept asking questions, leading him from one topic to another until he found himself relating a fairly embarrassing story from his freshman year at college.

"What can I say? At home, if a door was shut, you knocked before walking in."

"Totally not your fault," she agreed, scooping the last of her taco salad up with her fork and spoon. "If you ask me, though, she did it on purpose."

"My sisters and mom said the same thing." He groaned and rubbed his hand over his eyes.

"Smart women," she smirked.

"And so are you by a simple extension of logic." He enjoyed watching her face pink. He was having a great time. So much so, that it was getting harder and harder for him to remember that he was just pinch hitting for Ken.

"What?"

"Hmm? What what?"

"You said something just now." She crumpled her napkin and tossed it onto her plate. "Sounded like 'lucky guy'."

"Oh." He cleared his throat. "Well, yeah,

I," he tried not to squirm under her amused gaze, "I was thinking about Ken. That he was a lucky guy to be dating you."

"Dating?" She reached for her half-full water glass and drained it, but it did nothing to cool her flaming cheeks. "I'm not dating anyone."

Grant frowned. He might've been happy to hear that if the words hadn't come out flatter than the tortillas he'd just consumed. Suddenly anxious to correct any notion that he wanted to date her, he shrugged.

"Me, neither." He shook his head and tried again. "I mean, I'm not ready to date right now." He gestured at nothing. "Just moved. Bought a house. Y'know. Too busy."

He'd once had the opportunity to visit the grand opening of a museum exhibit where they'd demonstrated how to tell rare crystal pieces from basic glassware. Right now, his own words rang as falsely in his ears as any of the thuds the curator had produced from the cheap knockoffs.

"Good." She started to reach behind her to get her coat and had to stop to take a breath. Her back wasn't consistently better yet.

As if he could read her mind Grant was suddenly there, holding her coat for her. Across the room she saw Inez pressing a hand to her heart and sighing dreamily.

She rose slowly and slid her arms into her

coat sleeves, disturbingly aware of Grant's gentle touch as he shifted the coat to make it easier for her. Shivered when his fingers grazed the back of her neck as he lifted her hair out from where it routinely got trapped under her collar.

"Yeah, um." She stepped away. "That's great, thanks." Goosebumps were for amateurs at that point. It was two against three—her heart and body against her head. Whether or not she *should* date him, she wanted to.

"Sure." He touched her arm lightly and slipped on his own coat. Dropped some cash on the table, enough to cover the bill and a New York-sized tip. "My sisters are always complaining about their long hair," he told her as he escorted her to the door. "Beats me why they don't cut it."

"Because you can't do as much with short hair," she explained automatically.

"So they tell me." He laughed. "I just don't understand how it's worth it to keep something around when you're going to complain about it six days out of seven."

Harmony wished for a scarf as they stepped outside, a nice, thick one like Noella had. Since she didn't have one, she twitched her nose a few times until she was fairly sure it wasn't going to freeze.

"Have you got room for dessert?" Grant offered her his elbow but she shook her head and kept her hands in her pockets. He didn't blame her. It was so cold compared to inside the restaurant that he was having trouble breathing.

"Can't. I have deliveries tomorrow."

"Deliveries? Are you sure your back is up to that?" In his mind, he pictured her carrying twenty and even thirty pound boxes. Bending and twisting to get them in and out of her car.

"I'll be fine." She shrugged. "In fact, I'm less worried about the deliveries than I am about the drive."

"Hmm, yeah." He stood aside while she opened her car door tonight, needing a little space. "I have to tack ten or fifteen minutes onto the estimated driving time around here." It was nothing compared to trying to outguess public transportation in New York, let alone taxis, but he enjoyed grousing about it.

She grinned. "You'll get used to it. Won't be long before you don't need your GPS to get around anymore."

"Not for the local stuff, anyway." He agreed, then shook his head. "Can't believe I'm considering forty plus minutes away as 'local'."

"You'll get used to that, too. Thanks for dinner, Grant." Laughing, she got in her car and started the engine.

"Maybe I should go with you tomorrow." *Probably shouldn't have said that out loud.*

She quirked an eyebrow at him. "Why?"

"I dunno." Reaching up, he ruffled his own

hair and wished he hadn't. He really needed to start wearing a hat. "Keep you company? Hey!" A brilliant idea struck him. "We could sing!"

"It's a long drive," she cautioned, eyeing him almost warily. "It'll take most of the morning for just one stop." Why didn't she just say no?

"I've been spending my mornings sanding my floors." He grinned. "And my afternoons. And my evenings."

One corner of her mouth turned up. "You need a library card, amigo." Shoot. She was going to say yes.

"That's a great idea. I'll get one as soon as we get back."

She burst out laughing. "Okay, you win. But be warned. I expect you to carry every box and smile nicely at all my clients." Her heart flipped when he gave her a sample.

"Will this do?" It wasn't his standard schmooze smile. Nor did it feel like his casual, 'Glad to see you!' Glimpsing his reflection in her window, he had to admit that this was a special smile.

"Keep practicing." Where she could see him, she hoped. "Be at my place at 7 AM tomorrow."

"Yes, ma'am." He mock saluted her. Closed her car door and watched her drive away.

Seconds later, shivering in his vehicle, he

shuffled through his music until he found "Rewrite the Stars." A private school in Maryland, huh? He still hadn't decided if she was joking about that, but the memories of her voice as she sang sent chills through him. What was her dream, he wondered, and why did she sing as though it was as out of reach as rearranging the constellations?

He wanted to ask her about it the next day, but she was all business. Load the boxes. Explain the route. Make the deliveries and try to get them to place a firm order for next month. Calm, cool, and efficient. And just a wee bit grumpy.

"Okay, you can stop smiling now." Safely back in the car, Harmony elbowed Grant, waved at her client, and drove away.

"What was that for?" he asked, rubbing his arm.

"You're too happy."

"I'm what?" He laughed, then held up his hands defensively in case she tried to elbow him again. "Define too happy."

"You haven't quit smiling since we got in the car three hours ago." Why that bothered her so much was anybody's guess.

"I thought you liked my smile." He let it start spreading across his face again.

"I thought I did, too." She gave him a sardonic look.

"Oh, ouch." He gripped an imaginary sword

in the middle of his chest. "That hurts."

"Yeah, yeah." She rolled her eyes as he went into extended sound effects and drama. On the inside, though, she was cracking up. She didn't remember the last time she'd had so much fun. Especially while driving for endless miles making deliveries.

"Oooh, look at that." Dropping the act, he leaned forward, almost hitting his head on her rearview mirror. "Is it legal?"

"A green barn?" Putting one hand on his forehead, she shoved him back into his own space. "As far as I know."

"I thought all barns were red." He didn't, but he enjoyed the funny looks she gave him.

"You're kidding." She hoped he was kidding!

"Of course I am."

She gave a low roar of frustration. "If I'd known you were going to behave like a grade school kid on Halloween candy, I wouldn't have let you come!"

He sobered instantly. "I'm glad you did."

She drove half a mile before shooting him a sideways glance. Which was the real him? The goofball who'd been tormenting her the entire morning? Or the serious man staring thoughtfully into the distance now?

Or both? She wasn't always a grump, though she felt like one now.

"You have quite a business." He eyed a field

of snow mixed with dirt as they passed it. "How'd you get the idea for it?"

Slowly, she lifted one shoulder. "Relief Society. I'd only been here a few weeks and they had an evening event. They invited all the girls who were going to transition into Relief Society in the next year and, when it came time for us to sit down and eat, half the girls had brought their own meals."

He whistled softly. "Because of allergies?"

She nodded and turned left at the next crossroad. "They were all different, too. Nuts, gluten…" Her voice trailed off.

"That's a tough way to grow up, having to bring your own food to everything." He knew firsthand what it was like to stand out when you'd rather blend in.

"I know." She chuckled. "I have a mild nut allergy myself, so I joined them. They were so nice about it. Everyone offered to share their food and I think—I think they were just glad to have a so-called adult who wasn't a family member that got it. That got *them*."

He watched her face silently as she relived the evening in a few moments.

"I don't remember what the lesson was about, and I probably should, but that's when I knew what I wanted to do while I was here."

His mind ground to a halt. "While you're here?" His curiosity piqued further when she tensed visibly.

"In Cadmia." She forced herself to sound matter-of-fact.

"Does that mean while you're here on earth in Cadmia?" he questioned. "Or…"

"No, silly. It means until I leave."

"You're leaving? When?" Why did he feel like he'd just taken a cannonball to the stomach?

"Not sure, really." She grinned. "I might get myself a new town for Christmas."

Grant sat back and tried to breathe.

"Why?"

"Why not?" The sassy answer hung in the air between them longer than she'd expected. The strain in her shoulders intensified with each passing mile.

"Because…" His mind raced around, hunting for an answer. Every time he thought he had something, he ran smack into the wall of indifference surrounding her. "I don't know why not." Certainly not him. He was just a blip in her life. She wouldn't even miss him when she moved to…to…

"Where are you going?"

"Dunno." She tossed off the answer as casually as she could. Except something was bothering her. "Hey, how long have we been driving?"

He barked a laugh. "Three hours, give or take."

"No, I don't mean that." Checking her

mirrors, she brought the vehicle to a stop.

"Whoa." He sat up straight. "You can't park in the middle of the road!"

"Relax. We're fine for a few minutes, or hadn't you noticed we're the only ones on the road?" Pulling her phone out of the cup holder, she frowned at it. "Oh no."

"What?" He'd just started to accept the fact that there was literally no one within half an hour of them and now his pulse spiked again.

"We're lost." She rubbed her forehead. "I don't have a signal."

"Ah." Understanding dawned. "And it can't tell us where we are if it doesn't have a signal." He started at his right and scanned a full three hundred and sixty degrees before admitting defeat. "I don't see anything but empty fields."

"Welcome to the Ozarks." Someday, she was going to learn to print out a map for each new client. The fact that they were heading back toward Cadmia didn't make any difference. Being able to find Cadmia was one thing. Finding her new client's house was a whole different proposition.

Grant checked the signal on his phone. There was a big X where the bars should've been.

"So I guess we just keep driving until we're in range of a tower?"

"That's one option." She tried zooming in

on the map and the app balked, giving her a screen-sized error. "I know there has to be something this way if we go far enough, but I only have half a tank of gas."

"Well, that's what, a couple hundred miles?" he guesstimated.

"Do you have any idea how easy it is to drive past a town in these parts?" She glared at him. "And when we do find a town, there is no guarantee, *none* whatsoever, that it will be less than half an hour from a gas station."

"Seriously?" As he looked around again, the fields he'd been admiring took on a menacing air. He wasn't panicking. There was no need for that, right? He was just used to being able to see a building no matter which direction he looked. In some places he knew of, he could even reach out and touch a building with each hand.

"Grant?" She grabbed his chin. Forced him to look at her. "Breathe." She registered the warmth of his skin and how smooth it was under her fingertips. He must've shaved that morning.

Her mind abruptly time-tunneled back to her eleventh birthday party. Her dad shaved every day before her mother's death, and she still remembered being surprised that his cheeks were scratchy when he bent to kiss her happy birthday.

Grant forgot all about his burgeoning agoraphobia as her thumb moved slowly across his cheek.

"We…" Her eyes flicked over his face. Met his eyes and read the signs there. Dropping her hand in her lap, she tried again. "Um, we just need to go back the way we came."

Checking for traffic, she started a tight three-point turnaround. The ditches there were three or four feet deep and she wound up doing a five-point turnaround to keep her car out of them.

"Right." Grant tugged at his collar and wished he didn't want to kiss her. "We had a signal, we just need to go find it again."

"Exactly." Exhaling, she put the car in drive. She hated backtracking.

Grant juggled both of their phones for the next twenty minutes, anxiously checking them until his lit up.

"Got it!"

They huddled over his phone, plotting the rest of their drive, then reversed direction once more.

"That's why I wasn't worried about the gas," she explained, turning down the very next road. "I knew that I would be just ten minutes from the next station after this last delivery."

"Nice." He took a couple of deep breaths, grateful he was able to, and smiled at the fields they were passing. He needed to get out more!

Finally locating a trim little house in the

middle of next-to-nowhere, Harmony made the same little speech she always gave to new referrals, took next month's order, and got them back on the road.

"I think I could raise my rates if I had you as a permanent delivery driver," she teased, glad that the worst of it was behind them.

"I work cheap." His smile dimmed as he remembered that she was planning to leave. "Who's going to take over?"

"Huh?" She navigated one of Missouri's weirder, five-way stops, and headed down what she was ninety-five percent sure was the right road to the gas station.

"When you move, who's going to run your business?" She didn't answer and a suspicion started sneaking over him. "Harmony? You're not planning to just bail on them, are you?"

"No, I…ugh!" She pulled into the gas station. "You've got five minutes for a bathroom break if you need one." Hitting her seatbelt release, she hopped out and slammed the door behind her.

Startled, he just sat there. Climbed out and stared at her back, which she kept deliberately turned toward him as she gassed her car. The five minutes were probably up by the time he walked through the station doors, but he risked it anyway.

Shelves of junk food sneered at him as he meandered toward the corner where he hoped the restrooms were located. He hated junk food on principle, but hunger pangs were beginning to penetrate his shock.

Harmony found him crouching in front of a shelf of crackers, a perplexed look on his face.

"Hungry?" She was, too. It was nearly one in the afternoon, way past her usual lunch time.

"Starving."

"Yeah." She touched his arm as she walked past him. "I'll be right out."

Standing up, he started for the next aisle over, then paused to read some posters on the far wall. There was one for Cadmia's annual charity play. And one with a picture of a bowl of chili.

"Excuse me." Addressing the bored-looking woman behind the counter, he pointed at the second poster. "Is that today?"

Chapter 10

It didn't take much to convince Harmony to make another, smaller detour, and they ate their fill of chili and crackers at the local fundraiser.

"You can hardly blame him." Grant defended the friendly mayor on their drive back to Cadmia.

"I'm not wearing a ring!" She wiggled her left hand for emphasis.

"There are half a dozen perfectly logical explanations for why a married woman wouldn't be wearing her ring."

"Okay, okay." She gave in. It wasn't the mayor's presumption that bothered her anyway. It was the thrill she'd gotten at the idea of being married. To Grant. Specifically.

It was a pipe dream, of course. Even if she returned to Cadmia, how would she explain to Grant that she was an heiress? How would she know the prospect of marrying a few billion dollars wouldn't change him?

Grant was busy with his own thoughts and the rest of the drive passed in near silence. He roused himself enough to thank her for letting him tag along, reiterating that getting out of the house was exactly what he'd needed.

And promptly spent the next two weeks hard at work on his renovations. Cold meat sandwiches and frozen pizzas became staples in his diet, though he did add canned vegetables if he remembered.

When he couldn't work anymore, he studied the scriptures and prayed. Why couldn't he get Harmony off his mind? Was there something he was supposed to do? The closest he got to an answer was the reassurance that he should stay in Cadmia.

He still sat next to her at church, but they didn't talk anymore.

There didn't seem to be anything left to say.

Was it even any of his business? No.

Yet he came up with entire lists of things to say while he was painting or installing new shelves or doing whatever he found to keep his hands busy. He even started rehearsing them the second week, determined to try to persuade her to stay on.

The plumber he hired got a huge laugh out of listening to him talk to himself, but as soon as Grant saw her on Sunday, his mind went as blank as a fresh sheet of paper.

Finally, the Sunday before Thanksgiving, he got knew he had to do something. So, after giving her a strained smile, he sat down and took her hand in his.

From the corner of his eye, he saw her expression shift rapidly from a polite smile to surprise and half a dozen other reactions, ranging from confused to happy and back to the polite smile.

He released her hand long enough to partake of the sacrament and pass the tray along, then tentatively reached for it again. Held onto it when she tried to get up and leave after Sunday school.

"Grant, I…" She began blinking erratically, trying to hold back the tears stinging her eyes.

"What're you doing for Thanksgiving?"

"What?" She tugged at her hand, but if he noticed he gave no sign. "N-n-nothing, I guess."

"Wonderful."

His tone and eyes made the word a caress, weakening her knees so that she was glad she was still seated.

"Come to Massachusetts and have Thanksgiving with me and my family." He held his breath, waiting to see if she'd accept his invitation. Leading with his heart was a new experience for him, but he didn't seem to have a choice in this case. Two weeks of cold, hard logic had gotten him nowhere.

She closed her eyes against the intensity of his gaze, but that had no effect on the squadron of planes using her stomach for acrobatic practice.

"It won't change my mind."

"About leaving?" He ran his thumb across the back of her hand. "I know."

She didn't trust her voice, so she nodded

stiffly. She was an idiot. There was no other name for it. Nevertheless. She released a shaky breath. This once, she would allow herself to live a dream. Even though it might easily become a nightmare.

"Would you rather fly or drive?"

"Close to fifteen hundred miles?" She managed a breathy chuckle. "I'll fly, any day of the week." His forehead wrinkled and she had to sit on her free hand to keep from reaching up to smooth it out. "When did you want to leave?"

"Wednesday morning if we're flying. And," he hand-shrugged, "assuming I can get tickets." It shouldn't be a problem. Last minute tickets were more expensive, that was all.

"Don't worry about tickets. We can take my plane."

Wednesday morning, a little earlier than he'd originally planned, he parked outside a modern prefabricated building and hauled his suitcase out. The door tripped a bell as he entered and the little man behind the counter squinted at him over his spectacles.

"Help ya?"

"Yeah." Grant grinned a little at the taciturn greeting. "I'm looking for Harmony Wells?"

"Ain't seen her today." The man resumed his paperwork. "Find her plane in Hanger H, though."

"Thanks." Chuckling, Grant walked back outside and studied the layout of the buildings. Whistling a carol, he strode along, the gravel crunching under his boots.

"Back off, Bob."

Grant slowed at the sound of Harmony's voice.

"Awww, c'mon. Just a little one?"

Grant winced at the following thud.

"I recommend you stay there." Harmony's tone left no room for doubt that she meant it.

Rounding the corner, Grant peered into the dim hanger. Harmony was doing something to her plane, with her back very deliberately to one corner.

As his eyes adjusted, he made out a pair of legs on the ground, then a grimacing face.

"Hey. You found the place." Harmony closed her preflight list. "Is that bag all you're bringing?"

"We'll only be there a few days," he reminded her as he complied.

"I'm just kidding. Toss it in the back." She pointed at her duffel on the floor. "I always travel light."

A clattering sound drew their attention to the wall behind them. Bob knocked over a second item as he bent to retrieve the first.

"Leave it." Harmony snapped. "Go clock out and dry out."

Grant looked more closely at Bob, the man

who'd abandoned him for a bar after the drag race in Topaz. The lighting was still bad, but he could see now that Bob's clothes were rumpled. He was blinking rapidly, too, as if struggling to focus. That, plus a faint whiff of something that reminded Grant of rotten fruit, explained a lot. So did the way Bob was rubbing the side of his face.

Harmony noticed when Grant shifted, placing himself ever so slightly between her and Bob as the handyman left. Though she appreciated the gesture, it wasn't necessary. Bob was a mouse with the manners of an alley cat.

"Did you hurt yourself?"

"Hmm?"

"When you hit him." Grant took both of her hands and examined them. Brushed his thumbs over her knuckles.

"You think I punched him? Don't be silly." Scoffing, she moved away and secured the back door. "Would you mind giving me a hand?"

Together they pushed the plane out onto the runway.

"All aboard!" She opened her door.

"If you didn't punch him, then what?" he asked as he climbed in on the passenger side.

"Nosey, aren't you?" she grumbled.

"Very nosey."

"Fine. I slapped him." She glared at him. "Satisfied?"

"You slapped him? That's it?"

"That's all he needed." She shrugged.

"I see."

She put her hand on the starter, then hesitated. "I always say a prayer before I take off."

He stilled, the previous matter forgotten. "That's a wonderful idea."

They folded their arms and she offered a heartfelt prayer for their safety during the flight. Silently, she added her prayer from the last few days, that she'd get along well with his family.

"Ready?" she asked after the amen.

"You bet."

"Buckle up, then." Smiling, she put on her headset and checked in with the tower while she flipped switches.

He twitched when the plane started moving. After hundreds of flights, including in private planes, there still seemed to be more window in his window seat than he was accustomed to.

"Better put that on." She pointed at the second headset, which he promptly slipped on. "We're on our way."

"Fabulous." He blinked and they were suddenly a few feet off the ground. To take his mind off what he could see, he began rambling about his family. And continued long after they reached cruising altitude, talking nearly the entire three flight. His voice grew hoarse, but thanks to his nieces and nephews, he never ran out of things to say.

Harmony listened patiently, even encouraging him with questions. Years of practice learning new names made it easy for her to keep up with the antics of his five nieces and nephews. The identical twin girls, Eliza and Jane, apparently had a bumpy entry to mortality, putting their mother, his sister Renee, on bedrest and still arriving prematurely. Perhaps, if she were very careful, she would be able to tell them apart based on his descriptions.

After a smooth landing, she parked the plane in a rented hanger and found her way through airport security to the nearest restroom.

"I'm just going to…" She paused and shuffled her feet. "It was a long flight. Be out in a few."

The 'few' turned out to be nearly fifteen minutes. Not long as one figured time, but longer than he'd expected. The results, however, were absolutely worth waiting for.

He couldn't stop staring. She'd pulled her gorgeous brown hair back into a loose French braid. And yes, she was wearing a little makeup, a first since they'd met. More than that, though, he saw the vulnerability she didn't hide quite well enough. She was scared. Of meeting his family? Or of spending time with him? Maybe both? He fervently wished he knew how to reassure her. She was going to love his family. She might even start reciprocating the feelings growing in his heart.

Harmony blushed a little under his perusal and scolded herself furiously. She wasn't wearing makeup for his sake, it was for her own. It was a simple dusting of powder, a swipe of mascara, and a little lip gloss. Just enough to make her feel less like the hayseed she'd been playing for the last three years.

After all, she wanted to look nice when she met his family.

No matter what she told herself, though, a small, stubborn piece of her heart insisted on hoping that he liked what he saw. Judging by the warmth in his eyes as he came over and took her by the hand, he liked it a lot. Her resolve weakened still further when his gaze lowered to her mouth.

Grant closed the distance between them, coming close enough to kiss her. He wanted to, more than he'd wanted anything since he'd decided to become a doctor at ten years old. He searched her eyes for permission while his brain screamed at him not to be an idiot. She was leaving Cadmia for points unknown. Kissing her now would only guarantee a longer recovery time.

I could follow her. The idea sprang unbidden to his mind.

Harmony swallowed hard and dropped her gaze as the longing in his eyes intensified. *This was a bad idea!* She should've stayed in Cadmia. Should've bought a turkey sandwich and frozen pie from Stock's and holed up in her own little corner.

The moment passed in a blink and Grant gritted his teeth, wishing he'd kissed her first and asked for permission later.

Turning slightly away from her, he spotted a lineup of taxis. Maintaining his hold on her hand, he started slowly toward them.

As their taxi pulled up in front of a two story, cream-colored house, she wiped sweaty palms on her slacks and tried to get her breathing to settle down. She was dimly aware of Grant getting their luggage out of the trunk and paying the driver.

Pocketing his wallet, Grant opened her door. "Ready?" Her eyebrows came up in a "now or never" look and she put her hand in his, allowing him to help her out. He carried both of their bags in one hand, draping his free arm around her shoulders.

"You'll love them," he promised as they made their way up the short walk, passing two fairly lopsided snowmen. "Mom's a world class cook and Dad's got enough hobbies to sink a small battleship."

She had just started to relax when the front door swung open and kids started pouring out of it. Her stomach landed forcibly in her throat as she watched five children of various ages come pelting down the sidewalk toward them.

"Uncle Grant!"

The squeals and cheers hit Harmony's ears like they were coming out of a concert speaker directly overhead.

Grant, feeling her shoulders tense, let go of her and advanced toward the children. Roaring at a moderate volume, he scooped up the twins, felt his oldest nephew clamber onto his back, and laughed helplessly when the remaining two glommed onto his legs.

"Alright you guys. Don't break Uncle Grant on the first day." A slim woman with dark blond hair skipped down the porch and rescued Grant from the boy on his back.

"Thanks, Steph." Grant kissed his oldest sister's cheek and wriggled his eyebrows at her son, Peter. "What've you been eating, monkey? You weigh a ton!"

That made all the kids giggle.

"So, is that her?" Steph lowered her voice but didn't try to hide her meaning. Grant hadn't brought a girl home since community choir some fifteen years ago.

He rolled his eyes and turned to smile at Harmony. *Whoa.* A minute ago she'd been acting like a scared rabbit. Now she practically oozed confidence.

Her heart beating like a jackhammer, Harmony sauntered over to where Grant stood next to a lovely woman. Her best guess was that the children stuck to him were the nieces and nephews he'd told her about during the flight.

The oldest one had to be Peter, which probably made the woman holding his hand his mother, Stephanie. The twins in his arms were Eliza and Jane. He was right, they were *very* hard to tell apart. Two sets of curious eyes peered up at her from around his legs and she couldn't help smiling back at Joey and Phil. Joey grinned right back, but Phil, the shier boy, buried his face in Grant's pant leg.

How she wished she had the luxury of hiding somewhere!

Reaching the small group, she held out her hand. "Hi. I'm Harmony."

"Stephanie. Welcome to Tenby." She tried not to study her brother's guest too closely, but curiosity had been eating at her since her mother called on Monday to tell her there would be 'one more for Thanksgiving dinner.'

Grant watched the women as they shook hands. Harmony seemed perfectly at ease, a queen greeting an equal.

"Thank you." It took every trick her drama teacher had ever taught her to keep from getting the shakes. She was meeting Grant's *family*. It meant nothing, of course—except where it meant everything to her.

"Who wants gingerbread?" A perky brunette stood on the porch, a tray in her hands that was so fresh out of the oven it was still steaming.

Grant put the twins down as quickly as he could, but Eliza clung to his neck until he changed his mind and straightened up again.

"M'lady wishes to ride," he announced, grinning.

"You always were her favorite," Stephanie remarked with a smile. Taking Grant and Harmony each by an arm, she started for the house. "Harmony, I should probably warn you that Mom's got a room all picked out for you already."

"That's very thoughtful of her." She should've booked a hotel. *How had she not thought of booking a hotel?!*

"Mhmm." Stephanie slanted a look at their guest. Something was off, she just couldn't put her finger on what it was. Maybe Renee would have better luck. She had girls.

"Hey, bro." Renee, the brunette with the gingerbread, kissed Grant's cheek, tickled Eliza's stomach, then smoothed the little girl's hair.

"How's she doing?" Grant asked.

"Oh, she's fine." Renee poked him lightly in the shoulder when he gave her a skeptical look. "You'd be the first one we called, count on it."

"Thanks." He still held Eliza a little tighter. "Renee, this is my friend, Harmony. Harmony, my sister, Renee."

"How do you do?" Harmony told herself to knock it off, but she couldn't seem to shake the formal behavior. Not without falling apart in tiny, nervous little pieces, at any rate. She wouldn't have minded if she didn't think she sounded stuffy.

"I'm very well, thank you." Renee flicked a glance at Stephanie.

"No, you don't." Stephanie shook her head vehemently. "No lectures on formalities and comportment over the holiday or I give you my word, I *will* slip cranberry sauce onto your plate."

Renee made a face at her. Grinned at Harmony. "The most difficult thing about having siblings is that they know all of your weaknesses."

"No." Stephanie countered. "The most difficult thing about having siblings is getting along during the holidays."

Renee blinked innocently. "Didn't I just say that?"

They both laughed and Harmony was able to breathe. They were joking. Teasing. Yeah. Sisters did that.

Catching Grant watching her worriedly, Harmony composed her face. She was going to have to be more careful if she wanted to pull this visit off.

"Here, let me have those." Stephanie took the bags from Grant and went through the door Renee opened for her. "I'll just put these in your rooms."

Harmony continued smiling as she was introduced to the rest of the family. Four sisters meant four brothers-in-law. Add in two parents and five nieces and nephews and she had fifteen names to keep straight with faces. Theoretically, the challenge would keep her mind off her worries. It was ridiculous to worry about relentless paparazzi in an ordinary town like Tenby.

"It's so nice to meet you." Grant's mother, Genevieve Reeves, or Genny for short, welcomed her with a hug.

Harmony held onto her longer than maybe she should've, her senses reeling from the experience. She hugged Merry, Grace, and Noella routinely, but somehow this hug provoked a flashback to the hugs her mother had given her.

"Yes, indeed." Todd, Grant's father, patted Harmony gently on the back. "Always a pleasure to have friends join us for Thanksgiving."

"Thank you." Oh, now she really *was* going to cry. Why couldn't her father have been like the dear, sweet man before her? Todd's sky-blue eyes were kind, his smile genuine, and she nearly walked into his arms for a hug.

"Did I mention that my friend Harmony is a race car driver?" Grant, sensing that something was wrong, threw himself into the conversation.

Chapter 11

"She is?" Gingerbread crumbs dribbled down the side of Joey's mouth as he spoke.

"A *real* race car driver?" Peter stared up at her in awe, his gingerbread apparently forgotten halfway to his mouth.

Harmony suddenly found herself surrounded by wide-eyed little boys. Even Phil was there, peeking at her from where he stood behind Peter.

"She sure is." Grant winked at Harmony, who looked back at him uncertainly. "Let me show you a picture of her car."

Curious, Harmony leaned in to see, too. His cellphone must've had a good camera, because she couldn't see that much difference between the professional racetrack shots and what he had. Of course, the tiny screen left something to be desired.

"Wow."

But clearly the boys were impressed. Three pairs of innocent eyes turned toward her.

"What's it like to drive a race car?" Peter asked.

"Can we ride in it?" Joey blurted.

Peter shook his head at his little brother. "She didn't bring it with her."

"She might have," insisted Joey.

Harmony felt a hand on her knee and looked

down to find Phil smiling shyly up at her. Her heart melted and she scooped the little boy up.

"Would you like to see some more pictures?"

Joey raced over to the couch and jumped up on it.

Peter, with the superiority that a two-year gap makes at that age, took her hand and led her over, and didn't sit until she was seated.

From the corner of her eye, Harmony saw Stephanie give Peter a thumbs-up.

"Here she is." The boys crowded around to watch as she scrolled through some of her favorite shots.

"She's beautiful," Joey breathed. "Will you give us a ride someday?"

"Well, Joey." Harmony bit her lip. She'd never broken a five-year-old's heart before. "She isn't mine anymore."

"How come?" His forehead furrowed.

"I sold her. It's someone else's turn to drive her now." She could feel Grant's eyes on her.

"I wouldn't sell my race car in a million years!" Joey said emphatically.

She ruffled his hair lightly. "Not even if you were moving and couldn't bring it with you?"

"Wellll…" He brightened suddenly. "Are you going to marry Uncle Grant and move here?"

Grant choked on a bite of gingerbread, prompting his brother-in-law Bill to start pounding him on the back.

Harmony felt hot all over, like when she ate the spicy salsa at the Purple Skink. If Grant's family had laser sights for eyes, she would've had ten red dots right between her eyes. Her heart and her head fought bitterly over what the right answer was, and not just because she wanted to be polite.

"I don't think we're supposed to ask questions like that," Peter admonished his little brother. Turning back to Harmony, he asked, "But how can you be a race car driver without a race car?"

She didn't laugh at his statement like some in the room did; instead, she shifted her focus to answering his question. "Some drivers borrow their cars from rich people." At least this was safe ground.

"Lunch time!" A woman Harmony hadn't met yet came into the front room. "All the kids who want more gingerbread today better come and eat real food!"

Peter stayed with Harmony a moment longer. "I'm sorry you had to sell your car."

"That's very sweet of you, Peter." She smiled sincerely. "But I'm glad she'll be with someone who loves to race."

The boy considered a moment, then nodded and ran after the others.

Which left her alone with Grant. Or as alone as they were likely to be in a house overcrowded with curious people.

Grant couldn't help staring at her. She'd had the perfect opportunity to tell his family there was nothing between them. And she'd let it pass. Did that mean…?

"We better join the others." Dusting crumbs from Joey's gingerbread from her lap into her other hand, she rose and followed Peter.

Grant kissed Elisa's cool cheek. "You love me, don't you?" The little girl looked up at him and smiled around the three fingers she was sucking on. "That's my girl."

After lunch they adjourned to the backyard for a snowball fight. To the front room for cards or downstairs for air hockey and board games. Then to the kitchen for sandwiches and back to the front room for a short movie before bed.

Harmony found herself with a lap full of sleepy Phil, who snuggled into her arms and started snoring softly before the movie was halfway done. She rested her cheek against his hair and closed her eyes, pretending he was hers. The last fifteen years of dodging paparazzi were all a bad dream and the deep voice chuckling from where Todd and Genny sat was really her dad, who was a very proud grandpa.

Gabby, Phil's mom—and a spectacular shot with a snowball—waited as long as she could before coming to retrieve her sleeping son.

"It was nice to meet you," she whispered as she straightened away.

Harmony's heart broke as she watched Phil's parents lovingly wrap him in his coat then duck out the door.

"Hey." Grant sat cross-legged on the floor next to her.

"No thanks." She shook her head when he offered her the bowl of popcorn. "I'm still full from supper."

"Harmony." He caught her hand as she started to rise. "You've been avoiding me. And that isn't easy to do in a house this size."

"I shouldn't have come." She cut straight to the heart of the problem.

"Why not?" He put some popcorn in his mouth to keep from talking while she thought over her answer.

"It isn't real."

"Uhhh…" Glancing around the room, his eyes settled on the television. She couldn't possibly mean the animated show they'd just watched.

"I've dreamed of this. Family coming over. Kids being spoiled by their grandparents."

He slipped his arm around her shoulders. "Snuggling by the heater after a long day?" His smile vanished when a tear sparkled down her cheek. "Harmony?"

She tried to get up, to run away to the bedroom she'd been assigned. At least there she'd have a door to close between them.

Here, there was nothing but the hard floor, a semblance of privacy, and Grant's arms.

He set the bowl aside and turned her so that she could hide her face against him while she sobbed. Her hair tickled his neck as he rocked her, his heart breaking with her every whimper.

He sent up a stream of silent prayers for her; and for himself, that he might know how to help her.

The storm passed gradually, until she was left lying in his arms with all the energy of a wrung out washcloth.

He kissed her forehead gently and propped her up against the wall. Getting to his feet, he scooped her into his arms and carried her to her room upstairs.

Miserable, she held still while he deposited her on her borrowed bed.

His whispered, "Sweet dreams," as he left should've made her snort. She wasn't going to dream. She'd rest while she waited for the house to quiet, then she'd slip out and fly back to Cadmia.

Or would she? She had a small emergency kit on the plane. She could fly as far as the money took her, then start over. Send Lydia a new burner phone on the way. That would be best.

Weariness crept over her as she plotted her new life hauling air freight and soon her breathing slowed. Her imagination wandered to the life she wanted, so that she woke startled and confused by the sound of Grant's voice calling her name.

"Harmony?" He knocked on her door a third time, wishing that he'd left it open a crack the night before. "Are you in there?" Icy dread swept over him and he wondered why he'd said that. Of course she was in there. As the silence stretched thinner and thinner, his confidence faded.

"Just a minute." Great. Her mouth tasted terrible and she sounded like she'd swallowed one of Merry's wood rasps. Her lips twisted in bitter humor. Just as well she wasn't married to Grant with four children. Who'd want to wake up to that voice if they didn't have to?

They were beautiful children, though. Her heart ached at losing them, no matter how hard she tried to tell herself they were just part of a dream.

"No hurry." His heart surged with relief and he whispered a prayer of thanks. "I, uh," he closed his eyes and tried to remember why he was there. "Breakfast in ten minutes."

"Thanks." No time for a shower. She made a face at the mirror where she was watching herself brush her teeth. She hadn't plugged her cell phone in, either, and the battery was dangerously low.

Dropping to her knees for morning prayer, she reminded herself that Heavenly Father already knew exactly what had happened, and plunged into her thanks, followed by a heartfelt plea for the day to go well.

"As long as I'm still here," she murmured, "please bless me to be a good guest." The scent of roasting turkey and bacon vied for dominance all the way downstairs where she discovered a spread that would've put a commercial buffet to shame.

Over a hearty breakfast of Belgian waffles, fruit, her choice of fried or scrambled eggs, bacon or sausage, and a never-ending glass of milk, Harmony learned the loose schedule for the day.

"It seems to work best to let families have the morning to themselves," explained Genny, who ate while puttering.

"So we'll have scripture study after breakfast," continued Todd, "then a few hours to breathe before family lunch."

"Usually followed by naps." Grant grinned as he refilled her glass. "And probably sledding on a hill nearby."

"Leftovers for supper," finished Genny, her head in a cupboard.

"Wow, you guys have it all figured out." Harmony tried not to think of her last Thanksgiving at home, but couldn't help it. It was burned into her mind.

The straw that broke her back was when her dad's latest girlfriend tried to give Lydia a drink of her alcohol that day. Harmony had been content keeping her sister out of the house whenever possible, or entrusting her to the servants when absolutely necessary, but hearing their inebriated dad giggle while he told whatever-her-name-was to cut it out knocked her world on its ear. She knew then that things had to change.

"Unless you don't want to?" Grant watched Harmony carefully, noting her deliberately blank face as well as her lack of response.

"Sorry, what?" Harmony blinked away the bad memories and focused on the man sitting beside her.

He started over as if he hadn't said anything. "The local theater is showing *Holiday Inn* today and I thought we might go see it."

"Oh, um." Harmony blinked and Genny had somehow walked off with her empty plate and utensils. "Yeah, I'd like that."

Todd almost had to physically intercept Genny to get her to leave the kitchen, but soon the whole family was comfortably arranged in the front room.

"Do you need to borrow a Book of Mormon, Harmony?" Todd smiled at her from his recliner. "Or do you use one of those devices?"

"Could I borrow one, please?" She'd started to reach for her phone only to remember that it was plugged in upstairs. Rather than asking everyone to wait and then having to hunt for an outlet down here, she gratefully accepted the worn paperback copy Todd passed her.

"We're in Alma 17," Genny supplied helpfully.

Harmony's heart flipped when she glimpsed Grant's name written in a tight scrawl on the inside of the cover. The pages were heavy with underlining in red pencil.

They started with a prayer, and as they read aloud, the underlined tenth verse leapt out at Harmony: "And it came to pass that the Lord did visit them with his Spirit, and said unto them: Be comforted. And they were comforted."

And they were comforted, she repeated to herself. Even as they read on, her thoughts kept coming back to that verse. What would it be like to have that much faith?

"You're sure you don't want any snacks?" Grant put his arm around her and stepped closer to ward off a boisterous group of teens that thankfully parted and flowed around them on their way to their movie.

"No, nothing." Harmony squinted up at him. "I had your old Book of Mormon during scripture study today."

"You did?" He probably shouldn't have been so surprised. "I must have left it there when I headed to college."

"Yeah." She fidgeted. "You underlined a lot of verses."

"There's a lot to try to keep track of in there." Pleased that she was staying near him, he drew her along as the line moved forward.

"You used red pencil for most of it, but I did see some places where you used blue."

"Blue was for extra special things," he nodded. He traded some cash for two tickets and they went to the next line. "I should go back through it and see if what stood out to me then still stands out now."

"You're so lucky," she sighed.

"How do you mean?" He gave her nine-tenths of his attention, sensing that something important had prompted the declaration.

"Your life. Your *whole* life you've had the gospel. A supportive family." She threw her hands up, nearly knocking an extra-large soda out of the hands of a passerby. "Sledding."

He tightened his hold on her, partly to keep her from talking with her hands anymore in the crowded lobby, and eased her forward a few more steps.

"You're a convert?" he asked gently.

"No, not exactly." Closing her eyes, she rested her head on his chest. "Mom joined the church when I was about three, so I was baptized at eight. Dad couldn't get past the Word of Wisdom." She swallowed hard. "After her death, he became a full-fledged alcoholic. My sister didn't get baptized until she was ten." She'd let Lydia make her own decision, and was grateful for the dozens of wonderful phone conversations they'd had as Lydia took the missionary discussions.

"I'm so sorry to hear about your dad." He hugged her tighter and blinked back the tears threatening him. Learning this made her even-handed response to Bob all the more amazing to him. She could've panicked and really let him have it, but she'd settled for the necessary slap.

Someone behind them cleared their throat. "Hey, do you two mind? The line's movin'."

"Sorry." Grant whisked her along, smiling despite his irritation at the interruption. "We don't have to go to the movie if you don't want to."

"It's the one where she talks about her paragon of a father, right?" she sniffled.

"Okay, let's go take a walk or something." He knew exactly the dialogue she was referencing. Pulling her out of line, he headed for the exit.

"Aren't you going to return the tickets?"

"No need." Her face cleared when he showed her the tickets before tossing them. "I'd rather they keep showing retro movies than give me the ten dollars back."

She nearly stopped right there to kiss him. The thought made her cheeks burn and she was glad to step out into the cold, crisp New England air.

He slowed as they cleared the crowds. "I'd say something about how all these folks should be at home with family on Thanksgiving," he joked glumly, "if I wasn't right out here with them."

Slipping her arm around his waist, she gave him a shy squeeze. This was a new feeling. Attractive men were a dime a dozen, but a man who'd drop his plans to make sure she was comfortable, inconveniencing himself in the process—she hadn't known many of them.

Hoping to get her to open up again, he stayed silent as they walked along the sidewalk, dodging slush puddles and other pedestrians.

"I didn't mean to complain back there," she said in a small voice. "I'm much too blessed to complain."

He risked pressing a kiss to the top of her head while they were stopped at a corner. "I didn't think you were complaining."

She sighed. "I guess I just wonder sometimes what my life would've been like if…well, if it had been more like yours." She wouldn't be on her second passport, that much she felt sure of.

"What has yours been like?" he coaxed gently.

"Busy." She rubbed her eyes. Somehow she found herself telling him about her time on the cruise ship, including how she'd injured her back when Van Phillips dropped her. Explained that she'd earned seventy percent of her business degree via online courses.

As she talked, Grant wished there was somewhere they could stop and sit so he could watch her face. He found it strange that her tone was sad when he thought her adventures were marvelous. Her words almost echoed, as if they were coming from a hollow spot deep inside her.

"You've done a lot of traveling," he admitted as they arrived back at his parents' car. "Much more than I have." He opened the door for her.

"I've enjoyed the travelling. Mostly."

"Only mostly?" He resumed the conversation as soon as he was behind the wheel.

"It…gets tiring after a while." She bit her lip, but sternly refused to tell him the rest of it. How lonely she'd been when she tried living in the family mansion after the lawyers cleared her dad out of it. That she only stayed in one place until a reporter stumbled across her. About not keeping in touch with any of the friends she'd made over the years.

"That makes sense," he nodded. "How about your sister? Does she like to travel?"

Her heart seized and her mind flew back over all they'd discussed. *My sister didn't get baptized until she was ten.*

"Harmony? What's wrong?" Her expression was perfectly normal, but she had a white-knuckled grip on her own hands that worried him.

"She doesn't." Her eyes flicked in his direction. That was a terrible answer. If she didn't act normally, he'd be a lot more likely to remember her slip. "She's busy with school and friends and things."

"Oh." Perplexed, Grant focused on his driving for a while. Roused himself to point out a few local landmarks, yet couldn't shake the feeling that Harmony had withheld more than she'd shared.

"Looks like we're the last ones back," she observed as they approached his parents' house.

"Good thing we're early," he chuckled.

Chapter 12

"Do we…" Harmony looked down at her hands and willed them to stop twisting in her lap as Grant parked. "Do we have to tell them we didn't go to the movie?"

"Not if you're rather we didn't." Grant winked. "You talk about how hungry you are and I'll field the questions about the movie. Okay?" She rewarded him with a faint smile.

"Deal." She closed her eyes while she waited for him to come around the car and open her door, something he apparently liked to do. She didn't mind. It was quiet in the garage and she needed a moment to collect herself.

The moment turned into five. Then twenty. She cracked an eye open and there he was, patiently leaning against his mom's car, waiting for her to be ready. Somehow that settled her more than twenty minutes of silence could've.

Grateful for his consideration, she opened the door a smidge, then let him swing it wide for her.

As she got out, the toe of her shoe hooked itself on the lip of the car, sending her catapulting straight into his arms. The sound of her own gasp reverberated in her mind, keeping time with her pounding heart as she stared up at him.

The desire to kiss her hit him like a bolt of lightning. He'd never been opposed to the idea, but this was almost overpowering. The longer he hesitated, the louder the electricity between them crackled and buzzed.

"Uncle Grant!" Peter's voice hit them like foam from a fire extinguisher.

Harmony jerked in surprise. She'd forgotten there was a house full of family on the other side of the garage door. Forgotten that she couldn't risk falling in love. Forgotten…everything. Except Grant.

"Coming, Peter," he responded. His arms fell to his sides as Harmony backed away from him, her eyes wide with what he thought was fear.

"Okay. Please hurry. We can't start without you."

Harmony shook her head, the child's voice clearing away the last of her bemusement.

"Here we come!" Grant followed her at a discreet distance, as much for his sake as hers. Logically, he knew she hadn't intentionally fallen into his arms. On a more visceral level, he felt wounded by the way she'd retreated. He fought back the resulting inner turmoil and joked with his siblings at the same time. Realizing he was fighting a losing battle, he excused himself to go to the bathroom.

He paused at the top of the stairs and nearly went into his bedroom instead. Then, to keep himself honest, he entered the bathroom and closed the door behind him. Dropping to his knees by the bathtub, he poured out his heart to his Heavenly Father.

"I know so little about her. Why do I feel…so drawn to her?" As he prayed, the agitation seeped out of him. "I guess I'm scared, too," he admitted quietly. "Right now we almost know where we stand." Except when he didn't. "A kiss would change that."

Getting to his feet, he washed his hands as thoroughly as if he was about to operate. Shook water off his fingers and carefully dried them.

"There he is!" Joey pointed at him when he came back downstairs.

"Sorry everyone," he mumbled. He should've told them to go ahead without them. But since he hadn't… "Should I say the prayer, Dad?"

"That's alright, Grant. I've already asked someone." Todd folded his arms and everyone else politely followed suit.

Much to Harmony's surprise, it was Todd's deep voice that offered a humble prayer over the food and thanking Heavenly Father for his family. If her dad was anything like Todd… Her throat tightened. No use wishing for things she would never get.

Several times during the meal, Grant caught his mother watching either him or Harmony.

Like him, she knew something was wrong. But how? Harmony laughed at the stories, helped the children, ate her fair share, and was, on a surface level, absolutely fine.

"Will you go sledding wif us?" Phil asked Harmony, revealing an endearing lisp.

"I would love to." She probably would've agreed to go to the moon with this enchanting little boy.

He grinned and stuffed a forkful of pie into his mouth.

Chuckling, Harmony concentrated on her own coconut cream pie, pacing herself so that she finished when Phil did.

"We need our coats," he told her gravely as they got ready to leave.

"That's very smart." She helped him straighten his coat sleeves, which were partially inside out, found his knit cap hidden in his hood, and wiped the last little bit of pie off his chin before he struggled into his scarf.

"I can do it," he insisted when she offered to help, so she hurried into her own things and held his hand on the short walk to his family's car.

Gabby smiled invitingly, and Harmony gladly climbed into the back with the little boy. His non-stop chatter carried them to their sledding destination.

"A school?" Harmony shot Gabby a questioning look. There was no snow on the black asphalt of the parking lot, so was this a short stop on their way somewhere else?

"Sort of." Linking her arm through her husband's, Gabby beckoned for Harmony to follow.

The three-person sled in Roger's hand piqued her curiosity, and Harmony fell into line behind Phil, who hopped along in his parents' footsteps even though the snow wasn't very tall near the building they were skirting.

"Behold!" Gabby swung her arm out in front of her, indicating the view.

"Whoa…" A hill slanted away from the back of the school at an angle that even a parked car couldn't have resisted.

"Impressive, right?" Roger gave a moment of attention to the sled he was carrying and it pulled apart into two somewhat sturdy-looking plastic sleds. "Have you been sledding before?"

"I've been skiing." She accepted the sled slowly.

"There's nothing to it." Gabby promised. "Here, let's take the first ride together, okay?"

Harmony snuck a look at the people around them, but Grant hadn't shown up yet. "That'd be great, thanks."

"You sit down first." Gabby positioned her. "And I'll be in back so I can steer."

"Oh-oh-ohhhh!" The word became a paragraph as they sailed down the hill, Gabby expertly guiding the sled to one side as it coasted to a stop.

"Are you alright?" Gabby touched her arm, sounding genuinely worried.

"Sure. Fine." Harmony wobbled a little when she stood. "I always thought I'd hear it if I broke the sound barrier, though."

Roger hooted as he and Phil joined them. "It's a fast hill, but not that fast."

"Ride wif me next, Harm'ny!" Phil begged, seizing her hand.

"I'd love to." Harmony studied the other sleds racing down the hill, noting the way the adults used their hands and feet like ski poles to change direction or speed.

"You and Daddy go ahead," Gabby suggested. "Harmony and I are going to walk kind of slowly."

"Good idea." Harmony laughed even though she thought she knew what they were going to talk about as they walked. "Your son is so adorable."

"And he talks to you." Gabby's raised eyebrows said a lot about how unusual that was. "That's a pretty good recommendation in my book."

"Recommendation?" Harmony rubbed her cold nose to keep it from freezing.

"Yeah, he seems to think you'd make great aunt material." Gabby waited for her to respond, then pushed on. "What do you think of the idea?"

She shrugged. "I hope I'll have a nephew as sweet as Phil when I become an aunt."

"Hmmm." Gabby's eyes narrowed. "There's really nothing between you and Grant?"

Thinking back to their moment in the garage, and other times when there *could* have been something, Harmony hesitated.

"You don't seem very certain." Gabby squeezed her arm. "Look, I'm not sure what's where in your timeline. Everybody's different. So all I'll say is that you've got my vote, too."

Gabby's words brought a lump to Harmony's throat that refused to be swallowed. And she just happened to make eye contact with Grant as Gabby let go of her arm.

"Are you ready?" Phil hit her legs like a miniature whirlwind.

The lump in her throat got even bigger. *Was she ever.* But she wouldn't trade Lydia's future for her own. Lydia, who didn't need her high school graduation ceremony crashed by unscrupulous reporters.

"Let's go!" She hustled Phil over to the sled, where he obediently took the front seat. "One." She took a deep breath and focused on the hill. "Two."

"Three!" He shouted loud enough for the entire neighborhood to hear.

Laughing, she pushed off. They got passed twice before they reached the bottom, which was okay with her. They were both still in one piece and that was what mattered.

"Again, again!"

She managed to make the hike up the hill four more times before she knew she had to surrender.

"There you are!" Roger scooped up his son and swung him around in a circle. "I think you've worn your new friend right out, big guy."

Phil shoved his hat out of his eyes and sent Harmony a heart-melting smile. "Sorry."

"Don't be sorry." She pressed a kiss to his cold cheek. "That's the most fun I've had in a long time."

He giggled and ducked back behind his dad's shoulder.

"We only have time for a couple more runs, alright, buddy?" Roger winked at Harmony, plopped Phil onto the sled, and climbed on behind him. "Ready?"

"Set!" Phil shouted.

"Go!"

Harmony stared after them, smiling at Phil's giddy shrieks as his dad dug his hands into the snow, propelling the sled faster and faster until they flew off it to land in the soft snow well beyond where her more sedate rides had taken them.

"I'll have children someday," she promised herself.

"Of course you will." Genny peered anxiously into the young woman's face. "I'm sorry, I didn't mean to eavesdrop."

"No, it's okay." Harmony shoved her hands into her coat pockets. "I was just talking to myself."

"A private conversation if ever there was one." Genny smiled sincerely. Turning to watch her grandchildren again, Genny asked innocently, "How did you like the movie? *Holiday Inn* is one of my favorites."

Groaning inwardly, Harmony shrugged. She didn't want to lie to her hostess. Especially not to Grant's mother.

"You didn't actually see it today, did you?" Genny's lips twitched. "I wondered if you two might not have something better to do than go to a movie." Truthfully, she'd been disappointed that Harmony had returned without an engagement ring on her finger.

"Nothing like that." Harmony hastily corrected the misconception she heard in Genny's tone, then flinched. If *not* that, then what? She'd done it this time. "We took a walk. Downtown."

"Oh." For the next few seconds, Genny couldn't seem to decide whether to look at Harmony or watch her grandchildren. "Would you mind awfully if I got a bit nosey?"

Harmony shook her head. "I'd say it's about time. For the record, Sister Reeves, your son and I are just friends. We haven't even been that for very long."

"I...see." She did, didn't she? The enigmatic young woman her son had brought as his guest to their family get-together was just his friend. And barely that. Odd. With the signs they were giving off, she would've said they were falling in love. "Just friends."

Harmony's world gradually tilted. *Just friends... Just friends...*

"Everything okay over here?" Grant shot his mother a thinly veiled look of suspicion.

"Fine." Genny smiled serenely at him.

"Okay, pack it up!" Bill, Stephanie's husband, put his fingers to his lips and whistled to be sure he got everyone's attention. "Leftovers, cookies, and hot chocolate at Grandma and Grandpa's!"

The soggy, weary group tumbled into their cars, where Eliza began to cry for Uncle Gwant.

Grant, who'd had every intention of keeping an eye on his mother and Harmony, wound up riding with his sister instead.

"Dear Eliza." Genny waved mischievously at her mildly glaring son. "She does love her Uncle Grant."

"It's only natural after what he did for her." Harmony headed for the only remaining car, the others having swiftly loaded and left.

"Oh? He told you about that?" Genny had to hurry to catch up.

"Four hours in the air can be a long time in a small plane." Harmony ducked into the back seat and closed the door. Her phone buzzed with a new email and her jaw dropped as she read it. "I don't believe it!"

"Hmm? Don't believe what, dear?" Genny turned in the passenger seat to look at her.

Harmony reread the short email. "My friend in Cadmia is overseeing the annual Christmas play this year and, to help her out, I contacted an indie singer to see if she would sing in it." Holding up her phone, Harmony pointed at it. "She just said she'd be delighted to come!"

"That's wonderful!" Genny frowned slightly. "What's an indie singer?"

Sensing an opportunity, Harmony switched gears and pulled up some of Helen Montgomery's Christmas carols while she explained. She even handed her phone over so Genny could look at Helen's website. It turned out to be the perfect distraction, allowing them to complete the short ride back to their house without further awkwardness.

"And she's travelling all the way to Cadmia?" Genny asked, wide-eyed. Closing her car door behind her, she gave Harmony back her phone.

"Amazing, isn't it?" Harmony didn't bother to hide her disbelief as she added, "And she hasn't said a word about being paid for her time."

"There's hope for the world yet!" A beaming Todd wrapped an arm around his wife and politely herded them inside, where the kitchen was a veritable beehive of activity.

Turkey sandwiches, turkey and gravy, and even plain turkey was being dished up and served out to the hungry sledders. Betty and Wes, Grant's youngest sister and her husband, were making hot cocoa assembly line style.

Peter, as the oldest grandson, was tasked with serving mugs to his grandparents, then their guest, Harmony. Finally, with a great sigh of satisfaction, he accepted a mug that was all his, complete with *lots* of colorful mini marshmallows.

Harmony sat back and soaked it all in. She'd had a wild emotional ride on this trip, but being able to enjoy the friendly chaos was wonderful. She used to do things like this all the time. Somebody would find out she was spending the holidays alone and she'd let them rope her into their plans.

Like traveling, faux family events lost their luster quickly, and she had indeed gone to ground the past few years, hiding at home as much as possible until the last of the glitter blew away in January sometime. Maybe someday she'd figure out what made this visit different.

"How's the cocoa?" Grant slid onto the chair beside her, his arm coming to rest quite naturally around her shoulders.

"Better than Susan's." They shared a smile and she rested her forearms on the table to give herself some space.

"Listen." He set his cocoa on the table and mimicked her pose. "I don't know what my mom said out there, but I don't want it to worry you."

"Nothing to worry about." She took a sip of cocoa. Time to change the subject. "Hey, you didn't hear. We've got a genuine celebrity coming to this year's annual Christmas play."

Startled, Grant took the phone she was proffering and read, "Helen Montgomery." His forehead crinkled. "Why does that name sound so familiar?"

"Because she's a celebrity, Grant." Stephanie, who happened to be walking by in time to hear the exchange, threw a wadded up napkin at him.

"Har, har." He threw it back at her and tapped the icon that took him to Helen's song list. Turned on a sample and snapped his fingers. "I've got it! I heard this song playing at Stock's last week."

"And all over town." Harmony laughed and took her phone back. Everyone else had tuned in when he started playing the sample, so she turned the volume up a little and turned on her copy of the song.

"We all have our dreams. We all have our

fears." Helen's throaty alto spread through the now-quiet group. "So open your eyes! Open your ears! See what the world has to offer. And offer your hand to those around you."

"Wow." Gabby spoke for all of them as the song faded out. "That was amazing."

"A lot of heart in that song," Wes agreed.

"Helen Montgomery," Harmony slipped the name drop in, "definitely has a way with words." She could tell the sisters were making mental notes to look the singer up.

"And you say she's coming to sing in your play?" Renee sounded suitably impressed.

"Mmm." She set her mug down. "It's not my play, it's Cadmia's. My friend just happened to volunteer to be in charge of pulling the rabbit out of the hat this year."

They all chuckled at that.

"Still, it sounds terribly exciting." Genny caught Jane's napkin as it slipped off the table. "Are you going to be in the play?"

"I, uh…" Harmony faked a laugh and looked at Grant out of the corner of her eye. "Well…"

Genny clapped her hands, and the twins followed suit. "How exciting! We seem to have a celebrity at our table!"

"Nothing's settled," she hastily inserted. "I haven't even asked Grant if…" *Oh crud.*

He was staring at her. They were all staring at her, but he was the only one that mattered.

"Noella is having trouble finding volunteers to play the parents in the play." The words came out in a rush and she gulped hot cocoa to keep her heart from escaping through her mouth. It lodged in her throat, beating painfully.

"You'll do it, right?" Stephanie used her 'big sister' voice, which wasn't necessarily less scary than her "mom" voice.

"I…" Grant fumbled with his mug, nearly upsetting it. He met Harmony's eyes and thought he read a "please no" there. Except that didn't make sense. How, exactly, had he gotten into the conversation between Harmony and Noella in the first place unless Harmony wanted him there?

"Of course he will," interjected Genny. "It's for charity, isn't it Harmony?"

"Yup." She waited for Grant to speak, hoping he'd find a way to beg off. Hey, wait. "It's so close to Christmas, though, I'm she'd understand if you're planning to be out here again, visiting family."

"How close?" Gabby had a mischievous gleam in her eyes and an innocent smile on her lips.

"Really close." Harmony forced the words out. Why did she have the eerie feeling that Gabby knew exactly why she didn't want Grant to agree? There was just the one kiss at the end, to round out the family's story. Only…he wasn't the kind of man she could casually kiss and walk away from.

"It's just two performances, isn't it? And one's on the twentieth?" Grant nearly died from the twin lasers Harmony's eyes shot at him.

"Yeah." She took another drink and shifted so she wouldn't have to look at him.

"That's settled then." Genny added more miniature marshmallows to the twins' mugs, prompting Renee to protest.

"Mother! If you feed my children any more sugar, you can just come to the hotel and put them to bed yourself."

Genny's response was lost in the laughter.

Chapter 13

Harmony closed her eyes against the commotion surrounding her. Technically, *Grant* hadn't agreed to be in the play. So why did she sense a kiss looming in their future?

"Goodnight, Mom."

"Goodnight, Dad."

As she tuned back in, each fond farewell hit Harmony like a hammer. As she prayed for strength, though, the Holy Ghost brought a general conference quote to her mind. It came through crystal clear, right down to her hearing Elder Holland's voice as he said, "Furthermore, envy is a mistake that just keeps on giving. Obviously we suffer a little when some *misfortune* befalls *us*, but envy requires us to suffer all *good fortune* that befalls *everyone* we know! What a bright prospect that is—downing another quart of pickle juice every time anyone around you has a happy moment!"

"What's so funny?" Grant eyed her, not sure at this point whether to smile along or be worried.

"No, I...I thought of something." Something she couldn't possibly have explained without sharing a lot more than she felt up to right then.

"Well, kids, we're going to bed, too." Todd stifled a yawn. "All that sledding wore me right out."

Harmony rose abruptly. "Before you go, I'd like to thank you for having me as your guest."

Todd's forehead crinkled in confusion. "You say that like you're not planning to be here in the morning, Harmony."

Hearing him say her name as tenderly as he had any of his daughter's brought tears to her eyes.

"I…" She coughed. She could've made an excuse about not having packed the right clothes, but excuses were too easy to tear down. "I'm afraid I won't be. I have to leave tomorrow." She flashed an apologetic look at Grant. "I need to get back."

"I hope nothing's wrong." Genny looked pointedly at Grant, who rolled his eyes.

"No, I just…" She couldn't put it into words.

"We understand." Todd folded her in a daddy hug that she'd never forget. "And we're sure glad you could join us for Thanksgiving."

Genny smiled and hugged her, too. "Will you be alright flying all that way by yourself?" she fished.

"I won't be alone, Sister Reeves." Harmony gently wedged the formality between them. "There's always a radio tower nearby."

"How nice." Genny blew Grant a kiss and let Todd lead her away.

Alone in the kitchen, Harmony was keenly aware of Grant. "You don't have to be in the play if you don't want to."

"I don't mind." He watched her, wishing she'd look at him. "Why do you mind?"

"Me? What do you mean?" Draining her mug, she took it to the sink to rinse it before adding it to the dishwasher.

"I mean you obviously wanted me to say no."

She laughed and hunched her shoulders. "So why didn't you?"

He rubbed the back of his neck. "That's a good question. I guess my mom beat me to it."

"You can still say no." She watched his reflection in the darkened kitchen window. "There's, um, a kiss at the end."

"A…" He almost dropped his mug. "Oh. Is that why you don't want to be in it? Because you'd have to kiss me?"

"It's nothing personal." Hastily, she turned to face him. Her cheeks grew hot. It was, in fact, *very* personal. "No need to add fuel to the gossip fire in Cadmia, right?"

"Right." That wasn't very convincing.

Sensing that he didn't believe her, she added, "And Noella's already started rehearsals with the younger cast members…"

"That means she's running out of time." Grant watched her keenly. "I don't see how I can say no." He got to his feet and took her by the shoulders. His mind wasn't on the play. "I thought the plan was to stay until Monday."

"It was." The warmth coursing through her had nothing to do with the hot cocoa. "Plans change."

"What time should I be ready?" He conveniently ignored what she'd told his mother.

"I'll take off around dawn." The winter sun rose too late for her taste, but it was a practical choice given this colder weather. "You, however, should stay. Enjoy your family."

He brushed a tear off her cheek and asked helplessly, "What do you want from me, Harmony?"

"I don't know." Wrapping her arms around his waist, she pressed her cheek against his chest. "I mean, I know, I just…I can't…have you."

"You can if you really want me." Eyes closed, he whispered the words into her hair.

Time stopped as they silently reflected on their crazy relationship. They'd both insisted they weren't dating. Anybody, not just each other. Now here they were, huddling together in his parents' kitchen, murmuring things they would never have said in Cadmia.

"I'd be a fool not to." She resisted his attempt to kiss her.

"Harmony?"

Hearing the despair in his voice, she tightened her hold. "I'm not just moving at the end of the year because I'm bored. I'm ducking the media."

"The media? As in the paparazzi?" he teased. "Why would they be after you?"

"It's…complicated." Her gut churned as she withdrew a few steps from his embrace. Stood as straight as she could while her entire body tried to walk back into his arms. She still wasn't ready to tell him she was an heiress.

"It has something to do with…" She turned in a slow circle then, not finding a way out of it, she reluctantly met his eyes. "With my dad."

"Your dad? I thought you told me he was dead."

She shook her head. "The point is," she dragged in a deep breath, "when I leave Cadmia, I won't look back." An exaggeration, perhaps, but a very necessary one. He deserved to know to cut his losses now.

He slowly ran a hand over his face. "I'm guessing you haven't told a lot of people about this." He had several more questions, but they stuck in his throat.

"You're the first in a very long time." She clenched her fists and hugged her midsection. "I couldn't let you think…I didn't…care." Her words were punctuated with tiny gasps of agony. When he reached for her, she turned and sprinted up the stairs to her room.

Grant flopped into a chair and stared at the

empty space where she'd been. This was how it was going to be, then. Another month at the most and he'd have nothing but a few deliciously painful memories.

"Why, Heavenly Father?" He rested his head in his hands. "Why let me come so close only to lose her?"

Upstairs, Harmony curled up on top of the bed covers and whispered much the same prayer. "A couple of months, that's all. I couldn't have met him a couple of months from now?" She'd never yet been able to return to normal relations with people after the paparazzi 'revealed' her.

The sound of footsteps in the hall made her tense. Coming from the stairs like they were, they had to belong to Grant. The footsteps stopped in front of her door and she bit her knuckle to keep from calling to him. Thankfully, the footsteps resumed before she changed her mind and she was again left alone in the dark.

I can do this. I can hold out a few more months. Then Lydia and I can go home.

Her lips twisted bitterly at the thought of calling the house where she'd grown up 'home.' It was certainly too big for just her and Lydia. Swiping at her tears, she toyed with the idea of having it bulldozed. Or hiring someone to implode it. Might be fun to see it come down.

Except…she'd miss it. Had missed it for the

last ten years. The little library on the southeast corner. The huge playroom on the second floor, where her mother's laughter might still echo. She sniffled as she remembered spending summer nights in the attic, learning to use an expensive telescope. Her dad hadn't been much of a teacher, but he'd tried. Before the alcohol ruined him.

So, the house wouldn't come down. Not right away.

She made a mental list of other things she might do with the building, including turning the entire first floor into a casual library for the neighborhood children. Eventually, exhausted from the day, she dropped into a light doze.

Something—who knew what?—woke her after only a few hours. Scrubbing at bleary eyes, she packed her toiletry kit and stuffed her dirty clothes into the plastic bag she'd packed for them. Knelt in sorrowful prayer, then slipped down the stairs on cat feet, her shoes in her hand.

Making sure the door was locked behind her, she left the house.

"You've reached the New England taxi company." A brisk voice answered her call.

"Morning. I need a taxi." She gave her location.

"Got it. I'll have a driver there in ten minutes."

Ten very long minutes later, Harmony was

on the verge of doing jumping jacks to stay warm when a white taxi pulled up to one of the stop signs. She waved for him to stay there and hurried over to climb in.

"Say, you're a real early bird!" The driver, a middle-aged man who didn't look like he could outrun a jelly donut if he wanted to, gave her a once-over. "Traveling light?"

She ignored the impertinent question. "Where's the nearest open restaurant? Someplace that serves more than coffee and baked goods."

"Eh, that'd be… Torguson's on eighth."

She confirmed that on her phone and nodded. "Perfect. That's our first stop. Mind if I eat in your taxi?" With his okay, she placed a pickup order while he drove, then had him take her to a light rail stop.

"We go anywhere in Massachusetts," he told her as he pulled in. "Reasonable rates, too."

"Thanks." She wiped her mouth and handed over the fare, including a generous tip. "I like trains."

Especially when they helped confuse her backtrail. She'd studied the schedule between bites in the taxi, so she knew exactly which route she wanted. She bought a ticket to the airport and walked over to the modest overhang some overpriced architect had designed as a public transport 'shelter.'

Her cheeks froze first. Then her knees and shoulders. She was nearing popsicle status when the train finally pulled in, four minutes late.

Ascending carefully, she made her way to the second level. As she'd hoped, it was empty, nobody else having gone to the bother of climbing the stairs. Setting her phone on the table in front of her, she said a short prayer and started her scripture study.

And they were comforted. Mormon's description of the sons of Mosiah hit her so strongly that she turned to Alma 17 and reread that chapter. Her whole perspective seemed to change, allowing her to see herself in the story.

In the middle of the wilderness, on a mission to teach the Lamanites about their Savior, Jesus Christ, these young men had called upon the Lord for help—and received it.

Well, she was far from home, too. Nothing as noble as a mission, but she was doing her best to keep the commandments. The more she thought about it, the more her problems—past, present, and future—paled in comparison with imprisonment and starvation for believing in Jesus Christ.

By the time she got off the train at the airport, she felt supremely calm. If she could fall in love with Grant without realizing it, she could fall in love with someone else on purpose.

On a whim, she whipped her phone out and placed an order for three electric blue remote control cars to go to Brother and Sister Reeve's house. Then, not wanting to leave Eliza and Jane out, she got them each a hot pink remote control jeep.

Once she'd made it through airport security, she made a beeline for her plane. As she ran through her preflight list, she filed her flight plan on her phone.

A pang of regret filled her as she swung onto the runway. She hadn't even said goodbye to Phil.

Then she steeled herself and called the tower.

"Clear for takeoff."

Despite what she'd told Sister Reeves, she didn't speak to another mortal until it was time to land at the much smaller airport in Cadmia.

She prayed a lot, though. Told her Heavenly Father that she needed help deciding where to move next. It would only be for a little while, but for once she wanted to ask if there was a particular somewhere she *should* go.

She was still humming "I'll Go Where You Want Me to Go" an hour later when she set down in Cadmia.

The first thing she did, now that she was back in the same time zone, was call Noella.

"Hello?" The sounds of road noise filled the silence immediately after the greeting, telling

Harmony she'd caught her friend on one of her weekly commutes.

"I got an email from Helen Montgomery," she announced without preamble. "She said yes." Wincing, she held the phone away from her ear as Noella squealed in delight.

"Perfect! We have our draw! And…our parents?"

"Oh, good grief." Harmony groaned. "In a town of two thousand people you can't find someone else?" Getting Noella to let them off the hook was her last hope.

"It is short notice!" Noella paused. "Sort of."

"Yeah, I'll sort of…" Harmony looked up to heaven and reined in her frustration. "Does it have to be Grant?" Ugh, she was whining!

"There is someone else you would prefer to kiss in front of an audience?"

Harmony rolled her eyes and hung up. Blasted know-it-all… Kicking a tire gently, she hopped in her car and drove to her house, where she logged some sleep on her couch.

The afternoon sun was glaring through her kitchen window when she got up to take a turn in the bathroom. Since her holiday was over, she opened her business email and whistled softly.

"Better get some of this taken care of." Grabbing a cheese stick, she began assembling orders in her storeroom. When the stack of boxes in the corner was waist high, she finally gave into her growling stomach.

"Empty fridge for supper. My favorite." After the delicious, home-cooked meals at the Reeves', the frozen meals in her freezer were less than tempting. "Blinky's it is."

The crowded parking lot nearly changed her mind for her, but Fireclay was just too far to go tonight, even for a delicious meal at the Purple Skink.

"Harmony!"

"Noella!" She happily returned her friend's hug, then looked around for the boyfriend. Danny, she thought his name was? "Are you alone tonight?"

"Oui, just me." Noella bumped her shoulder. "And you?"

"Just me." Harmony shrugged and hoped her smile was believable.

"Then we should eat together. Catch up."

Harmony let her do most of the talking, interrupting only to place an order for the meal she'd seen Grant eating there.

"You want all of that on one plate?" The teenager behind the counter clarified.

"That's the idea. Oh, and pico de gallo, too." She handed over her debit card and the girl swiped it.

"We'll bring it right out."

They snagged a booth just as the bus boy finished cleaning it, and Noella heaved a heartfelt sigh.

"What's wrong?" Harmony jumped at the chance to redirect Noella's attention from Thanksgiving. "Is it the play?"

"Yes. Or rather, the community center." Leaning close, she muttered, "It stinks of fish."

"Fish." Harmony stared at her blankly. "That's weird." An understatement at best.

"It gets worse."

Harmony listened in astonishment as Noella related the entire incident, from the tremendous stench at the community center to watching Mrs. Arnold drive away.

"The way you describe it," she interrupted, "I'm surprised Mrs. Arnold didn't wave at you on her way past." She'd never liked that woman. Too manipulative.

"Perhaps she will next time." Noella massaged her temples and shot a dark look at the noisy teenagers in the far corner.

"*Next* time?" Harmony scowled as she stole a fry and dunked it in ketchup.

"Oui." Shoving her half-eaten burger aside, Noella put her elbows on the table. Ticked off the events on her fingers. "First, I get committee approval with no help from the committee. Next, someone mysteriously takes down all my flyers. *Just* as mysteriously, they go back up, which I do not understand. But third, people go out of their way to tell me how sorry they are Mrs. Arnold's children will not be in the play."

"Serves them right for not showing up at the audition," Harmony muttered.

"And now, this! This…rotten shrimp."

Harmony smothered a smile in her napkin. It wouldn't have surprised her to see smoke coming out of Noella's ears.

"With her conveniently on hand to watch the results of her sabotage." Harmony twisted the straw of her shake. "Yeah. She probably will try again if she figures it's the only way to stop you."

"Wait. This is an idea." Noella perked up. "Yes, I think it will work. Father Tom will let us keep using the kitchen, I am sure of that."

"Hello?" When she didn't explain quickly enough, Harmony waved a hand in front of her face. "*What* will work?" She listened intently as Noella outlined her very simple plan. "I like it." She shoved Noella's burger back in front of her. "Now eat. Tomorrow's fast Sunday."

Her eyes narrowed as she watched Noella demonstrate a peculiar interest in the arrangement of her remaining pickles.

"You have asked Grant about the play?" Noella peeked at Harmony through her lashes.

"Actually." Harmony's stomach fluttered as she wiped her mouth, then her fingers, stalling. "I did." Her eyes flicked toward Noella. Returned to studying her own plate. "And he said yes." She cringed away from Noella's triumphant squeal and the attention it garnered.

"Magnifique!"

Harmony glared at everyone who turned to look. Next, she glared at Noella. "We are not kissing at rehearsals," she hissed. The last thing she needed was to get used to being in his arms, to feeling his lips on hers. *Get a grip!*

"No problem." Noella winked. "I'm sure you get enough practice as it is."

Harmony crumpled her napkin savagely. If it had been any of Noella's business, she might have told her that Grant had never kissed her. Not even when she wanted him to.

Instead she asked, "When are you going to clean out the building?"

Noella shuddered dramatically. "Monday. *Very* early."

"I'll help you." Harmony shrugged off Noella's thanks. "I guess I'm just a glutton for punishment, that's all."

Chapter 14

"Didn't realize I was volunteering for the dawn patrol," Harmony yawned as she pulled up to the community center on Monday. It wasn't just that it was *early*. She hadn't slept well last night. And when she did, she dreamed of Grant, down on one knee.

"We must not be seen." Noella drummed her fingers on her knee. "It was very selfish of Mrs. Arnold to sabotage the entire community center to regain control of the play. Luckily for us, I have checked and no one is scheduled to use this building for another week."

"Lucky, right." Harmony yawned again. "Are you going to talk to her about it? I mean, about any of this? If she figures out the place is useable again, she might do something even worse." That sounded vaguely familiar, like she'd said it before.

"What could be worse?" Noella flinched. "Never mind, I don't want to know."

Harmony chuckled as she guided one tire up onto the sidewalk so they were as close to a door as they could get. "Let's get the stuff inside. Then I'll move my car to the other side of the park just in case."

It took a little effort, but Harmony found some humor in the stinky job.

"I do not know how you can sing in this

smell." Noella pulled her ladder over to the next light fixture and started climbing.

Harmony shrugged. "The olfactory sense adapts more quickly than the others." She gave the fixture she was cleaning one more swipe to remove any lingering shrimp juice, then slid down her ladder like a firefighter. "Oof. Hey, we're done in this room."

"Oui, only fourteen more to go."

Harmony made a face at her, then headed into the next room. Up and down she went for the next two hours. Her nose became the least of her worries as her knees started whining, then grumbling, and finally screaming.

"Got to quit skipping leg day," she muttered.

Tired and hungry, she didn't complain because she didn't want to discourage Noella, who was still going strong.

"Mine's full." Harmony slid down and tied off the bag. "Want me to take yours out, too?"

"Yes, please! Oh, another bag, please?"

Harmony tossed a new bag up to her. "Leave it to the queen bee to pick such a ridiculously expensive sabotage." Harmony hefted the bags full of rotten shrimp.

Noella shoved damp hair out of her face. "The price, it is nothing." She leaned casually against her ladder. "What I find most difficult to believe is that she climbed up and down ladders this many times."

Harmony snickered as she left, but it was a valid point. They'd gotten lucky in the sense that the community center had two ladders tall enough to reach the hanging light fixtures, so they could share the climbing. On the flip side, they had to check *every* light or risk missing a shrimp. They'd discovered quickly that there was just enough of a lip on top to hide the tiny shrimp from a distance.

The clean air outside smelled weird to Harmony. Either that or the dumpster needed cleaning as badly as the building. She pinched her nose as she dropped the bags inside, then put the lid back.

She made one more trip out to the dumpster while Noella distributed partially open boxes of baking soda throughout the building.

"I outsmarted myself this time," Harmony sighed as they made their way over to her car, street lamps winking on around them as the dusk triggered their sensors. "Should've just parked at the corner there, by the bank." She pointed. "Nobody would've noticed except Officer Jones."

Noella laughed at the face Harmony made, but didn't disagree. The whole town knew that Jones had a rulebook for a heart.

"You poor thing." Harmony patted her car apologetically when they arrived. "We are so sorry."

Despite the chill, they rolled all four windows down partway on the drive back to Noella's.

"Thank you so much." Noella rested her head against Harmony's shoulder for a moment, then propelled herself out of the car.

"Anytime." Harmony shifted into reverse. "Just…not anytime soon, okay?" Noella was still laughing when she backed out.

Rubbing a hand over her face, Harmony grimaced. Even wearing the heavy dishwashing gloves Noella provided hadn't protected her fingers from the shrimp stench.

She shed her clothes in the bathroom and took a hot shower, then used toothpaste to get the last of the shrimp odor off her hands. Heating a frozen chimichanga for her supper, she stayed awake long enough to eat it, then collapsed on the couch, where she slept better than she had in days.

Her alarm went off at the usual time in the morning, startling her out of a weird dream about a giant seagull chasing her—because she looked like a shrimp?

She gasped in pain when she tried to roll onto the floor for morning prayer. "My knees!" She shifted to her back and massaged her aching muscles. "I don't even think I can drive with these!"

Somehow she dragged herself onto the couch again, then lunged into a standing position.   In the kitchen she found her painkillers and took two with a swig of water. Smacked her forehead as she realized she hadn't eaten anything for over twelve hours.

"Chimichanga for breakfast?" she muttered, opening her freezer. "Why not?"

Eventually, she settled herself on the couch for scripture study, her heating pad wrapped securely around her knees.

"Found another one!" Her first smile of the day came as she highlighted Alma 42:27— "Therefore, O my son, whosoever will come may come and partake of the waters of life freely; and whosoever will not come the same is not compelled to come; but in the last day it shall be restored unto him according to his deeds."

She marked the whole verse in yellow, then underlined 'will' and 'may' in brown. She was keeping up with the Sunday school and Relief Society lessons, but her personal study topic for the year was the concept of agency, particularly as it was used in phrases like this one.

Gingerly, she stretched and tried kneeling again. Putting one of the couch cushions under her knee helped and she made it through her morning prayer, again asking where she should move this time.

Her head jerked up in surprise when the doorbell rang. "What in the world?"

Cautiously, she peeked through the blinds without disturbing them. And found three teenagers shivering on her front porch.

"Hello?" Harmony opened the door and the conversation with a question.

"Good morning!" they chorused, far too cheerfully. "We're with the Cadmia Cadets!"

"We're sophomores," inserted the shortest one, getting a semi-friendly elbow for her efforts.

"And we're selling eighteen kinds of frozen cookie dough as a fund raiser," rushed the tallest.

"They come in one pound containers. How much can we mark you down for?" Finished the last girl, her words faintly muffled by her face-enveloping scarf.

Despite everything, Harmony laughed. Waved at the two mothers she could see inside a van parked on the opposite side of the road.

"Well, what flavors do you have?" Harmony needed cookie dough like she needed another hole punched in her favorite belt, but she admired their moxie. "And what're you raising funds for?"

"Chocolate chip, snickerdoodle," began one of them. She kept going even as the others started answering the rest of her questions.

"The Children's Hospital in Springfield has patients over the holidays," answered another.

"We want to get them activity books and kits so they'll have something to do *and* gifts to give to their families." The shortest one smiled shyly.

"Wow." Harmony cleared her throat. "That's a wonderful…yeah, that's wonderful." Who cared if she could use the cookie dough? "How much would it cost me to get one of each?"

Two of the girls looked at the third, who must've been doing the math in her head.

"Ninety dollars," she squeaked.

"I see." Harmony did a little math of her own. "So five dollars per pound and you make what, three dollars profit? Four?" She could almost sense the panic radiating off them as they exchanged wide-eyed looks. "Girls, it's okay. You're *supposed* to make money with a fund raiser."

"More than three dollars. Not as much as four." The girl with the scarf said finally.

"Okay. Put me down for two pounds of each flavor." Harmony made a mental note to call her dentist as she got her wallet from her coat pocket. "I'll give you half the cash now and half when you deliver the cookie dough on the…" She let the sentence hang while she started counting out ninety dollars.

"On the fourteenth," mumbled the shortest girl, her eyes following each ten dollar bill as it moved from Harmony's hands into hers.

"Good deal." Maybe she could use some of them as parting gifts to her clients. They each had a few family members without allergies. "You did a great sales job. Now keep smiling,"

Harmony shook hands with each of them, "even if someone else slams their door in your faces, okay?"

"Okay!" They chorused.

"Wait!" The tallest girl very solemnly handed her a receipt pad. "I marked it as half paid today and signed it."

Harmony countersigned it just as solemnly and gave it back so the young entrepreneur could tear off the top copy for her. She'd been about to ask about a receipt and decided they'd just earned a ten dollar bonus when they returned.

"Bye!" They waved and raced off, two of them heading for the van before the third got them rounded up and headed for the next house.

Chuckling, Harmony closed her door, shivering. "I'll say this much for Cadmia. It sure has some nice people in it."

With a great deal of groaning and griping, she loaded her car with the boxes she'd filled last night. Tired of chimichangas, she heated a bowl of chicken noodle soup for an early lunch. Knowing it wouldn't keep her full for long, she put some cheese sticks in her pocket and headed for the garage door.

Ding-dong!

"You're kidding." The front doorbell rang again, so she changed course.

Harmony's heart leapt into overdrive when

she looked out and saw a man in a thick coat, his face mostly hidden by a balaclava. She could just make out a flower delivery truck in her driveway and she struggled to remember if she'd ever seen the one like it in the area before.

The doorbell rang again as she typed the florist's name into the phone, making her shaking fingers miss a letter. She hit enter anyway and exhaled in relief as the search engine autocorrected the mistake. There actually was a florist by this name in Fireclay. Aaaand, yes, the design on the truck matched the design on their site.

Still, she could never be too careful.

"Who is it?" Harmony called.

"Bell's Floral. I have a delivery for Harmony Wells."

She searched her feelings and found only peace. As she opened the door, he took a step back.

"Hey, it's a pleasure to finally meet you." He jerked his balaclava down off his face and thrust a vase of roses at her. "I came by twice yesterday." Jerking his thumb toward the truck, he added, "There's more. Be right back."

"More?!" She took a deep breath to steady herself and ended up with her nose in the flowers. She loved roses! But who could've sent them? They looked like a pale orange. No, peach.

Digging into her memory for the six months

she'd worked at a florist's, she finally dredged up the meaning for peach roses—gratitude.

Were they from one of her clients? She searched for a card and found none.

"And here you go!" The delivery man was back at her door with another dozen roses!

White, yellow, and *crimson* roses shouted at her that these were *not* from a client.

"Oh, and the cards."

Harmony showed him that her hands were full and backed up enough to set the flowers on a counter behind her. Accepting the cards, she dug in her pocket for what was left of her cash. She'd have to stop by the bank today, too.

"No, no." He held up both hands. "I've already been tipped." His tone indicated the tip was roughly the equivalent of an early Christmas bonus. Grinning, he backed away. "Have a great day!"

Operating on muscle memory, Harmony closed and locked the door. Sagged against it as she stared at *two* dozen of the most gorgeous flowers she'd ever seen.

The desire to know where they'd come from overcame her shock at length and she opened the card on top.

"Thank you for the cars and jeeps!" Her lips curved up as she read the names of all five of the children printed on the bottom of the card.

Which left the second card. The second

bouquet. Of course, she was just guessing which card belonged with which bouquet. Nevertheless…her eyes touched each rose, noting the three different colors. White, yellow, crimson—by chance? Or intent?

She frowned as she tried to recall the meanings of the colors. White, for purity. Yellow, for friendship. Yes, she thought so.

Crimson. Her cheeks colored to match the brilliant red roses as she considered whose signature she hoped was on the card.

Tucking it into her pocket for later, she transferred the vases to the kitchen table and reluctantly started out on her deliveries.

It was like carrying a live coal around with her. The card burned her while she drove. It scorched her whenever she stopped to chat. Seared her hand as she held it when she got back to her house.

Tearing the envelope open, she took a deep breath.

"Harmony. I don't know how to say what I'm feeling. I hope the flowers will say it for me." As she finished reading, she swiped at a tear, but it hadn't come alone. Its friends played a grand game of chase down her cheeks. Some chose the faster, inside course and landed on the corners of her mouth in salty defeat. Others chose the curve of her cheeks and slid down to the point of her chin, from whence they dropped onto her bare feet.

Getting up, she took the vase in her hands. Twisted it right to left, then left to right, trying to pick a color. Her fingers grazed the yellow petals. Stubbornly bypassed the crimson. Settled on the stem of a perfect, white rosebud.

She kissed it softly.

Appetite gone, she skipped supper and changed straight into her pajamas. Stared unseeingly at the television while the same cheerful German man talked about baking something or other.

When she couldn't tolerate the noise any longer, she shut it off and sat in the dark. Knees against her chest, she whispered prayer after prayer.

"Am I wrong? Should I stay in Cadmia? What does Lydia want?"

Lydia. They'd spoken just two days ago on Sunday and Lydia had no more clue where they should go than she did. Visiting the lawyer was on her list, but not at the top of it. Not on the bottom, either, exactly…

Heaving a sigh that was half sob, Harmony curled up under a blanket and began quoting the Articles of Faith to herself in order.

"We believe in God, the Eternal Father, and in His Son, Jesus Christ, and in the Holy Ghost.

"We believe that men will be punished for their own sins, and not for Adam's transgression."

She stumbled over the seventh, which listed

various gifts of the Spirit, then proceeded quietly on. A yawn escaped her on the tenth, but she made it through all thirteen and started over before sleep overtook her.

She turned off her alarm the next morning and rolled over. There was nothing to get up for. In fact, she might as well stay in bed until Friday.

Well. Her storage room was abysmally out of order. And her fridge was still empty. The arrival of the roses yesterday had driven most non-essential things from her mind.

Also, she'd feel better if she got up and prayed. Read her scriptures.

Her to-do list growing longer by the heartbeat, she threw the quilt off and trudged into the bathroom. The tube of toothpaste felt as heavy as if it was made of lead when she tried to lift it. Her hairbrush found every unlikely knot and snarl that morning. She shoved a foot through her favorite sock and dropped a spoon down the disposal in the kitchen when she put her dishes in the sink after scripture study and breakfast.

Dropping to her knees right there, she asked again what she should do. Hearing no answer, she drug herself to her feet and reached for her copy of the *Ensign*, a church magazine.

As she pulled it toward her, intending to read for a while, a piece of paper fluttered out and onto the floor. Stooping, she saw that it was a receipt from Stock's.

Was that an answer?

She picked up her keys, then hesitated. Given her track record that morning, did she dare drive? Going over to the sink, she peered into the mouth of the disposal. She had a natural aversion to sticking her hand into something designed to pulverize its contents, so she got her long pliers from the garage.

In a matter of seconds, she stood triumphantly holding the wayward spoon.

Okay. She could do this. Right?

She was so relieved to arrive safely at Stock's that she didn't charge through the store at her usual get-it-done pace. Today, she browsed. Up one aisle and down the next. Repeat.

It was getting boring when she turned a corner and found herself in the store's Christmas section. Wreaths and wrapping paper, ornaments and canned pie filling as far as the eye could see.

Well, as far as the wall stretched, anyway.

"Hi." Grant stood watching her, his hands wrapped tightly around the handle of a mostly empty basket.

"Grant."

The sound of his name on her lips drew him a step toward her. The sadness in her eyes stopped him there.

"Your flowers are lovely. Thank you."

Harmony wished she could look away. His eyes seemed to be boring holes in her, seeking answers she too wished she had.

"I'm glad you like them." Frustrated, he raked his fingers through his hair. Moved closer and lowered his voice. Stock's looked empty, but the walls there had ears. "Is this all there is going to be between us? Formalities and the polite exchanging of phrases?"

"What did you expect?"

Her answer was so wooden Grant recoiled from her.

Harmony started to move past him and he reacted as though his future was slipping through his fingers.

Grabbing her arm, Grant twirled her to face him. Pulled her close. He might've kissed her, except that he caught sight of Miss Birdie, Stock's only bona fide employee, gaping at them from the front register. *Of all the luck!* He'd needed that kiss. Needed something tangible, something besides the theory and conjecture about the non-relationship that had taken over his normally logical, rational thought process.

Harmony was left to stand, bewildered, as he stalked away.

Chapter 15

Lydia. Her sister's name popped into her mind like a neon sign. Harmony didn't know why, but she needed to see Lydia. To talk with her in person. Hurrying to the checkout, she emptied her cart and reloaded it as fast as Miss Birdie could scan and bag.

"Everythin' okay, darlin'?" Miss Birdie squinted at her over the tops over her rectangular spectacles.

"Is everything ever okay all at the same time, Miss Birdie?" She managed a smile that would hopefully take the sting out of her atypical reply.

Miss Birdie blinked. Scratched the tip of her nose. "Come to think of it." She scanned a bag of produce. "Guess not!"

Harmony channeled her impatience into pulling up a static website that she co-owned with Sister Adams, the friend-of-a-friend Lydia was staying with until she finished high school. There were hundreds, probably thousands, of defunct websites sitting idle online, which made this the perfect cover for them. Delving into the background of the site, she added alternate text to an image and saved it. The site would now send Sister Adams an alert that something had been changed and voila, communication.

"Hope your day gets better." Miss Birdie

patted her arm and glared behind her.

Harmony winced. She opened her mouth to say it wasn't *his* fault—For who could be behind her but Grant? The rest of the store was empty, she'd just meandered through the whole place.—then closed her mouth. Best to act as if she had no idea what Miss Birdie was talking about.

"It will." She gave her best fake smile as she transferred the last bag to her cart. "They always do!" Her face smoothed out as soon as she left the building, but she'd stopped hurrying.

Sister Adams wasn't expecting to hear from her and, no matter when she replied, Harmony wouldn't leave until after movie night on Friday or very early on Saturday. She might even split the difference and go at midnight. She'd slept in her plane before.

The breeze shifted, bringing Grant's cologne to her. She turned to face him.

"I'm sorry." Wearily, he shrugged. "I'm not thinking well these days."

"Don't apologize." Hands in her coat pockets, she braced herself against her car. "I'm the problem."

He sighed and came to lean beside her. "I understand you have to leave. I don't understand why you can't come back."

"Maybe I could." She squeezed her eyes shut and willed her stomach to stop flopping around like a cartoon water hose. She knew better than to think she could run a multibillion dollar empire by herself. But the lawyers and boards of directors had been in power for far too long. She and Lydia needed to assert themselves as their grandfather's heirs. Evaluate and reevaluate how things were being run and, where things had gotten off course, bring them back in line with family values. She'd have noticed anything overt, even at this distance. It would take an up-close-and-personal review to find and fix things. And that would take time.

"Then let's plan on it." His voice was soft. Inviting.

She rested her head on his shoulder. "You don't know anything about me. Why in the world would you want to wait for me?"

Grant took a deep breath and let it out. "Because it feels right." Gently, he kissed the speck of her forehead that wasn't covered by her knit cap.

Without moving her head, she looked up at him. "Then there are some things you deserve to be told."

He followed her back to her place, where she motioned for him to take a seat across from her at the kitchen table.

"I am…" She stopped. Swallowed hard. "Would you mind offering a prayer? I'm going to need help with this."

He put his hand on the table, palm up, and she slipped hers into it. There was no spark this time. No crackle and buzz like a lightning storm was building in her kitchen. Just the steady hum of controlled electricity coursing through a closed circuit.

Grant didn't know what to say, so he kept it simple. "Heavenly Father, we come before Thee today to ask for a blessing upon our communication. Give us the words to speak that will allow a correct understanding between us." He closed in the name of their Savior and she added her amen.

The first thing she saw when she opened her eyes was their joined hands. It felt right. *They* felt right, more than she ever would've imagined.

"I am Harmony Adelaide Wells, daughter of Cecelia Faith DuBois, and granddaughter of Miles Owen DuBois." She could tell from the way Grant's eyebrows drew together that he didn't understand the significance of the relation. "Of Global Tech."

Grant knew it had to be important or she wouldn't be leading with it. "Is he a computer engineer?"

She shifted a little uneasily. "When he died, my grandfather wholly owned the company." She squeezed his hand and released it so she could open her laptop. Turned it so he could see the financial page she'd accessed. "This is today's stock price."

Grant's head started to pound and his vision started to go in and out.

"Hey." She waved her hand in front of his face. "Grant!"

"Huh?"

"Snap out of it!" She caught his face in her hands, forcing him to look at her. Their eyes met and, if there hadn't been more to tell, she would've kissed him right then.

"How…" He paused to clear the rasp out of his throat. "How much of…the company…"

"All of it." When his eyes flicked to the computer, she closed the lid. "Per the terms of my grandfather's will, it was to be divided equally between his blood descendants."

"Okay, so…" The rasp had moved to his brain, which was desperately trying to process the information. "So. That's you and your sister and…?" He raised his eyebrows hopefully. Not that there was that much difference between inheriting fifty percent or thirty percent of the several billion the company had to be worth.

"It's just us." Knowing he needed a minute, she got up and poured them each a glass of water.

"Cadmia will never be your home. Will it?"

She paused, finished setting the glasses down, and retook her seat. "It's highly unlikely."

"Where is home for you?"

Her shoulders hunched as she brought her elbows to rest on the table. "I was wondering that just the other day."

Surprised, he waited for her to continue.

"We own four or five residences, scattered around the world." She sipped her water. "I really only have memories of one. Emotionally, though, I guess I don't have a home."

Her small voice broke his heart and he reached across the table to take her hand in his. "We'll make a home. That's a promise." She blushed adorably and he almost got up to kiss her.

"It's a little early for promises." Shifting uncomfortably, she withdrew her hand. "When my mother died, the media was warm and sympathetic. When my dad started with his…shenanigans," she grimaced, "they milked it for all it was worth. Lydia and I were dubbed billionaire orphans, poster children for at risk rich kids, the works."

"And now I understand why you're hiding from the paparazzi." He grimaced with her. He'd actually forgotten about that.

"Things only got worse when I decided to petition the courts for custody of my younger sister, Lydia. Between the media and the servants, who I suppose were only trying to help," she sighed, "I was faced with a lose-lose situation. A life in the quicklime-light and a spoiled brat of a sister."

"Quicklime-light?" His eyebrows jumped to his hairline. That stuff could cause nasty burns when it was mishandled.

"Like it? I coined the phrase myself." She could feel her face turning red. "It's terrifying how knowing that everyone thinks they know all about you eats away at you. Makes you second and third guess yourself until you start to believe they really do know you better than you know yourself."

He covered her hand with his and took a deep breath with her when their eyes met.

"How did you get out of it?"

"We snuck out of the country and into Canada." His touch had a steadying effect on her, so she left her hand in his. "Lydia stayed there with friends while I played decoy in…elsewhere." A bitter smile played at her lips. "When I was fairly certain they wouldn't find her, I ducked out, too."

He waited, but she didn't seem to have anything else to say.

"That's it? That," he hunted for another way to put it, "brings us up to date?"

"More or less." She took a sip of her water. "I brought Lydia back into the country a few years ago. She'll finish high school this year and I'm relieved to report that she's a healthy, happy young woman."

"I'm glad to hear that." He meant it, too.

He'd seen enough tragedy for one lifetime during his time at the E.R.

"Harmony." He hesitated. "About your dad. How long has it been since you've seen him?"

"Ten years." She met his eyes steadily. "And if you're hoping he's changed, I haven't found any evidence of that."

His heart sank. "You've kept an eye on him, then?"

"My lawyer has. And, once in a while, I'm foolish enough to look him up online."

The pain in her eyes cut him to the quick.

"Let's just say that when he makes the news, the stories are never positive."

"Harmony, I'm so sorry." Recapturing her hand, he gripped it firmly. "Of course you've tried…"

She gave him the ghost of a smile. "How would you know that, Grant Reeves? We barely know each other."

He opened his mouth. Closed it and regarded her thoughtfully. "We know each other a lot better than we did yesterday."

"True." Her heart did a funny little flip, as if approving her decision to confide in him. Her brain sternly reminded her that greed could grow in a person.

"And, unless you have something else to disclose?" Relief coursed through him when she shook her head. "Then I have something to say."

She tensed. *Don't propose. Don't propose!* The last thing she wanted was for him to make some dramatic gesture that she'd have to turn down because their relationship wasn't there yet.

"I'm starting to see how much I still have to learn about you. And," he laughed weakly, "I'm afraid I'm going to seem very boring. Nevertheless." He held up a hand when she started to protest. "I'd like to give us a try."

Happy tears flooded her eyes, making it impossible for her to see.

"I'd like that, too."

Reaching into his pocket, he produced a handkerchief, which he used to tenderly dry her eyes.

"Let's start today." His heart soared at her enthusiastic nod. "Give me an hour to get things squared away, then I'll be back to pick you up for our first official date. Alright?"

She sat there for several seconds after he left, trying to wrap her mind around what had just happened. Then it clicked in her head that she *only had an hour* and she bounced to her feet.

Her groceries received the minimum amount of attention. She entered the disorganized storeroom with a grimace and marched past the chaos to her closet.

What am I going to wear? Her present wardrobe consisted primarily of tees and jeans. Grant knew that, right? Of course, she did have a couple of dresses and a few blouses to pair with her skirts for church. She got the blouses out and held them up next to the two pairs of jeans she wasn't already wearing.

Blue? Or cream? Stonewash? Or navy? Sneakers? Pumps?

Exasperated with her indecision, she took a break for a hot shower. Arranged her freshly washed hair in soft waves around her face and applied just enough makeup to make a noticeable difference. If there was one thing she'd learned from wearing stage makeup on the cruise, it was that too much makeup was not a look she liked.

Giving in to her pragmatic side, she chose her navy blue jeans and comfortable black sneakers. The cream-colored blouse broke up the otherwise dark outfit, and she added modest clip-on earrings for the fun of it.

Ten minutes to spare.

Could a person go crazy in ten minutes?

Not willing to take a chance, she started pacing. Checked her phone and came to a sudden halt.

Sister Adams had already responded. In short, she thought Harmony's idea was brilliant.

Harmony's heart twisted as she read on to where Sister Adams sweetly declared they would change their Saturday party plans to a surprise party for Friday night.

[Lydia will be all yours on Saturday!]

The message ended with a smiling emoji that had hearts for eyes.

"Crumb." Harmony resumed pacing, though more slowly. "How am I ever going to pay this woman back?" They owed her so much! For the last four years she'd kept Lydia safe. Worried about her. Mothered her. She'd practically adopted the poor kid.

She exhaled shakily as she tapped out her response. [Thank you! I'll be there before noon.]

That was as far as her plans had gotten, so she sent the message without further detail. Still fidgety over her debt to the Adams', she composed a message to her lawyer asking him to renew the offer to fund adoptions for the Adams', who weren't able to have children.

They'd adopted two children since taking Lydia in, and while her sister often complained about her "younger siblings," Harmony could tell she loved them.

What a crazy life they led. Lydia would never be whole without the Adams in her life, and Harmony was so used to living alone that the thought of seriously dating someone gave her the jitters.

Smirking at herself, she stopped at the sound of a car door closing outside. Ran through the breathing exercises her acting teacher taught her in high school and counted to ten after Grant's knock before opening the door.

"Wow." Grant made an unhurried perusal of her, enjoying the way her chin came up while her cheeks turned the same shade of pink as the rose he held. "Hi, I'm Grant Reeves." He held out the rose. "I'll be your date today."

"All day?" She peeked at him over the rose. He was devastating in inky black slacks and a rust-colored button-up shirt that made his hazel blue eyes pop. The look in those eyes made her heart start doing backflips.

"What's left of it."

She shivered at his tone and ducked back into her house to put the rose somewhere safe.

"And where are we going?" she asked as she locked the door behind her.

"The moon." He kissed her cheek and hovered for a potent instant before offering her his arm.

"Ah." She tucked her hand in the crook of his elbow. "That's one place I've never been."

The 'moon' turned out to be Monte Blanc, a quiet restaurant in Fireclay where they ordered from an impressively diverse menu.

"Is this lunch or supper?" Harmony didn't really care, she just needed to say something.

"Does it matter?" Picking up her hand, he laced his fingers through hers.

"No." Delightful prickles rushed up and down her nerves as she considered the man she was holding hands with.

"Good. Because we have important things

to discuss."

She squeezed his hand involuntarily. "Sorry."

Winking, he pressed a kiss to the back of her hand.

"Let's start with your favorite book."

"My…" Startled, she studied his eyes to determine if he was serious.

"It's a difficult decision, I know." Amused, he had to discipline a smile. "I'll go first. My favorite book of all time is *Norby, the Mixed-Up Robot*, by Janet and Isaac Asimov."

"*The* Isaac Asimov?" At his nod, she leaned forward. "I missed those somehow. Tell me about Norby."

Grant happily spent the next ten minutes explaining to her why he liked the books so much.

"I wouldn't say all eleven books in the series are equally entertaining, but I do have the entire collection," he finished. Looked at her expectantly.

"I guess…for me it was the Great Brain series." His puckered forehead prompted her to continue. "Tom Fitzgerald was not your average kid." Without giving away the details on any of Tom's clever escapades, she sketched the cagey young man and the late 1800s setting of his stories.

Their conversation paused while the waiter brought their food and Harmony offered the prayer.

"Okay, that was the easy one." Grant narrowed his eyes in mock menace. "Now tell me what your favorite color is."

They went back and forth with his questions until Harmony interrupted.

"My turn." She washed the last of her breadstick down and took a deep breath. "You have to get a sack of corn, a chicken, and a fox across a river, but your canoe will only hold you and one of them at a time." She outlined the rest of the brain teaser and sat back to wait.

"Riddles, hmm?" Grant chewed a final bite of chicken parmigiana and wiped his mouth. He knew the answer, he was just tickled that she'd asked! "You take the chicken first."

Her smile grew into a grin. "You've heard it before!"

"One of my uncles is the king of riddles." He shrugged. "Here's one for you. How many animals did Moses take on the ark?"

"None." She wrinkled her nose in disdain for the old trick. "Noah, however, took at least two of each."

They traded riddles through dessert, alternately laughing and pondering until their plates were empty.

Grant reluctantly waved at their waiter, who brought them their check and a portable card reader.

Harmony's heart started pounding in her ears as she watched the portable card reader approach. How Grant would handle it now that he knew she…

Grant set the check aside without looking at it and inserted his card in the machine. As he'd expected, it populated his total and a suggested tip amount. Since they'd monopolized the table for literally hours, he tripled the tip and hit enter.

"Prices here never cease to amaze me," he remarked casually as he helped Harmony into her coat. "A meal like this in New York would cost enough to rent a small house here in Cadmia." That was quite possibly his overstatement of the year, but he hadn't missed Harmony's apprehensiveness. A little humor seemed like the right move.

"Let's take a walk," she suggested as he reached for the doorknob.

Opening the door, he tested the temperature.

She saw his mouth twist to one side and sighed inwardly. "You're right," she agreed before he could speak. "It's too cold for a walk tonight."

"So," he caught her arm as she moved to walk past him, "let's take the long way home instead."

Pleasantly surprised, she nodded. Helped him pick a roundabout route back to Cadmia, then settled in for the ride.

They edged through city traffic, heading for the edge of town, where the street lights faded and cars thinned out until it was just them and a long, empty highway.

"I have another important question for you."

Her soft, serious tone told him she was in earnest and he motioned for her to go ahead.

"How much do you want to stay in Cadmia?"

Miles flew by while he thought about it. Realizing he was exceeding the speed limit, he eased off the gas.

"I'd never choose a place over a person, Harmony."

Chapter 16

He made breakfast burritos for two the next morning and had to stop himself from panicking every time he remembered he was out of milk.

"Have to love a woman who insists on contributing to the meal." He chuckled as he looked over the kitchen with a critical eye.

Knowing his own limits, he'd hired a local contractor to replace the stove and fridge, and another one to take care of all the plumbing. Gleaming chrome appliances now stood out against eggshell blue walls. White cupboards with royal blue trim lined the wall over the counter, their yellow knobs standing out like tiny suns in an evening sky.

The kitchen table was new, too. Solid walnut, temporarily hidden under a forest green tablecloth, and large enough to seat four.

His lips twisted wryly. Maybe he *was* planning to flip this place. He ate most of his meals on the TV tray he'd set up in the living room. After over a decade of snatching food whenever—and wherever—he could find time to chew, it would take some pretty hard work to make eating at the kitchen table second nature again.

His whole being stilled at the sound of a tentative knock on the kitchen door. His shoes squeaked on the linoleum floor as he walked over to answer it, the sound loud in his ears.

"Hi." Harmony held up the milk jug as if it was her ticket to the breakfast he'd offered to make. "Am I early?"

"Perfect timing." When she didn't come through the door he was holding open for her, he held out his hand. "Step into my castle, fair lady."

Her eyes widened and her lips twitched, but she put her hand in his and allowed him to draw her inside.

"It looks amazing!" She felt him take the jug of milk from her and slipped out of her coat, automatically hanging it on the back of the nearest table chair, then started exploring the kitchen. "And a pantry? You've been working hard!" It was empty, but it was the thought that counted.

"I'm no carpenter," he laughed. "I did help design it, though. See how the shelves swing out from the wall?"

"They do?" She experimented and whistled. "Hey, that's perfect. You can load the new groceries from the back instead of having to rearrange things every time!" She pulled her head out of the pantry to look at him suspiciously. "What's so funny?"

"Oh, I don't know." He deftly transferred a baked burrito onto a warm plate and handed it to her. "I guess I didn't expect you to be more interested in my kitchen than—" He paused when her fingers brushed his. He'd hate to have his pulse taken right then. "Than in the food."

"Sorry." She waited while he dished up a second plate. "I've just never actually been in the old Palm…" She broke off, blushing. It wasn't polite to stand there in his house and call it the Palmer place. "In your home before."

"It's okay to call it that." Smiling, he deposited his plate on the table and held her chair for her. "The longer I work on this place, the less like home it feels." Saying it out loud made it so real.

"Really?" She brushed her loose hair back over her shoulders. "I thought renovating a place was supposed to make it seem more like home."

"So did I." He shrugged and offered her his hand for prayer, which he voiced. Held her hand a moment longer and looked into her eyes. "I guess I just needed something to do while I figured out what was next." Her hand felt so right in his that he gave into an impulse.

His lips on the back of her hand sent her heart catapulting through her chest. Suddenly shy, she withdrew her hand and reached for her fork.

"These, um…" She needed to get a grip. "Look delicious." She started to cut into her burrito and came close to shoving a piece of it off into her lap. *More grip. Less force.*

"Thanks."

She darted a look at him and the light in his eyes told her he knew exactly what his touch had done to her. It didn't make any sense, though. They were both adults. She'd done her fair share of hand holding and even some kissing. She lowered her gaze. Perhaps too much kissing?

One of the reasons she'd left the cruise line was that she'd finally seen what the casual, week-long romances were doing to her. She'd never gone beyond hand-holding and a few kisses, but it still dulled her appreciation for those things. They became ordinary. Boring.

So why did her heart turn handsprings every time she met Grant's eyes? Oh dear. He was speaking to her and she hadn't heard a word!

"...think better while my hands are busy, so I've gotten an awful lot done upstairs these last two weeks." He paused to pour milk for them both. "What I'm trying to say is, we should have fun with this."

"This?" She hated to have to ask, but she didn't want to try faking it all day.

"Us." He gestured back and forth between them. "Which is why I have arranged the perfect date today."

"For example?" She'd spent what little time they'd had apart since dinner trying to figure out what he had up his sleeve. He'd been so confident last night.

"I'll tell you after breakfast." Whereupon he calmly ate a bite of burrito. He continued to smile like a Cheshire cat while artfully dodging her questions about what he had planned.

She handled it pretty well until he poured himself a second glass of milk.

"You can be quite aggravating when you put your mind to it," she accused crossly. Scooping up her final bite, she popped it into her mouth and folded her arms across her chest while she chewed.

"Good girl." Jumping up, he stacked all the dishes and carried them over to the sink. "Now, let's play!"

She laughed as he caught her hand on his way back past the table. "Where are we going?"

"All the way," he crossed the threshold into the front room, "in here."

"Wow, this is huge!"

"Don't mind the mess." He rubbed the back of his neck, looking askance at the pile of lumber on the far side of the room. Wished he'd put a sheet over the half a dozen paint cans directly to his left.

"What a beautiful tree." She ran her finger over the tips of the soft Douglas fir needles. "You sure know how to pick them." Christmas music started playing softly, bringing her around to face him.

"I set it up a few days ago, but never got around to decorating it. Want to help?" He picked up some paper bags.

"I'd love to." It was a little tricky, remembering that this was their first official date, when she kept finding herself more or less in his arms as they worked. And liking it.

"Oops, sorry." Ugh, he was an idiot. "Hold still." Carefully, he removed the Christmas lights from where they'd tangled in her hair. "Maybe I should wait to do the lights until after the decorations."

"No, that's okay." She stepped to one side. "If you do that, then you'll never get the lights on without knocking off ornaments." She'd thought she was being clever, putting ornaments on the top half of the tree while he strung the lights on the bottom half, but apparently not so much.

"Yeah, good point." He'd never bothered to wonder why his dad taught him to do it in that order. "I'll hurry."

"Take your time." She managed a smile despite the awkward situation. "I'll…get out the rest of the decorations."

"So." He cleared his throat and resumed working with the lights. "What's your favorite thing about Christmas?"

"I don't know." She shrugged, feeling suddenly tired. "Everyone always asks me that and…I don't think I have one. But that makes people uncomfortable," belatedly she flicked an assessing glance at him, "so I usually say I don't know."

"Uh-huh." He plugged the lights in and they lit up the tree.

She gasped. "I…I didn't think I'd like plain white lights." Leaving the bags, she came to stand squarely in front of the tree. Even with the weak mid-morning sun shining through the window behind it… "Grant, that's stunning."

"You like it that much?" He tentatively settled his hands on her waist from behind. She didn't pull away, so he relaxed. "We can leave it like that. Just the lights."

"What about the other ornaments?" She couldn't get over the effect of the pure light sparkling at her from the otherwise bare tree limbs. The few baubles she'd managed to hang on top looked so out of place now.

"I'll donate them. To Noella's play."

"You don't have to do that." Without thinking, she turned to face him.

"But I could." No longer sure what to do with his hands, he stuffed them into his pockets while he shrugged. "Alec was telling me they had to get a new tree for the play and they could probably use some decorations for it."

"Good thinking."

His practical answer robbed the moment of some of its magic, so she refocused on the beautiful tree.

"That's what we'll do then." Rubbing his hands together, he grinned at the back of her head. "Now for the surprise. This way, Miss." He mock-bowed and motioned for her to precede him through another door.

Curious, she started down some stairs and found herself in a fully finished basement-game room. An open door at the far side of the room let her see into a bathroom. A bookshelf, piled with boxes of games, sat near a card table. An air hockey table stood opposite a hanging TV large enough for a T-rex to rampage through. And right next to the door was a pool table, calling her name.

"Whoa." Her fingers itched to pull a cue down from the rack and get a game going.

"What do you want to play first?" Oblivious to her ogling of the pool table, Grant made a beeline for the shelves of games. "We've got chess. Checkers. Upwords. Skip-Bo." He continued listing off the options.

She wriggled her toes. Swayed slightly as the laughter bubbled up, up her legs to her torso, and then out of her mouth.

"What?" He smiled and folded his arms protectively across his chest at the same time. This seemed like such a good idea last night.

"Nothing, I just…" She laughed some more as she crossed the room and picked up the top two boxes. "Parasailing. Scuba diving. Dancing. I've been on a lot of creative dates, but this is definitely a first." She didn't mention roller skating because she was terrible at it and didn't want him to think she was hinting.

I've been on a lot of dates. Grant grabbed at his imagination when it tried to run away with him. *She said she's been on a lot of* creative *dates,* he told himself sternly. *Scuba diving? How am I supposed to compete with scuba diving here in Cadmia, Missouri?*

"How about this one?" She held up a box and swallowed the laughter that was threatening again.

"Yeah." He shifted, then moved to hold her chair for her.

Shaking the top off the box, she searched the contents and came up empty. "I don't see any instructions?"

He put a hand over his heart and drew himself up in an air of offense. "You don't know how to play this?" Using that as an excuse, he slid his chair much, much closer to hers. "Today is the day you learn!" She responded by bumping her shoulder against his and he took that as a good sign.

His corny lines and exaggerated flirting kept her laughing so hard that the rest of the morning flew past.

"I get it." Harmony rolled the dice and came up empty again, which meant her token was still trapped in limbo. "I finally get why Lydia hates this game." The games they'd already played were piling up to her left and now she wished she'd stuck with UNO a little longer, despite Grant's crazy 'house rules.'

"I'd say it's more fun with more people."
He rolled the dice and moved his piece around
the board, landing with a groan on one of her
holdings. "But it really isn't."

"Shall we adjourn for lunch?" she suggested
hopefully.

He paused in the middle of figured out the
points he'd lost and made eye contact. "I
thought you'd never ask."

The room suddenly shrank to closet
proportions and she could barely breathe. Her
thoughts scattered to the four winds, but most
of them centered on the hope that he was going
to kiss her.

Grant swallowed hard. *I've been on a lot of
dates.* Which meant a lot of kisses, probably.

How many kisses? he wondered. Realizing
he'd held the exact same position for at least
ten seconds, he scrambled for a way out of the
now-embarrassing silence.

Dropping the pencil and pad in the middle
of the game board, he folded the board in half.

"Hey!" Startled, she watched him upend it
into the box, tokens and cards and dice clinking
together into a big mess.

"I'll organize it later," he promised
cheerfully. Unless he found a trash bag first. "I
think we can agree you won, though."

"Um, okay." She flushed a little as she
added her point-heavy notepad to the box.
Had she imagined the discomfort on his face a

moment ago? Or did it help explain his abrupt ending of the game?

"C'mon." He got to his feet and winced. Shook his left leg. "Nice. My foot's asleep."

She managed a laugh and got up as well. "Want me to drive?"

"No, that's okay." He stomped his foot and grimaced as a thousand cold needles stabbed his sole. Gritted his teeth. "It's already waking up."

She tried holding his hand on the way to his vehicle and noticed that he was quick to let go. Of course, it wasn't a long walk and he *did* open the car door for her immediately after taking his hand away.

Then he turned on the radio. Odd. In all the driving they'd done together, they'd never needed a filler. Her conviction that something was bothering him grew with every wordless inch he drove.

"Here we are!" He slid a sideways glance in her direction and found that she was still watching him, brow slightly furrowed. "Do you know what you want for lunch?"

"It's Blinky's, Grant." She tilted her head to one side. "I've eaten here two to five times a week for the last two years." That was a little harsh, actually.

"Right." He hadn't forgotten, he just… He should just write a book on how not to impress a date. Deflated, he reached for his door latch only to find her hand on his arm.

"What's wrong?"

"Nothing." That was technically true. Nothing *would* be wrong once he wrapped his head around her dating history. It was history, right? *Parasailing. Scuba diving. Dancing.* He knew for certain he'd never taken a woman on a date that involved a swim suit.

He's lying. Her heart sank slowly toward the pit of her stomach and she let go of his arm. Heard his door open. Flinched when it shut, the noise loud in the enclosed space. Whispered a prayer as he came around to her side of the vehicle.

"Harmony?" He studied her. She stared straight ahead through the windshield. Hadn't even looked around when he opened the door for her.

"I was wrong." She gave him a tight smile. "I'm not hungry after all." She watched his frown deepen. He seemed to be struggling with something…a decision?

Moving closer, he reached around her and unbuckled her seatbelt. "Come inside and we'll talk." He didn't have a clue how to say what he felt. Not without embarrassing himself into next year, at any rate. But experience with his mother and sisters told him that continuing to insist it was 'nothing' would only make things worse.

Her gaze slid over to his face. To his eyes.

Something in his eyes drew her out of the vehicle and she followed him inside, though she kept her hands in her pockets.

He'd never seen Blinky's this empty. "Over here." Pointing toward an empty booth, he walked beside her and wondered how she could feel so far away when he could've reached out and touched her.

Except…she didn't want him to. Yes, that was it. She didn't want him to.

She didn't even scoot over when she sat down on the bench, further evidence that she'd closed and locked a door between them. No, he had. Well. *They* had.

Frustrated, he scrubbed a hand over his face and took the other bench. He hadn't meant to shut anything. He'd just taken a step back to try to adjust what he thought he knew about her. That's what dating was all about. Learning new things and deciding how—or if—they changed how you felt about someone.

He took a deep breath and opened his mouth to say…something.

"Hello, you two!" Susan bustled up to their table. "What're you doing hiding a-way back here?" She clucked at them. "I train folks the best I can, but you'll still get better service if you sit up front where you're easier to see."

Harmony was suddenly all smiles. "You're right, Susan, we are hiding." She lowered her voice to a conspiratorial whisper. "From the cold air by the front door." Harmony didn't mind Susan's harmless snooping most of the time. Today, however, she wasn't in the mood.

Susan's eyes flicked back and forth between them, as though trying to decide how to take Harmony's statement. And why they weren't sharing a bench.

"Seriously, though." Harmony shrugged and leaned against the back of the booth. "We're in no hurry."

"All time in the world." Grant agreed, forcing his old "everything's fine" smile.

"Uh-huh." Susan squinted suspiciously at them and asked, "What can I get you?"

"Number five for me, please." Harmony slipped out of her coat and folded it on the bench beside her. "Orange soda, no ice."

Grant hastily scanned the menu taped to the booth wall. "I'll take a number seven." At Susan's quirked up eyebrow he added, "With root beer, please."

He discarded his fake smile as soon as Susan turned her back. Reached across the table and touched Harmony's hand. She didn't pull away, so he gathered his courage and tried again.

"Wrong is a big word. It means different things to different people." He blew out a breath. "So, nothing is wrong—but, something *is* bothering me."

"What?" He didn't answer quickly enough

and she straightened. "What blew in out of nowhere and spoiled our fun?"

He waited gratefully while the server placed two large glasses of soda and platters of delicious, greasy food on the table between them.

"Enjoy." The teen faked a smile and vanished as suddenly as she'd appeared.

By mutual agreement, they offered separate prayers over their food.

Grant picked up the ketchup and squirted some on his fries. Set the bottle down and sat there, hands on either side of his plate.

"The first thing you did when I told you what I had planned for our date was compare it with other dates you've been on."

She blinked. Unbent a smidge. He was right. She hadn't meant anything by it, but she could see how it might've hurt him.

"And…it got me to thinking." Needing something to do with his hands, he started slowly rotating his glass, watching the bubbles slide up the sides.

"About?"

He hand-shrugged, then became absorbed in his drink again. "Things."

Exasperated, she moved his drink and took his hands in hers. "For example?"

"All the…things I haven't done." She started to withdraw her hands and he gripped them more firmly. "The last time I asked someone on a date, she laughed in my face.”

"What?" The word escaped before she could even think about it. "Why?" She cocked an eyebrow at him. "Was she crazy?"

He didn't have to see his reflection to guess his face was as red as the ketchup on his fries.

"Because I'm socially awkward." There. He'd said it.

She inhaled sharply and started to respond. Compelled herself to consider her words first.

"I never noticed."

Wearily, he released her hands and sat back. "This isn't the kind of social I mean." His vague gesture seemed to take in most of Cadmia. Possibly even the four-state area. "I was what they used to call a child prodigy. Not the creative kind." He ran his fingers through his hair. "I graduated high school at nine. While other boys my age were discovering hair gel and shouting that girls had cooties, I was usually nose-deep in a nonfiction book."

Chapter 17

She waited for him to go on, but he seemed to have slipped away, into his memories. Bad ones, judging by the sad look in his eyes.

Getting up, she moved to sit beside him, even going so far as to nudge him over to make room.

"Couldn't have been easy, straddling two worlds like that," she coaxed.

"I had good days," he shrugged, "and not so good days."

Afraid he was going to lapse into silence again, she touched his arm. "Did you get all these muscles carrying encyclopedias around?"

Amused, he shook off the ancient past. Picked up a fry.

"Not exactly. My parents could tell I was catching it from the other boys my age, so they paid my sisters to play with me. Hopscotch, basketball, soccer, basically much any game that required me to be on my feet without a book in my hands. And, they started me on a modest weight-lifting schedule." He nodded when she gave him a doubtful look. "They were strict about it, too. I couldn't have my library card until I'd checked off the entire routine."

Her laugh cracked the gloom surrounding him and let in a gust of fresh air. His breathing became easier and he started to relax.

"I slacked off a lot during med school, then started up again when I found out that the hospital had a small gym." He shrugged as if that explained that.

"And…your killer smile? Your smooth lines?" She thought back to the day he'd come along on her delivery route. "Your road trip chatter?"

He started to reach for another fry, then reached for her plate instead, pulling it over so that she could get to her food.

"You can blame my smile on my first boss." He wiped his fingers on a napkin. "I made the mistake of standing out, you see. Of being right too often. He rewarded me by making me give lectures to the rest of the staff."

"Reward for him, torture for you," she guessed, gently rescuing the napkin from his white-knuckled grip.

"That sums it up. When someone told me I had all the personality of a tongue depressor, I started practicing my smiles in front of a mirror." He saw her flinch and shrugged. "It's more or less much the same story with any smooth lines you might've heard. I started getting invited to the fancy luncheons and charity events, where they introduced me as their 'rising star.'"

"Ouch," she commiserated softly.

"You've never really seen me with strangers. People I don't know or want to know or have anything in common with." His mouth twisted into a bitter smile. "After a few miserable evenings, I knew something had to change. I could either get a different job or find some way to mingle without feeling like I was being dragged across hot coals."

"That makes sense, but how…?" She was genuinely curious. Her social education after leaving the protective confines of the neighborhood where she grew up had been rough and tumble at best. Learning when to smile and who to trust and who to avoid hadn't come easily.

"I studied the greats. Comedians, romantic leads, tough guys of the screen. I even took an acting class." He grimaced. "First class I ever failed. On paper. Personally, I thought I made great progress."

She tapped her fingers on the table. Turned her plate halfway around. Took a big bite of her sandwich.

"One thing I learned in that class is that body language is a huge part of how people communicate." He paused for a sip of his drink. "If I had to guess, I'd say that right now you're not particularly comfortable."

She looked away while she finished chewing. "I was just wondering." She lifted a shoulder. "How good at acting you've gotten since that girl turned you down."

"Not that good, Harmony. Toss me into a

den of lab coat lions or a charity dinner filled with rich harridans and I can put up a decent front." He covered her hand with his. "Leave me alone with someone I actually want to get to know and there's no telling what will happen."

The timbre of his voice made her shiver involuntarily and she looked at him, wide-eyed.

"You've seen the real me. At church. On the road trip. The plane trip." He rolled his eyes, embarrassed. "Our time with my family. That's part of where I got the courage to push for us to date." He laced his fingers through hers. "I thought you liked me."

"I do." She swallowed some soda to clear her throat. "That's why I agreed to date you."

"How're we doing back here?" The teenage waitress burst into their bubble. "Can I get you anything? Refills?"

"No, thanks." Harmony lifted the glass she was still holding to show her it was still mostly full.

"Alrighty then. I'll be back to check on you in a bit and if you need anything in the meantime, just give us a holler."

Alone again, they shared a soft laugh.

"I'm sorry it sounded like I was comparing you with guys I used to know." She squeezed his hand.

"Does that mean you weren't?" This time he was the one who took a big bite.

"Of course not, silly." She pushed the idea

away with her free hand. "I don't even remember most of their names." She toyed with a fry. "Now that we've talked through what was bothering us, I have to ask you something."

He choked on his drink. Got his breathing back under control, no thanks to her hand on his wrist.

"Yes?"

"Are there any other games in that stack that we're both going to be sorry we played?"

In his relief, he laughed so hard that Susan peeked around the corner at them. Ducked back when Harmony waved at her.

"It's a pretty mixed bag, isn't it? The last owner left all of that down there and I only discovered it last week." Wiping his mouth, he tried to think through the games that were left. "Let's see." The basement was one of the few pleasant surprises of renovating that place, though he'd arranged to have someone else give it a thorough cleaning because he just couldn't face it.

While they ate, they discussed their plans for the rest of the day. He almost forgot their earlier awkwardness until she hesitated before getting into his car.

She put her hand on his chest and closed the distance between them. Most of the men she'd known would've taken the hint and at least tried to kiss her. But Grant froze. She could feel his heart rate accelerating, see his neck muscles tensing.

"Thanks for lunch." She brushed her lips across his cheek, then folded herself into the car. She had time to put her seatbelt on before he slowly closed her door. *Wow.* If he was faking that, he deserved an Oscar.

She deliberately gave him space the rest of the day, skipping over Twister in favor of Upwords, which he won. Beat him at three out of four games of pool. In the end, it was the effort of keeping her distance while trying to act casual that wore her out.

"Hey, I saw that." He tapped her arm lightly as she covered a yawn with her hand. "Are you trying to tell me something?"

"Mmm, sorry." She put her cue away and did a quick forward flip. Then a backflip. "Okay. I'm awake now."

Grant reached up and pushed his mouth closed with his index finger, making her laugh.

"Oh, c'mon. You've seen people do flips before, haven't you?"

"Sure…just not in my basement." He pursed his lips. "Not that I can remember, at any rate."

"Ha, ha." She put a fist on her hip. "Want to learn?"

"Wha…me?" He held up both hands. "No, no. Thanks, but I just don't think an ER trip is how this date should end."

She tossed a handful of popcorn at him. "You wouldn't end up in the ER."

"Me? I was talking about you!" He calmly picked a piece of popcorn off his shirt and ate it.

The games forgotten, they talked about nothing in particular for another half an hour before she yawned again.

"I'm sorry." She twisted side to side, stretching her back, which was starting to complain about her sitting for most of the day. "I should probably go, though."

"Already?" He glanced around for a non-existent window, then remembered that it got dark around five during the winter anyway, and checked his phone instead. "It's early yet."

"I know, but I have a long day tomorrow." She shuffled and stacked the oversized Go Fish cards. "I'm going out of town Saturday and…"

"And you played hooky today." He finished for her as he put the cards back in the box. "Which means you'll be spending tomorrow making deliveries."

"Right." She bit her lip, unwittingly drawing his attention to her mouth. "*After* I box up the orders." She'd really been slacking off.

"Can I help?" He got up when she did.

"You?" Her breath caught as he crowded her space, making her look up at him. "Want to help?"

"I'd love to." He assured her as he opened the door to the stairs for her. He had a lot of wasted time to make up for. Their first five weeks of acquaintance, plus his whole life up to that point.

"You would?" She believed him, yet she hardly dared think what she wanted to. She hadn't agreed to date him just so they could become better friends. Would spending another entire day with him help him past his bashfulness—if that was the right word?

"Absolutely." The sight of her coat on the back of the kitchen chair reminded him it was cold outside and he picked it up. "I'll get there dark and early, as they say in these parts."

"You'll have a long wait," she teased as she let him help her into her coat. "The sun doesn't even start thinking about getting up until seven at this time of year."

"You don't want to get a head start on it?" He was honestly surprised.

"The side roads don't get plowed around here." She turned to face him, maintaining her proximity.

"Good point." He put his hands on her shoulders and worked hard to scrounge up the courage to kiss her tempting lips. Settled for a hug and walked her out to her car, intending to try again.

"You better get back inside," she prompted when he'd stood, staring down at her, for several heartbeats. "You're not even wearing a coat." She came up on her toes and the stubble on his cheek as she kissed it sent prickles down her arms.

Awkwardly, he released her and began backing toward his door. "See you tomorrow."

"I'll make breakfast this time," she promised. His answering grin lit up the space between them, which relieved some of her disappointment that he hadn't kissed her—again.

"Yeah? I'd like that."

"Remember you said that." She pointed at him and laughed. Once in her car, she exhaled. "What a ride!" She thought over the day as she let the engine idle to warm up.

Remembering his honesty in the diner, she amended that to, "What a man."

Maybe there was more than one way to measure the progress of a relationship after all.

By the time she reached her rental, she was giving serious thought to inviting him along on her trip to see Lydia. They'd have to meet eventually. Why not sooner than later?

The pros and cons of the idea chased each other through her dreams, producing preposterous and occasionally frightening scenarios.

"Ugh, no." She swatted at her phone when it went off in the morning. "Not yet." Unfortunately, she managed to hit its edge and send it spinning across the room. Suddenly the six foot charging cable she'd purchased for convenience wasn't so convenient.

Prying one eye open, she glared at the outlet by the foot of the couch. She couldn't even use the cable as a tow rope because it was out of reach, too.

Next she glared at her phone, which was still going off.

Out of nowhere, a laugh bubbled out of her.

"I give up." Rolling off the couch, she gave her phone a measured smack that shut off the alarm, then dragged herself to her feet. "And so it begins."

A cold shower opened both eyes wide, but she was afraid to sit down for scripture study. She'd probably fall asleep if she got that comfortable.

Her phone vibrated, alerting her to a text.

[Be there in twenty!] Grant ended his message with a smiley emoji.

She stuck her tongue out at the text, then gave herself a good shake.

"Under the circumstances, I think a compromise is in order." She answered his text with an emoji that matched her weird mood and turned on general conference while she got breakfast going.

By the time he arrived, carrying the half-empty jug of milk she'd taken to his place the morning before, she was ready for him.

"This is incredible!" He held his fork over his plate, not sure where to begin. The pancakes, fried potatoes, scrambled eggs, bacon, toast, and jam all seemed to be taunting him to just try and eat them all. "I haven't had a breakfast like this since I was a kid!"

"Well, don't get used to it." She blushed. "That is, I don't always cook like…this." She gulped some ice water before her face burned to a crisp.

"To many future breakfasts." He held out his milk glass and they toasted the thought. Now if he could just get up the nerve to kiss her.

Not that the morning provided any opportunities along those lines. She stationed him halfway across the room and they passed items back and forth to each other in something of an assembly line.

"Soy-free shampoo, three bottles." She read from her list and he handed them over.

"Egg substitute, two boxes." He read from his list, taking the items from her and packing them carefully.

And so on, until he taped off the last box and threw his hands in the air.

"Time!" He squared his shoulders to the point of pain and doffed an imaginary ten-gallon hat to an equally imaginary crowd.

"Good job, cowboy." She winked and labeled the box with a wide-point permanent marker. "Now we get to load the car."

Wanting to impress her, he pitched in without complaint.

"Okay." She slammed her trunk and tested it. Satisfied that it was securely closed, she jingled her keys. "Now for the best part."

"Oh?" He matched her progress to the front of the car and slid in alongside her.

"We get to sit down before we have to unload all of that."

"Yippee."

"I just have one question for you."

"What's that?" He struggled with his seatbelt, then remembered the trick she'd showed him last time.

"Have you ever played I Spy?"

The game didn't last long, due largely to the fact that soon all they had to choose from was empty fields and telephone poles.

"Where are you going this time?" he asked after a few miles of comfortable silence.

"Going?" She still hadn't made up her mind whether or not to invite him along.

"Yeah." Shifting so that he was facing her, he reminded, "You said you were going somewhere this weekend."

"Oh. That." Should she? Or shouldn't she? She could trust him, which was the most important thing. Lydia would be safe. *That* was the most important thing.

"Yes, that." He peered at her curiously. "Don't you want to talk about it?"

"I want…you to come along." As soon as the words left her mouth, she knew they were true. Beyond logic, beyond rational thinking, she *wanted* him to come along. "To meet my sister."

Speechless, he gazed at her, the countryside slipping by unseen.

"Really?"

"Really." Her heart sang with relief. He'd taken so long to answer that she'd half-convinced herself he was trying to find a nice way to say no. Getting the hang of his thought patterns was going to take some doing. A whole lifetime, even.

"I'm honored." That was the best word for it. He'd never understand what she'd gone through to keep Lydia safe. He could recite what she'd told him, but that wasn't the same as living it for ten years. And now she wanted him to meet her sister!

"We'll miss the rehearsal." She hand-shrugged. "Noella's okay with it, if you are."

"I've looked over the script and it's a simple enough role." He shrugged as though the thought of kissing her in front of an audience didn't unnerve him. "The dress rehearsal should be enough." And surely he could manage to kiss her before then, right?

"I think so, too. Of course," she added the last in a rush, "we'll have to leave at five."

"In the morning?" He balked. "What about

about the roads?"

"The roads to the airport are in great shape," she laughed. "And there are no roads in the sky."

He nodded. "The weather?"

"It's clear for now." She slowed and turned on her signal even though there wasn't another car in sight. "I'd rather wait until after sunrise, but they're expecting me around noon."

"Noon? It's a seven hour flight?" He combed through his memories, trying to think of somewhere in the contiguous forty-eight states that they couldn't reach in four hours or less from their central location.

"Put your calculator down," she laughed. "We're heading east."

"East?" It hit him. "Time zones."

"Exactly." Putting her car in park, she shut it off. "Leave at five, get there around nine, give or take a headwind, and by then it's after eleven their time."

"Exactly," he repeated. "It makes perfect sense when you put it that way."

"Morning, everyone!" Diane poked her head out the door, eyeing Grant with undisguised interest. "Need a hand?"

"We've got it!" Harmony called back. To Grant she murmured, "I should warn you. She's going to make some assumptions about us."

He hefted the first box out. "Smart woman." He almost made it this time. She was so close. He bent toward her. Got as far as her forehead—and no farther.

A slow smile tugged at the corners of her mouth as she watched him walk away. He'd kissed her on the forehead, like they were kids in an old movie or something. How sweet!

Chapter 18

"Okay, I understand why I'm nervous." He caught her hands and pulled them away from her hair. The taxi driver was making him crazy, for starters—and not just their terrible taste in Christmas music, either. How many times could they cut off a delivery truck and not die? "Why are *you* nervous?"

"What makes you think I'm nervous?" She tugged at her hands but he kept a firm hold on them.

"Maybe the way you've rearranged your hair six times since we left the airport?" She'd asked him what he thought every time, then taken it down and started over anyway. A braid, a bun, a ponytail, a…no, he'd lost track about there.

Her attention zeroed in on him when he edged closer. The taxi wasn't big to begin with, yet he'd managed to keep squarely to one side up to this point.

"Tell me," he invited.

"It's been eleven months since I've seen her." She watched the buildings whip past the taxi for a moment. She missed Cadmia already. Or at least, the wide, open spaces in and around the tiny town. "And she's not expecting me today."

"A surprise visit?" Releasing her hands, he put an arm around her shoulders. "You know she's going to be thrilled, don't you?"

"I suppose she will." Her mind darted toward the second source of her concern. She hadn't had a chance to prepare Lydia for…

Her ambivalent tone made him back up and take another look at the situation.

"But I'm the real surprise. Is that it?"

Harmony tried to think of a way out of answering him directly, but had to nod. So much for 'no boys' in her life.

"Don't worry." He winked. "Just tell her you bought me on approval."

Rolling her eyes, she snuggled closer, resting her head against his chin. His coat was slick under her cheek and made his shoulder seem softer than she knew it was. He'd hauled and hefted all day yesterday without so much as a whimper.

He might've imagined it, but he thought he heard her whisper, "She better approve."

"Here we are!" The taxi swung into a parking spot with all the finesse of a rhino taking a mud bath.

Grant gradually released his hold on his seatbelt as he realized the car had come to a complete stop. Reluctantly handed over his credit card.

"Tips are appreciated." The driver smirked as she gave him his credit card and the key pad.

"Tips? Me?" He punched the button for ten percent, the lowest choice. "I was a pediatrician, not an optometrist." If he had been, however, he would've suggested she get her vision checked so she could see the other cars on the road.

Harmony giggled and opened the door. She could feel the driver's puzzled eyes on them briefly before the taxi peeled out and vanished into the traffic.

"Did you just tell her she needed glasses?" Harmony turned her collar up but the undaunted icy breeze swirled around her ankles instead. Of course he had. Optometrist, indeed.

"Professionally," he took her hand, "that's not a diagnosis I'm qualified to make."

"You said that, too." She turned to look up at the imposing apartment building her sister had called 'home' for the last four years. Cold as she was, she stalled on heading inside. "Still, I gather that personally you have a very emphatic opinion."

"Indubitably."

Her laugh rang through the lobby, prompting the people there to look up briefly from their electronic devices.

Her grip on his hand tightened as they rode the elevator up, so that he was close to calling 'uncle' when the doors finally opened. Retrieving his hand, he put his arm around her shoulder instead. Much safer that way.

"Coming!" someone called from the other

side of the door Harmony knocked on.

Harmony blanched and he guessed that was her sister's voice. Releasing her, he stepped back just in time. The faint sound of Christmas carols became suddenly loud as the door was flung open.

"Harmony!" Lydia burst through the opening and into her sister's arms.

"Lidie." The word, as uttered by Harmony at the moment, was nearly a prayer of relief.

Grant stood by awkwardly while they hugged and sniffled. Appropriately, the carol in the background was Perry Como's "Home for the Holidays."

"I can't believe you came out just for my birthday." Lydia fanned her eyes. "Now I'm going to cry."

"You're already crying, doofus." Harmony gave her one last squeeze, then looked to Grant. In a whisper, she added, "And I sort of brought a birthday present."

Lydia's eyes went round as saucers. "You have a boyfriend?"

Grant felt Harmony's pain but couldn't help laughing at the same time. Lydia's incredulity was just so overdone!

"I refuse to answer that question while we're standing in the hallway." Catching her sister by the elbow, Harmony propelled her into the apartment. She reached for Grant with her free hand and he joined the tow line.

"Okay, okay, we're inside." Lydia shut the door behind them. "Now. Are you her boyfriend or not?"

Harmony buried her bright red face in her hands, which left the introductions to Grant.

"I am Grant Reeves, erstwhile pediatrician and ER doctor. I am presently between occupations and as such," he put his arm around Harmony again, "free to woo your sister."

Harmony's shoulders started to shake with laughter at his goofily formal speech. When she peeked through her fingers, she laughed even harder at the sight of Lydia's sagging jaw. But he wasn't finished.

"You must be the Lady Lydia, sister extraordinaire and birthday girl." He swept up one of Lydia's hands in his free hand and bent over it with all the savoir faire of a duke greeting a princess.

"Oh, I like him." Lydia dropped his hand and came in for a group hug. "Can we keep him?"

"That's up to him." Harmony instructed herself not to be embarrassed. Because, after all, that was how it worked, right?

Lydia pulled back and studied their faces. "Well, how about that? Your first official boyfriend in four years and you want to marry him."

Grant had a vivid flashback to the first—and last—time he'd voluntarily acted as the soccer goalie in a game with his sisters. His throat tightened, his stomach muscles clenched, and he struggled to breathe.

"Ohhhhkay." Harmony peeled Lydia off of them and sat Grant down on the lovely indigo couch. "Stay with me, doc." His mouth was close enough to provoke some interesting thoughts on how to get him breathing again, but she could wait. Something told her it was important to him to initiate their first kiss.

"I'm fine." Grant recovered quickly enough to be embarrassed by the lapse. "I think my stomach just caught up with me, that's all."

"Your stomach?" Lydia's lips twitched. The elevators in that building were infamous for their docility.

"He doesn't like flying in a small plane. Here, give me your coat." As she helped him out of it, Harmony gave him a wink that Lydia couldn't see, then shucked her own coat and draped both coats over the arm of the recliner. Sat down beside him. Belatedly, she asked, "Where are the Adams?"

Lydia turned a peculiar shade of pink. "They…went out."

"Out as in…?" Harmony let the sentence dangle.

"As in they're not here."

Grant's training kicked in and he inadvertently began assessing the young woman's unspoken communications. Her voice had pitched higher and while she was smiling, she refused to look at them. Her feet shifted slightly, too, like she wished she were elsewhere.

"If you two need a few minutes to catch up," he offered, ready to clear out so they could have a heart-to-heart, as his family called it, "I can wait outside."

"Does he need to wait outside, Lidie?"

At Harmony's use of her nickname, Lydia's shoulders slumped. "No, that's okay. I might as well tell him since he's here." She paused, expecting Harmony to say something the way that Tara, um, Sister Adams, usually did, but her sister just smiled invitingly.

"I was going to run away today."

And just like that, it was Harmony's turn to stop breathing.

"You…what?!" She choked out.

"Time!" Grant found himself between them, his hands tee'd in the traditional referee signal. *What was he doing?* Getting between sisters was a guaranteed way to shorten one's life! "You," he pointed to Harmony, "breathe. In and out. Good." He felt vaguely like a rookie lion tamer, wondering how much longer they'd put up with him telling them what to do.

Lydia watched him curiously and he had to work hard not to flinch under her gaze.

"You." He pointed at the third seat on the couch. "In your own words, Lady Lydia," he genuinely hoped the corny nickname was gaining him points, "tell your sister—whom you've scared to death, by the way—why you would risk leaving a safe place."

Lydia sat where he'd indicated and took Harmony's hand. "I decided to come find you."

Harmony closed her eyes. Opened them and wrapped Lydia in a hug.

Grant did his best to fake an interest in the artwork while they chatted quietly. Johnny Mathis's golden pipes were cheerfully "dashing through the snow" by then.

"I'm finally eighteen. I'm literally old news now." Lydia smirked at her pun.

"You're right about that." Harmony couldn't help snickering a little. Nevertheless, she started shaking her head. "I still don't understand why you'd risk leaving the Adams', though."

"I wanted to see you!" Lydia clearly thought that was a silly question.

"And I'm here because I wanted to see you." Harmony interrupted gently. "I think what I'm trying to ask is… Why did you feel like you had to run away?" She held out her free hand, palm up. "All you had to do was say something to me. We could've made arrangements for you to come out for a few days. Had a nice visit." She hurried on when Lydia opened her mouth to speak. "You didn't even know where to find me. You would've missed a lot of school, Sister Adams' and I would've been scared out of our wits, and someone a lot worse than a few amoral photojournalists might've gotten ahold of you."

"Give me a little credit, sis." Lydia finally got a word in. "I wrote a detailed letter to Sister Adams. And I have the brains I was born with." She smiled smugly. "You're in Jefferson City, Missouri."

"Not bad." Harmony slowly sat back. Not bad? It was unnerving. If Lydia had gotten that much out of their monthly phone calls, how close would a professional knows-all, tells-all get? "Not precisely correct, but probably close enough that, with time and a little luck, you could've found me."

Lydia wilted slightly.

"You've overlooked one small problem. By the time you found me, I wouldn't have been there anymore." Harmony waited for Lydia to look at her. "I would've been here, turning mountains on their ears trying to find you."

Lydia's face fell still further. "I had a whole plan for getting away. I don't think you would've found me anytime soon."

"Yeah. That's what I figured." Harmony smoothed her sister's hair and let her nestle her head against her shoulder. "We'll be together soon, Lidie. You just need to finish school first."

"Oh!" Lydia popped upright again, nearly breaking Harmony's nose in the process. "I'm done with school." She beamed at them both. "I got my GED two weeks ago."

Harmony wiggled one finger in her ear as if she thought she'd misheard. Nat King Cole's dulcet tones singing "Joy to the World" came through loud and clear, so her hearing was fine.

"Does that mean I can come with you now?"

Grant sucked in a breath, surprised yet again. Harmony's eyes sought his, prompting him to lower his chin and raise his eyebrows. He was the wrong person to ask.

"When are the Adams going to be home?"

Though Grant couldn't really follow their rapid-fire conversation, he got the gist. Lydia was all packed and rarin' to go. Harmony didn't think it would be appropriate to kidnap her own sister.

"That's final." Harmony's voice was firm.

"But they'll be gone for hours!" Lydia nearly wailed.

"May I make a suggestion?" Grant interjected.

The corner of Harmony's mouth quirked up, but she nodded anyway. He certainly hadn't asked permission before, just barked orders. It was a good thing he had gone with the take-charge approach earlier, though. Her brain positively exploded when Lydia casually announced her plans.

Grant shuffled his feet, then stopped and smiled. He felt guilty for telling them both what to do previously.

"Why don't we go have lunch?"

Amused, Harmony tilted her head at Lydia, who shrugged and nodded.

"If we're not leaving yet, we might as well do something. I'll get my purse."

Harmony mouthed a "thank you" at Grant, who just smiled.

"I'll go call a cab." He handed Harmony her coat.

"On a gorgeous day like this?" Lydia chortled. "The best restaurant in town is just a ten minute walk away."

"Swell." Harmony suddenly hugged her coat closer to her. *Gorgeous to whom?*

"You're not still a cold weather wimp, are you?" Lydia proceeded to regale Grant with stories of her time in Canada, where snow was always—according to her—head high and perfect for making snowballs.

Grant recognized a tall tale when he heard one, but they were having such a good time that he let it go. After all, if he remembered correctly, she hadn't been to Canada for the last four years. She, and consequently 'head height,' were a lot shorter back then.

He was just about to suggest that they take the stairs when Harmony gasped.

"I'll call you." And with that, she was gone.

Lydia recovered before he did and 'stumbled' into a strange man who rushed past them.

"Watch it!" The stranger shoved her aside, patted the camera to make sure Lydia hadn't damaged it, and chased after Harmony.

"What in the…?" Grant started to ask.

Lydia pushed the elevator button and leaned closer. "As soon as the door closes behind that guy, we're going back to the apartment."

"We are?" He lowered his voice to match her volume. "Why?"

"To wait for her, of course."

"Shouldn't we go help her?" he suggested, thoroughly confused.

"How?" Lydia shook her head. "Her best bet is to shake that camera-toting gossipmonger." Looking around his shoulder, she confirmed that the man was gone. "You probably didn't recognize him," she said in a normal voice as she pivoted and headed for the Adams' apartment. "But that's 'Uncle Terry,' the conniving lowlife who made friends with us, 'protected' us from the other reporters, and then did an exposé on us that nearly turned Harmony gray."

"Charming." Horrified, Grant stared at the door to the stairwell.

"Trust me." Lydia tugged at his arm. "We'd

just get in her way."

Harmony was already halfway down the stairwell by then, but only because she cheated. She slid down the banister. On the fifth landing from where she'd started, she stopped long enough to check the hallway door, but it was locked. Just like it was supposed to be.

A door slammed above her and she jumped on the banister again. She'd just started sliding when the door behind her opened unexpectedly.

She wrenched her wrist hauling herself to a stop and dashed up the stairs.

"Thanks!" she told the startled building resident as she breezed past him, shutting the door firmly. "Let's see you talk your way past a locked door, Walsh."

Ha. Knowing him, he'd bribe the guy and be hot on her heels in a matter of seconds.

Darting down the hallway to the stairwell at the opposite end, she continued traveling by banister, her wrist whimpering every inch of the way.

Pausing to smooth her jacket and hair, she entered the lobby as casually as she could while keeping an eye out for Walsh. *There he is.*

She ducked behind a fake plant and took a deep breath. Walsh went out the front door but returned almost instantly. *Great, now what? If he keeps hanging around, I'll be stuck here forever.*

She glanced at the door she'd just exited.

Ten flights of stairs? There were worse fates, right?

"Excuse me." A faintly familiar voice brought Harmony's head around. In the middle of the foyer stood a tall blond in a crisp pantsuit. "I believe you're in violation of a restraining order."

Harmony covered her mouth and watched in supreme delight as a junior member of her company's law firm quoted chapter and verse, so to speak, of the restraining order.

Every time Walsh tried to interrupt, the lawyer stared him down.

Harmony ventured out after Walsh gave up and left the building.

"Nice job." She offered her hand.

"Thank you, Miss Wells." The lawyer didn't smile. "I'm Antonia Woodwright, of your…"

"From the law firm, yes." Harmony's heart sank. "I'm guessing you've got bad news."

"It isn't good." Antonia nodded at a set of couches. "Shall we sit?"

Harmony sat, but she didn't relax.

"I'm often told I'm too direct." Antonia set her briefcase on the floor by her feet. "I just don't see how talking around something is supposed to make it easier."

"I'd actually rather you didn't beat around the bush." Harmony interrupted her apology.

"Oh?" Antonia smiled. "That's a relief. For

me, I mean." Shaking her hair back over her shoulders, she said, "Your father is quite ill, Miss Wells."

"How," she cleared her throat. "Um, how ill?"

"He's been admitted to a hospital." Antonia handed her a business card. "His doctors aren't optimistic."

"Now I know we promised we'd be gone until…" Sister Adams came in the front door of the apartment building and came to an abrupt halt when she saw Harmony sitting in the foyer. "Well, what's all this?"

Chapter 19

"Hard to believe." Tara Adams shook her head as she hung Harmony's coat in the apartment closet. "Walsh found us after all this time."

"Thanks for saying 'us,' Tara." Harmony sighed. "I'm sure it's my fault."

"What makes you say that?" Lydia leaned against Tara's shoulder without noticing it.

"A handful of things." Sitting down beside Grant, Harmony was glad for his arm around her shoulders. "I got my picture splashed all over the internet a few weeks ago. Someone recognized me in New Orleans, or thought they did." She bit her lip. "And I should've left Cadmia six months ago."

"I'm glad you didn't." Grant adjusted the position of the ice bag on her wrist.

"I'm curious how your lawyer knew where to find you." Brother Will Adams broke in.

"And why today," added Tara.

"I mentioned it to the firm when I told them I'd be in their general vicinity today." Harmony shrugged. "Antonia said Dad left a message nearly two weeks ago about his condition, but I guess the person he called had to take emergency leave. Their assistant kept working down the standing to-do list without checking their mail or calls—until yesterday."

Hmm. Perhaps the mix-up had something to do with Walsh's jack-in-the-box appearance.

Will winced. "I'd hate to have to clean up after that mess!"

"I can't speak for the rest of you," Tara eyed the envelope Harmony had tossed onto the coffee table, "but I'm more than a little anxious to know what your father wants."

Harmony drew a slow, steadying breath. "Half of me wants to shred it."

"Don't you think it might be important? I mean, your father's lawyer did hand-deliver it to your lawyer," Tara reminded her.

"Part of me wants to know what it says," mumbled Lydia. She snuck a look at Harmony, who shrugged.

"Go ahead."

The sound of Lydia ripping the envelope open was loud in the silent room. She rubbed the back of her neck and flipped open a card.

Harmony's jaw tightened as Lydia's face paled. She should've been the one to read it first. Who knew what their father had written in there?

Grant's fingers slid over Harmony's good wrist. His light touch held her in place while Lydia finished reading.

"He says he's dying." Lydia sat down suddenly as if her knees had given out. "He wants to see us."

"It's a trick." All eyes turned to Harmony.

"It has to be."

"Why?" Grant met her gaze without flinching. "What would he gain from it?"

"I…don't know." Harmony tried wrestling with the subject, but the habit of assuming the worst was too strong to be beaten in a few measly seconds. "What do you think?"

Grant scratched his chin. "Does he say what hospital he's in?"

Lydia consulted the card. "Brooks' Memorial. He's included a phone number where we can call him."

Tara inhaled as if she was about to speak, then paused. "It's probably not my place to have an opinion."

"No, go ahead." Lydia shifted her entire body so that it pointed toward Harmony.

Harmony managed a small smile. She'd been right about Lydia being close to Tara.

"Well." Tara clasped her hands in front of her. "It's hard to trust someone who has hurt you so much. And yet, it should certainly be possible to at least verify his claim without putting yourselves at risk of another media circus."

"The firm could check it out." Harmony scrubbed a hand over her face. "Except everyone knows that we're their largest client. Wouldn't take much to connect the dots."

Grant cleared his throat and showed them he was on his phone. "Hello, Brooks' Memorial?

Yes, this is Doctor Grant Reeves. I'm calling to get some information on a patient."

Harmony rested her head against his shoulder as he indulged in obligatory niceties. If he was doing what she thought he was doing, he was absolutely brilliant. Ignoring the mild pain from her wrist, she typed her father's full name and date of birth onto her phone's notepad in case Grant needed it.

He provided the information he had and waited patiently. "Room 413?"

Harmony looked up, not liking the change in his tone.

"Yes, I… Thank you, I'm going to have to call back. Yes, something's come up. Terribly sorry." He dropped his phone into his lap and massaged his temple. "He's telling the truth."

"You can tell that from his room number?" Lydia cocked her head to one side and tried to sound more curious than disbelieving.

"Brooks' Memorial isn't your average hospital," he explained quietly. "Staying there long enough to get a room number is not a good thing."

"Now what?" Torn between reaching for Tara or reaching for Harmony, Lydia wrapped her arms around herself.

"Now we talk." Harmony got up, took the card from Lydia, and put it carefully on the table. "More specifically, you talk. To Tara."

Flustered, Lydia made a few false starts before blurting, "I was going to leave today. To go find Harmony."

Tara and Will exchanged glances. "We know."

"But…how?" Aghast, Lydia put her hands on her hips. "I was so careful!"

"Sorry, that's a professional secret." Will winked at her.

Lydia groaned. "That's almost as bad as saying you'll tell me when I'm older."

Tara gave her a small smile. "Remember how long it took us to leave this morning? We wanted to make sure you'd still be here when Harmony arrived."

"Then…you don't mind?" Lydia reached under the cushion she was sitting on and produced a pink envelope. "I wanted to tell you, except…"

"Except you wanted the adventure more." Grant supplied when she fell silent.

Shamefaced, Lydia nodded. "Yeah."

"Hey." Harmony tugged gently on her sister's hair. "There are plenty of adventures left in the world. Is it okay if we skip this one?"

"Course." Getting to her feet, Lydia gave Harmony a big hug. Then Tara. Then a group hug.

Grant was starting to feel left out when Harmony rejoined him on the couch while the others got Lydia's things together.

"Have you had time to transfer your things

to the new suitcase we bought you?" was the last thing they heard Tara say before they all disappeared into another room.

"How bad is he really?" Harmony asked quietly.

"On that floor in that hospital?" Grant smoothed her hair. "It's only an educated guess, but I doubt he'll live to see spring." He kissed the top of her head and prayed silently for her while they waited for Lydia.

Lydia bid a tearful farewell to the Adams, promised to come visit for their children's spring break, and left with one arm securely around Harmony's waist. She bounced back quickly, though, volunteering to sit with the driver when the taxi arrived.

"I've never ridden up front before!" Besides, she figured this way Harmony could sit with her boyfriend!

Once they were safely in the taxi, Harmony's mind wandered to her dilemma again—what to do about her dad's request. What a muddle. Every time she'd gotten sentimental in the past and looked him up to see how he was doing, he'd been involved in some new scandal. She'd never given Lydia details, though the inquisitive young woman could no doubt find the headlines as easily as she did.

"Are you in there?" After a few silent blocks, Grant tapped one finger against her forehead.

"Yes." She slipped her arm through his. "Still thinking."

"Harmony?" Lydia turned from where she was sitting up front with the driver. "Will you teach me to fly an airplane?"

"Absolutely." Harmony answered with more enthusiasm than she felt.

The next ten minutes passed in similar fashion. Lydia's wish list was apparently a long and complex one.

"Tell you what." Harmony held up her hand with a laugh. "If you enroll in a good online college and keep your grades up, we can go wherever and do whatever you want."

Lydia's cheer was still ringing in Grant's ears when they walked into the hangar. Or maybe it was just the squeaking wheel on the luggage cart they'd rented for her things.

"If you two will load the gear, I'll get started on the preflight." Harmony opened the cargo door for them. It would take her a little longer with her sore wrist, but the pain killers had kicked in so that helped.

"Deal!"

Lydia's chatter kept Grant so busy that he didn't have a chance to be nervous on their return flight, a fact that astounded him.

"It's so beautiful here!" Lydia bounded out of the plane and took her first, deep breath of Cadmia air.

Harmony removed her headset and hung it,

then laughed as she watched Lydia twirl in ecstatic circles like a puppy after a long trip.

"Don't take this the wrong way." Grant put his hand on her arm. "But I am extremely glad I drove myself this morning."

"I'll bet you are." She swatted him playfully. Let him keep her hand when he caught it.

"Seriously, I think she may be the first ever recorded example of perpetual motion."

"Eh, she's just excited. She'll crash pretty soon." Neither of them were watching Lydia anymore.

"Please." He edged closer. "Don't say 'crash' while we're sitting in an airplane."

"Uh-oh." She drew back and flicked her eyes in Lydia's direction. "We're on candid camera."

Suddenly, he smiled. "Saved again." And he was gone, chasing a giddily shrieking Lydia across the runway.

"Well, that was almost exciting," she murmured to herself. Maybe it was for the best, though. Lydia had just met him. Catching them kissing—even if it was for the first time— might start Lydia planning their wedding.

Her cheeks a trifle pink, Harmony climbed down and used two fingers to give an ear-splitting whistle. Pointed at the plane. "A little help?"

Despite his earlier declaration, Grant followed them back to her place and helped them unload the car.

"I can walk around the block or something," Lydia offered cheekily when it came time for him to leave. "If you want."

"How about you make yourself useful and pull the bed out of the couch?" Harmony instructed.

"Oh, yay!" Lydia fake-cheered. As she left the kitchen, she put one hand up beside her face and mouthed, "All the details." With her other hand, she pointed at a very self-conscious Grant.

Grant motioned for Harmony to follow him outside. "You have got your hands full."

"No kidding." She paused to lock her car. "Thanks for all of your help today."

"Wouldn't have missed it." Tenderly, he tucked a loose strand of hair behind her ear.

"And…thanks for not trying to tell me what to do about my dad." She shifted from one foot to the other, more than a little worried. They'd started dating in earnest all of…three days ago? Four? She wouldn't blame him if he decided he'd rather back off in light of everything that had just happened.

He wrapped his arms around her and pressed his cheek against her hair. "How can I tell you what I don't know, either?"

She closed her eyes and clung to him, absorbing the moment. His cologne had faded since that morning, but she loved the way the scent of cedar lingered. If he wanted some space, he was definitely sending the wrong signals.

Grant rubbed her back in small, slow circles and felt her begin to relax. They'd had quite a day.

Spotting Lydia watching through the kitchen window, he chuckled.

"Again?" Harmony deduced what was going on and grimaced. "We're going to have to set some very clear ground rules."

"One more thing." He walked her the few steps back to her kitchen door. "When you promised to take Lydia anywhere, were you planning a trip for two?"

"I think we'll stay in Cadmia for the first little while. We need to get used to each other." She had to stop and think. "What are you asking me?"

"Nothing yet. But hopefully soon." Winking, he kissed the tip of her nose, waved to Lydia, and walked away.

"That man is going to drive me batty."

"Only if I don't beat him to it." Lydia observed nonchalantly from the other side of the door.

"Okay, that's it." Harmony marched into the kitchen. "We are going to have a long talk over a large pizza."

"Hawaiian?" Lydia suggested eagerly.

"Ew, you like pineapple on your pizza?"

Harmony compromised on the order, requesting half with and half without pineapple, but her plan to discuss serious things got completely derailed.

Hours later, teeth brushed and comfy pajamas on, she gave up and went to bed.

"So." Lydia yawned and snuggled under the heavy quilt. "You don't like sausage, of any kind, but you do like liver and onions. How does that make sense?"

"Ask me in the morning." Harmony gave Lydia's head a gentle push into the pillow. "Sweet dreams, Lidie."

"You, too, Nornie."

"What did you call me?"

"Nornie. That's what I used to call you when I was little." Lydia blinked sleepily.

"I'd forgotten that."

"Me, too." Lydia nestled close. "Remember when you used to let me sleep with you—" a giant yawn interrupted her, "—after I had a nightmare?"

"Yeah." Harmony reached behind Lydia to make sure the quilt was tucked up around her. "I sure do." Lydia's nightmares usually got worse when their dad brought a new girlfriend home.

Lydia's breathing slipped easily into the deep, regular pattern of peaceful sleep, leaving Harmony alone to contend with her feelings.

Well. Not alone. Both of them had offered

a prayer before climbing into bed tonight, but now Harmony said another one. A long, thoughtful prayer as she examined their situation.

How long could she hate her own father? Except—was she sure she did? She'd believed she did. Now, in the safe, quiet confines of her own space, all she could scrounge up was pain. Resentment.

Doctrine and Covenants 64:10-11 prodded her mind and heart.

"I, the Lord, will forgive whom I will forgive, but of you it is required to forgive all men.

And ye ought to say in your hearts—let God judge between me and thee, and reward thee according to thy deeds."

Forgive? Was she strong enough? She pondered on that until at last she fell into a deep, and mercifully dreamless, sleep.

Her eyes flared open at the sound of someone in her kitchen. Relaxed as she realized they were humming a hymn.

A smile stretched across her face. It was Sunday. Specifically, the Sunday after the Saturday when she brought her sister home.

"Morning, sleepyhead." Lydia greeted her with a hug. "Hungry?"

"I better be." She grinned as she surveyed the pancakes, eggs, and bacon waiting on the table. Grant had taken seconds and thirds of the potatoes, so those were all gone.

"I found most of this in your fridge. Were you saving it for something special?" Lydia asked.

"It's your fridge, too, Lidie." Harmony pulled her sister's anxiously twisting hands apart and kissed her cheek. "Now, let's eat and talk about ground rules so we don't have to worry, okay?"

"Do we have time? I mean, before we go to church."

This time Harmony moved past the wringing hands and hugged Lydia instead. "Spill it."

Lydia laughed nervously. "I just... Would you mind...?"

"I probably won't." She gave her an extra squeeze for confidence.

"Do we have to go to church? In Cadmia?" Neither of them spoke for a moment, then... "I thought maybe we could have some time for," Lydia's words slowed and her voice got softer, "the two of us." Her arms tightened around Harmony's waist.

"We'll have the whole week," Harmony promised, making a mental note to text Grant not to sit by them today. "A few friends are coming over for a movie night on Friday and we can duck everyone until then."

"Great."

Hearing the disappointment in Lydia's voice,

Harmony pulled back to study her face. "That isn't it, is it? At least, not all of it."

Lydia gave a mini shrug. "If we go to your usual ward today, your friends will be there."

"And?" Harmony prompted, sensing she still didn't have the full story. Why was that okay for Friday, but not today?

"You'll be Harmony, and I'll be…" Lydia's voice trailed off.

Understanding finally dawned.

"Not ready to be Harmony's little sister, huh?" Harmony returned Lydia's shy smile. "Don't worry, there's another ward not too far from here." She glanced at the clock. "We'll have to hurry, though."

"You don't mind?"

"No, of course not." Harmony sat down at the table. "It's hard enough figuring out who you are without everyone expecting you to be me."

"Yes, exactly!" Lydia heaved a sigh of relief. "I didn't know how to say that."

They had a wonderful time visiting a ward in Fireclay, where Harmony was as much a stranger as Lydia. No preconceptions, no hidden expectations, and a spiritual feast they happily spent the rest of the day reviewing.

"Now, tomorrow I'll have to pick up some things from the post office, then after that we can do whatever you want."

"I think…" Lydia rinsed her toothbrush and

set it to dry on her hand towel. "I think I want to get some things for your place. Sort of…housewarming gifts."

"You're getting yourself housewarming gifts?" Harmony teased as she brushed her hair out.

"It sounds silly when you put it like that." Lydia wrinkled her nose. "We won't be here very much longer, but a few things wouldn't hurt. We can have a Christmas tree, can't we?"

"That would be nice." Harmony's heart melted. Was it strange that her little sister should be the one to make her house into a home?

"Can we keep this place?" Lydia asked out of the blue. "I sort of like it."

"If we want to." Harmony cocked her head to one side. "You know we're—" Was there another way to say it? "—rich, right?"

"Yeah, I know." Lydia picked up a pillow as they walked into the front room and threw it at her.

They paused the conversation for a brief pillow fight simply because they could. Harmony surrendered relatively quickly in case it became a competition.

"I don't know how rich, though." Lydia stuck her hands in the pockets of her homemade pajama pants.

"I think it's time for you to meet our lawyers." Harmony tossed her pillow on the bed and held out her hand.

Together, they knelt for prayer, then got up to sketch out their week. A whole day in their hometown of Patria for lawyers and shopping and fun. Another day fixing up 'their' place. Wednesday would be a work day, and finally movie night on Friday.

"Wait, what happened to Thursday?" Lydia giggled.

"We'll think of something." Harmony had a suspicion that Lydia would need a day off by then, if not sooner.

Chapter 20

Grant held the bouquet carefully as he made his way up Harmony's front walk Thursday night. They'd exchanged a few texts throughout the week and he had a feeling that today hadn't gone well. So here he was, unannounced, trying to convince himself to knock on her door.

Which was opening. On its own.

His fake smile slipped when he saw Lydia's puffy eyes and red, damp nose. Discreetly plucking the card for Harmony from the side of the bouquet, he gave Lydia a genuine smile.

"I have a delivery for the Lady Lydia?"

She took the flowers, sniffled, and leaned into him, her head resting on his chest. "Thank you."

"Won't you come in?" Harmony's grateful eyes met his over the top of Lydia's head. "Both of you?" she teased.

Lydia managed a small laugh at that and came in. "I'll go put these in some water."

Grant stepped inside and handed Harmony the card he'd written to accompany the flowers. "For you."

"Thanks." Understanding lit her eyes and she wrapped her arms around him.

He didn't hesitate to return the hug, and they lingered there, drawing comfort from each other.

"Missed you." He touched his lips to her hair. Her cheek. Cradled her close.

"Is that what the card says?" she joked.

"Mhmm." He chuckled. "I like telling you this way a whole lot more, though."

"Me, too." She put one hand against his chest so she could feel his laugh better. Christmas music floated in from the kitchen and she sighed.

"Rough day?" He stroked her hair.

"She misses the Adams and her home in Rhode Island." Reluctantly drawing away, she led him over to the couch. "We flew to Patria on Monday. Um." She closed tired eyes. "That's our hometown. Saw our lawyers." She'd literally seen the weight of their inheritance settle on Lydia's shoulders as she signed paper after paper until her hand cramped. "We did some shopping, too. We had so much fun that we spent the night at…" Her throat closed up and she couldn't finish.

He took her cold hand in his warm one. "You stayed in your mom's house?"

She nodded and swiped at a tear. "Big mistake. For both of us. Worse for her, I think."

"Yeah?" He wiped away another tear for her. "Are you sure?"

Harmony gulped and nodded. "She hasn't been the same since we got back. Yesterday we had work to distract us, but today, well. She's been crying off and on since breakfast."

Lydia came in then and he scooted closer to Harmony so there was room for Lydia on his other side.

"Thanks for coming over." Lydia snuggled against him on one side, tucking her knees up to her chest and somehow reminding him of a puppy he'd had years ago, who always hid next to him during thunderstorms.

"Yes." Harmony sighed and relaxed to his left, head on his shoulder.

"Any time." He kissed the tops of their heads and eased his left arm around Harmony with a little help from her. "Have you two had supper yet?" In his experience, hunger was a major contributing factor to low spirits.

Lydia shook her head and didn't loosen her grip on the edge of his coat. She seemed eight, not eighteen, in that moment. Emotional trauma could do that to a person.

"It's early." Harmony reached around with her right hand and threaded her fingers through his left.

"Nornie?"

"Hmm?"

Grant looked back and forth between them as they conversed around him.

"I want to see Dad."

He felt Harmony flinch, but her voice was perfectly even when she responded.

"You're sure?"

"Yeah."

"We'll go on Saturday morning, okay?"

"Thanks." Lydia sighed and drooped a little in relief.

Grant squeezed Harmony's hand. He had in no way foreseen his, um, role in their decision, but he was happy for them.

"Will you come?" Lydia looked up at him and tightened her hold on his coat.

"If it's okay with Harmony." He felt a slight nod against his shoulder before she spoke.

"I'd like that."

"Then wild horses couldn't keep me away." He hugged them both. "Now, how about supper?"

Harmony laughed, a deep throaty sound that still had a few tears in it. "Is that the real reason you came over? You were hoping to schmooze a meal?"

Lydia giggled and he felt like he was halfway to his goal of cheering them up.

"Actually, I thought we could go over to the Blue Plate Café."

Harmony narrowed her eyes at him. "You're serious?" He wanted to sing karaoke? Now?

Lydia watched their conversation with interest.

"It won't be as fun as last time," he admitted, a smile tugging at the corner of his mouth.

"Oh, don't be cute." She poked him in the ribs.

"What, would you rather go to the Purple Skink?" He captured her hand before she could poke him again.

"Absolutely."

"It's a deal." He grinned triumphantly.

"Does this mean we're going out for supper?" Lydia frowned. "I don't know…"

"You'll like Inez." Harmony, trapped against him as she was, still managed to lean around him to promise.

"Inez?" Lydia rubbed her eyes. "I'm confused, are we going out to eat or to meet one of your friends?"

"Both." Grant ginned and jerked his head toward the bathroom. "Now go wash your face and put on a clean shirt. The bus leaves soon."

Lydia giggled and hopped to her feet. "You're crazy."

"Thank you!" He got up to call after her as she left, pulling Harmony with him.

Harmony cleared her throat. "Are you going to give me back my hands?"

"That depends." He loosened his hold so she could get away any time, but she didn't.

"On what?" She tilted her head to one side in case he wanted to kiss her.

"On this." Slowly, he lowered his lips to hers. Released her hands and gathered her closer.

She clung to him, half afraid that she'd fallen asleep on his shoulder and this was all a dream. A wonderful, fantastic dream. She followed him up onto her toes when he tried to straighten away, unwilling to let it end.

"Harmony." He stroked her cheek with his thumb and rested his forehead against hers. "I love you."

"I love you, too." She managed a watery smile.

"You don't have to say that." He pressed a finger to her lips. "You're under a lot of pressure right now and I'm not looking for anything from you. I just needed to tell you."

"I appreciate that." She brushed her lips against his and her heart flipped. "But I do love you. I have for a while now, I think."

He didn't contradict her that time, just claimed her soft lips again.

"On second thought." Lydia's voice invaded their bubble. "I should pick a different shirt."

Laughing, Harmony kept a hold on one of Grant's arms as she turned to face her sister. "You look fine. Let's go."

"No, I think this shirt is too…pink. Yeah, that's it." Lydia allowed Harmony to snag her arm and giggled all the way to the door. "You two are so adorable together."

"Thanks." Grant wrapped an arm around each of their waists and carried them to his car.

"You're pretty nice yourself."

He turned on Christmas music for their drive over, just loud enough for them to sing along if they wanted to, and made a point of driving down Fireclay's main street, where Lydia tried to notice all the decorations at the same time.

On the way back from Fireclay, Harmony glanced at Lydia and made a soft, maternal noise.

"She's asleep."

"You've had a big week."

She didn't miss that he'd included her in the statement and nodded slowly. "So have you. How're you holding up?"

"Me? Let me think. I started dating my best friend in Cadmia, who turned out to be an heiress with a little sister and says she loves me back." He rolled up to a stop sign and leaned over to kiss her softly. "I think I can stand it."

"Oh yeah?" She looked down at their joined hands. "You've still got to meet her dying father on Saturday."

"And kiss her in front of half of the town Saturday night." It was just the dress rehearsal, but still…

"Now that I think I can help you with."

"Promise?"

They shared one more kiss after he half-carried a sleepy Lydia in to the couch, then he let himself out.

"You should marry him." Lydia started to lie down on the couch and Harmony jumped forward.

"Come on. You have your own bed now, we just have to get you there." It had taken some serious re-arranging, but they'd shoehorned two beds into the bedroom and put her allergen-free merchandise behind a curtain in the front room.

Lydia stumbled along beside her. "Are you?"

"Am I what?" She focused on getting Lydia out of her coat.

"Gonna marry him!"

"He has to ask me first." Harmony sat her down and knelt to take off her shoes. Thank goodness it hadn't been snowy out tonight!

"He will." Lydia slumped over onto her pillow, yawning furiously. "He will."

Harmony gave up with a laugh and pushed her sister's legs up onto the bed. Carried her shoes out to the kitchen door and toed off her own.

Whispered a prayer. "I hope so."

They slept in on Friday since they didn't have anything planned until the movie night later that day.

"How do you think they'll react to me?" Lydia poured milk over her late, *late* breakfast cereal.

"Merry's a worrier, so she'll be polite but

distant.   Grace will accept you without question," Harmony smeared peanut butter on her toast, "and Noella will be the sister you never knew you were missing."

Lydia laughed. "I like them already."

"And they're going to love you." Harmony said their prayer, then made sure they had scripture study after breakfast.

"Who're you texting?" Lydia snickered. "As if I didn't know."

Harmony hit send and ignored the question. "C'mon. If we're going to make tinfoil dinners for tonight, we need a few things from Stock's."

"Does that mean I get to meet Miss Birdie?"

"It sure does."

They took their time over their preparations and Lydia squealed when the doorbell rang.

"I'll get it!"

Harmony laughed and let her answer the door all three times, even though it meant she was stuck in the kitchen with an incredibly curious Noella.

"You have a sister?!"

"The one and only." Harmony lifted a tray of tinfoil pouches out of the oven. She hated to admit it, but she was a little nervous. "Hope you're hungry."

"Harmony!" Noella at once pleaded and snapped in frustration. "You never told me you had a sister."

"She never told anyone." Lydia led their next guest into the room. "Which we'll explain once we're all here."

Harmony glanced at the clock, wishing Merry would hurry up. She was never the last to arrive.

"I'll get that," Lydia announced as the doorbell rang.

Harmony shook her head. "Have to give the girl credit for dramatics." She held up both hands when Grace and Noella started to talk simultaneously. "Bear with us, please. We've…we've earned the right to a little recreational drama." Her use of the word 'drama' reminded her of their trip tomorrow and her stomach twisted uncomfortably.

"Merry, thank goodness you're here!" Grace grabbed her friend's hand and hauled the startled woman over to the table. "They refused to tell us anything until you came."

"A whole three minutes." Harmony's lips twitched. "Gather round, folks. We'll talk while we eat."

As succinctly as possible, the sisters filled their guests in on why they had lived apart for so long—and why they were together now.

"How long before you leave?" Merry set her fork down though she'd barely touched her food.

Noella gasped and Grace frowned.

Harmony took a deep breath. Cocked an

eyebrow at Lydia, who made a 'go ahead' gesture with her fingers.

"We've decided to stay right here for a while." She leaned back while the others protested briefly, then explained. "It turns out that Dad is sick, ironically as the result of his degenerate lifestyle." They'd gone the extra mile and had their lawyer arrange the meeting. "Anyway, he's sick enough that the doctors aren't making any promises. We've agreed to see him tomorrow." *For the first time in ten years.*

All their heads swiveled toward Lydia when she spoke. "We won't make any long-term decisions until after we've met with him." Lydia made an effort at sounding cheerful. "At the moment, we hope you're in the mood for a silly movie."

"You got it." Merry promised without hesitation.

"I second the motion to adjourn to the living room." Grace picked up Merry and Harmony's paper plates, stacking them on top of her own.

"Motion carried!" Noella snagged Lydia's plate with a wink. "Let's go watch a movie."

Nobody had to fake laughing at Danny Kaye's antics in *The Court Jester*. Merry and Grace even sang along, especially at the cheesy ending.

Harmony loved hearing Lydia's laugh. Grant was right. They were both under a heavy load right now.

"We'll all pray for you tonight," Grace promised as she gave Harmony a second hug.

"Yes, of course!" Noella agreed from where she was clipping the leash back on Caesar's collar.

"And tomorrow." Merry gripped Harmony's hand.

"Thank you." Harmony and Lydia shivered on the kitchen stoop until all three friends were safely on their way.

"You have the most amazing friends *in* the world," Lydia announced as they re-entered the kitchen.

"Yeah?"

"No question. How many people can you drop a new sister and the fact that you're rich on and have them offer to pray that your visit with your dad'll go well?" Lydia's smile was genuine, but didn't quite cancel out the worry in her eyes.

"You've convinced me," grinned Harmony.

"Can we watch another show?" Lydia twitched the cuff of her long-sleeved shirt. "I'm not tired yet."

"Go climb into your pjs and I'll pull out the couch, okay?" Lydia rewarded her with a hug and kiss on the cheek, making her smile.

They stayed up much too late, but neither of them were ready to sleep. They had too much on their minds.

"What do you think he'll be like?" Lydia's memories of their father were fragmented at best.

Harmony hesitated. "Older." She wished she could say 'wiser,' too. At this point, though, she was afraid to hope for that.

"Did you used to like him?"

The question caught Harmony off-guard and she couldn't breathe for a moment. "I used to love him."

"And you don't anymore." Lydia didn't have the words to express how much that thought hurt her.

Harmony patted the pillow beside her and Lydia put her head on it. "I don't know him anymore, Lidie. I'm in the same boat you are." Her heavy eyelids were starting to close when Lydia spoke again.

"Do you think you can ever forgive him?"

"I'm trying to. I really am."

Those words circled round and round in Harmony's mind the next day as they rode the elevator to the hospital's fourth floor. *I'm trying to. I really am.* It was like having a hamster wheel in her head.

Grant held her hand as they walked to her father's room. And Lydia's, too. Acquiring yet another younger sister was a bonus to his relationship with Harmony as far as he was concerned.

He winced inwardly when Harmony's hold

tightened to a death grip as they approached Room 413 and a young, slender woman rose to greet them.

"Harmony Wells?" The woman didn't bother trying to shake hands. "Lydia Wells?" At their stiff nods, she introduced herself. "I'm Eileen Walker, your father's lawyer. He'd like to see Lydia first."

"No way." Harmony glared at her. "He can see me or he can see both of us or we can leave."

Eileen smiled thinly. "He said you'd feel that way." Turning, she knocked on the door.

A faint voice called, "Come in."

"Mr. Wells is a very weak man." Eileen directed the words at Harmony, then let her gaze slide over to Grant. "Too many people might tire him."

Grant dropped Harmony's hand and put his arm around her shoulder. They'd each said a prayer before leaving the airport in Cadmia and again when they touched down. He'd known something like this would happen.

"I'll be right outside," he promised.

The door clicked shut behind them and Eileen smirked. "They're in no danger. He can barely lift a pen anymore."

Grant bit back the words that sprang to his lips. He'd attended enough wealthy patients to know that at this stage, the 'family' often became more concerned with who got what than how.

Deciding to ignore the insinuations, he focused instead on praying for his girls on the other side of that blasted door.

Harmony had to squint against the bright sunlight that poured into the room, taking ordinary objects and turning them into blinding white spots.

"Harmony? Are you there?" Kenneth Wells' voice, familiar even after ten years, broke the silence.

"I thought you wanted to see Lydia first." Her eyes gradually adapted and she looked at the bed backed up to the far wall.

He gave a hoarse chuckle. "I didn't actually believe you would let me."

"I'm here." Lydia stopped just short of saying 'Daddy.' She wasn't sure what to call the shriveled stranger before her.

"Lydia." He sighed. "I wanted to apologize. For..." His hands, which were gripping the bedclothes, slowly relaxed and he lifted one of them, palm up. "For everything."

Tears stung Harmony's eyes and she closed her mouth tightly against the anger that wanted to escape and wreak havoc.

"Why did you do what you did?" Lydia wanted to know.

"Which time?" Sighing, he motioned to two comfortable chairs. "Sit down, won't you?"

"We're not sure how long we're staying."

Harmony was torn between needing to protect Lydia and needing closure for herself.

"I understand." He leaned back against a small mountain of bed pillows. "Have you ever spent the night in a hospital?"

Harmony had just enough patience to check with Lydia before she answered for both of them. "No."

"It's terrible. The bed's wrong. The noises are completely wrong. And the smells." He grimaced. "Don't get me started on the smells. I like a clean place, but you should be able to smell something besides the antiseptic, am I right?"

"Sure." Harmony didn't know what else to say.

He stilled. "My point is, it got me to thinking. About heaven."

Chapter 21

Lydia hid her face against Harmony's shoulder and tried not to cry.

Harmony had the same reaction, combined with a suddenly turning stomach. Despite everything, she still suspected a trick.

"Come closer, girls. I can't see you way over there."

Lydia nodded, so Harmony complied.

"Beautiful. Just like your mother."

Lydia was openly crying now, but Harmony dug her fingernails into her palm and refused to give in.

"I wasn't the man your mother thought I was. When she died…" He swallowed. "Could you get me a drink of water, please? My throat gets dry so fast now."

His plea softened her heart and Harmony poured water for him. Held it and helped him drink.

"Thank you." Wiping his damp lips with one finger, he started again. "When your mother died, she told me she knew I would take care of you. And I told her I would. I'm not making excuses, but I also told myself I needed help."

"So you started drinking?" Harmony's voice was bitter.

"Resumed." He sighed. "Sober for thirteen

years. I never told your mother."

Harmony recoiled a step as if he'd slapped her. It made so much sense! She'd wondered more than once over the years how her father could go from a firm non-drinker to incapable of caring for his children so quickly.

"Needless to say, my life went downhill after that." He pushed shaking fingers through wispy gray hair. "Taking your sister and leaving was the right thing to do."

"That's not what you told Mr. Lawrence." Harmony spoke quickly, determined to keep her head in control of her rapidly softening heart.

"Your lawyer? No, I didn't. At the time, I was furious. You were a child, *my* child, and I wasn't going to let you get away with…being right about me."

Harmony looked away, trying to hold back the tears, but they came faster than she could blink. She'd hurt him, too. Funny she hadn't realized that before.

"And you know what your lawyer told me? He said that the only way to prove you wrong was to stop drinking." He laughed harshly. "The proverbial red rag to a bull. Nobody was going to tell me what to do. Stupid."

Lydia timidly made her way to the side of the bed opposite Harmony. Slipped her hand into his. "I wish you had stopped, Daddy. I missed you so much."

He drooped visibly, his daughter's simple words stripping him of any remaining pride and leaving only the hollow shell of a man that he'd become.

"Liddie. My sweet baby."

Impulsively, Lydia wrapped her arms around him and hugged him as tightly as she dared.

He rested his cheek against her hair, his thin frame trembling with repressed sobs.

Harmony watched her hand move away from her body. It hesitated at the edge of the bed when her mind tried unsuccessfully to call it back—then reached out to touch her father's arm. The fabric gave under her fingers until she finally found his frail, bony arm.

He looked at his older daughter, fear and hope warring in his eyes.

Harmony's heart and head aligned in sudden, almost violent resolve. In an instant, she was on the bed beside him, sobbing against her father's shoulder.

"My girls." Kenneth wept openly as he did his best to rock them. Speaking to his deceased wife, he whispered, "Cissy, our girls are here."

They hugged and cried and talked, crazy talk where they all spoke at the same time and still managed to understand each other.

He wanted to know everything he missed and everything they were doing so that for quite a while they took turns answering his questions until he asked, "Harmony, what about you? Are you dating anyone?"

Harmony felt her cheeks warm and was surprised when Lydia didn't innocently answer for her. "I am," she answered haltingly, "seeing someone."

"That's wonderful." Kenneth's sigh was heartfelt. "I've lost track of the hours I've spent worrying that I soured you against the idea of romance in general."

"I thought she had something against romance, too," Lydia piped up, "until she introduced me to Grant."

"Grant?" Kenneth nodded approvingly. "I'd like to meet him sometime, if…if that's alright."

Harmony tried to catch Lydia's eye, but it was too late.

"He's out in the hallway now, Daddy."

Harmony retreated behind the mask of a polite smile, perfected over the years.

"Well, now." While it hurt Kenneth to sense Harmony's withdrawal, he didn't blame her. How could he after all he'd put them both through? "It's a good sign that he was willing to come."

Harmony's mouth opened. Closed. The thought of Grant meeting her dad filled her with fear *and* elation. It seemed that mixed emotions were the order of the day as far as her dad was concerned.

"Do you feel up to meeting him?" she asked at last.

"I'd like that." Kenneth left it there, the decision in her hands.

"Alright." Her conviction that this was the right thing to do grew as she got to her feet. "I'll ask him in."

As she walked over to the door, Lydia's voice followed her saying, "I really like him, Dad."

Grant leaned against the wall opposite Mr. Wells' door, praying silently.

What's-her-name, the lawyer, had taken off ages ago to make a phone call or something, leaving him to wait in relative solitude. He'd already tuned out the ambient noises of the hospital, though some sixth sense kept him alert in case his name came over the loudspeaker.

He stiffened when the door to Mr. Wells' room reopened.

Harmony, her pale face accentuating her wide, red-rimmed eyes, beckoned to him.

"I want you to meet my dad." She drew him into the room.

A glance at the bed showed Grant that Mr. Wells was wholly absorbed in talking to Lydia, so Grant held Harmony at the door for a moment. Wiped a tear off her cheek and raised a questioning eyebrow.

"It's alright." She closed hot, tired eyes and rested her face against his palm. "It was a happy tear."

"Oh, honey." He bent and kissed her eyes softly. "I'm so glad."

"Young man." Kenneth's attempt at sounding stern was foiled by a coughing fit.

"Mr. Wells?" Grant strode over to the bed, only a step ahead of Harmony. Out of habit, he helped the man with the glass of water on the tray beside him. Began automatically assessing him as if he were a patient. "Mr. Wells, I realize I'm not your doctor, but I'm concerned that you've overtired yourself."

"Should we go?" Lydia half-asked, half-offered.

Grant could tell from the tender way she was holding her father's hand that she didn't want to leave. Still…

"We should probably let him rest for a few hours." Grant helped Mr. Wells lie back on the pillows, which Lydia hastily rearranged to make him more comfortable.

"Don't go." Kenneth held out his hand to Harmony, who took it.

"Dad, this is my boyfriend, Grant Reeves. He's a doctor."

"Sorry to hear that," Kenneth rasped.

Grant flashed him the smile he saved for exasperating patients. "Perfectly understandable."

"I'm sorry, everyone." A middle-aged woman stepped into the room, a chart in her hands. "Mr. Wells has some tests today."

Kenneth scowled. "I don't want any more tests."

"Now, Mr. Wells…"

"One moment, please." Grant looked Kenneth in the eyes. "Mr. Wells, will you authorize your doctor to discuss your case with me?"

Kenneth glared at him briefly, then nodded. "Sure, go ahead."

Grant introduced himself to the woman, Dr. Watkins, and got a severely abbreviated version of Mr. Wells' case history. He also bought the man a few more minutes with his daughters before he returned to stand by Harmony.

"Well? I suppose you're going to tell me to listen to the doctor, Doctor." Kenneth scowled.

"Actually, I just came to ask if I could borrow Harmony for a moment." Grant had a daring—or possibly crazy—idea.

Surprised, Harmony allowed him to lead her over to Dr. Watkins.

"Dr. Watkins, this is Mr. Wells' oldest daughter, Harmony Wells." Grant cut right to the chase. "Now, if I understood you correctly, Dr. Watkins, your primary treatment goal for Mr. Wells is to keep him comfortable."

Dr. Watkins hesitated. "Yes, though we do have hope that these tests will…" Her voice trailed off as Grant's eyebrow slowly lifted.

"With all due respect to yourself and this excellent hospital, is there anything Mr. Wells is getting here that he couldn't get at another hospital?" Grant wanted the truth on the table.

Dr. Watkins cleared her throat. Pushed her glasses up on her nose. And, at length, shook her head.

Harmony sucked in a breath. "Does that mean we could have him transferred to another hospital?"

"I don't recommend it." Dr. Watkins was adamant. "Your father's condition is fairly good at the moment, but a move like that might be too much for him."

Harmony turned on her heel and walked back to the bed. Her stomach twisted and flipped as she held a murmured conversation with Lydia, who nodded emphatically.

"Dad." Harmony put her hand on top of his. "Would you like to transfer to a hospital closer to where we're staying?"

Tears welled up in Kenneth's eyes. "If you want me."

"We've been without you for ten years." Harmony bent and kissed his forehead. "And that's much too long."

"Alright." Grant took Harmony and Lydia each by an elbow. "We need to let him rest now. Also," he spoke firmly to Mr. Wells, who seemed about to object, "the sooner we leave, the sooner we can start the transfer process."

"I'm afraid there is a considerable amount of paperwork." Dr. Watkins frowned just thinking about it.

Harmony and Lydia kissed their dad goodbye, promised to call in the morning, and let Grant coax them over to the door.

"Just a minute." Kenneth pointed at Grant. "I want to talk to you."

"I want to talk to you, too." Grant ignored Lydia's giggle and squeezed Harmony's hand. "Dr. Watkins will get you started and I'll be along as soon as I can, alright?"

"Well. Alright." Harmony had a funny feeling she ought to stick around and listen to what they said, but she really did want to get the paperwork over with. "You'll be able to find us?"

"I'm sure I'll be able to get directions to Dr. Watkins' office."

"He's right." Dr. Watkins did her best to smile. "If you'll follow me, please?"

As they left, Grant returned to Mr. Wells.

"I mean what I said, sir." Grant used a paper towel to blot the sweat from the older man's forehead. "You need to rest so you'll be in shape for your trip."

"Don't," Kenneth shook his head, "call me sir." He took a deep, wheezing breath. "We both know you'll be part of the family soon."

Grant's heart forced its way into his throat and he had to cough to clear it. "I haven't asked her yet."

"You will." Kenneth patted his hand. "I saw it in your eyes when you looked at her."

"Yes, sir, I definitely plan to. If you have no objections." The words slipped out almost of their own volition and Grant was surprised at how he'd phrased it. It sort of sounded like he was going to ask Harmony no matter what her father thought about it.

Kenneth's head moved wearily from side to side. "Not my place to object."

Grant considered the statement. "Harmony has told me enough that I understand what you're saying. However, I don't think she'd mind if you gave me an honest answer, man to man." He saw Kenneth's eyes move toward the water and helped the man get another drink. He'd have to speak to a nurse about bringing in a glass with a lid and straw, which would be easier for Kenneth to manage when he was on his own.

"Man to man?" Kenneth's eyes bored into his and he seemed to gain strength from somewhere as he considered Grant closely. "All I know is how you've treated her here today. Keep on respecting her, loving her, and you'll do fine."

"Thank you." Grant took his time making sure Kenneth was as comfortable as possible, then rejoined his girls.

Harmony stifled her curiosity over what he'd wanted to discuss with her father and filled him in on their progress thus far.

"I think we're just a few signatures away from a jailbreak," she joked, flexing her writing hand.

"Wonderful." A strange sense of confidence flooded him as she smiled at him. "Dr. Watkins, whom do you recommend for transportation?"

She barely looked up from the papers she was organizing. "Between states? There aren't many companies that would be comfortable working with someone in Mr. Wells' delicate condition."

"Does that mean Daddy won't be coming with us?" Lydia hated that she sounded so helpless.

Harmony put an arm around her shoulders. "We'll find a way." They were billionaires, right? That should help?

Grant caught Harmony's eye and pointed out the door. "I'm going to make a quick phone call."

Harmony pushed aside a feeling of disappointment as he disappeared from view and focused on smiling for Lydia. Who could they call? Her lawyer? Hmm, yes, that might work. If the firm didn't know of a company firsthand, it would be able to find one.

In answer to Dr. Watkins' question, Harmony demurred, "No, thank you, I'm sure we can find the exit ourselves."

They shook hands all around and the girls found themselves out in the hallway. Just in time to hear Grant finishing his call.

"Thanks, I owe you… What? Well, sure, but…" Grant paused to listen. Chuckled. "If you say we're square, then we're square. Good deal. Bye."

"What was that all about?" Lydia slipped her arm through his and smiled when he offered his other arm to Harmony.

"That was about transporting your dad." He walked them over to the elevator where Lydia pressed the call button. "I worked for a private hospital for a while and they use an elite transport service."

"And they're willing to let us hire them for just this one job?" Harmony was genuinely astonished. Overwhelmed, too.

"Ordinarily, no." Grant stepped back to let them enter the elevator first. "But he owes me a few, so I thought I'd ask and he's agreed to do this sight unseen, so to speak."

"Wow." Harmony pushed the floor for the lobby and folded her arms. Staying at the front of the elevator, she unintentionally created a much-needed pocket of space for herself.

Grant hung back and talked with Lydia, who held onto his arm like he was the big brother she'd always wanted. At least, that's what he hoped. Because he'd made up his mind to ask Harmony to marry him.

As they approached their destination level, Harmony edged over to them and took Grant's hand.

"When does your friend think they can move Dad?" Lydia asked.

"They'll be in touch with Brooks' Memorial in the morning. Technically, they could start the transfer as soon as they all agree your dad is stable enough."

Harmony squeezed Grant's hand without meaning to, tried to pull away, and found that he wouldn't let go.

"Hey." He raised their joined hands and kissed hers. "It'll work out."

The elevator doors opened silently and they stepped out—into a fury of camera flashes.

"Ms. Wells, are you here to visit friends or family?" A microphone was unceremoniously shoved in her face.

"Are you dying?" Someone else shouted.

"Who's your boyfriend?!"

"Is that your daughter?!"

Spotting an opening in the pack, Grant wrapped an arm about each of the girls and carried them bodily through it.

As her feet touched the ground, Harmony's reflexes kicked in. Grabbing Lydia's hand, she bolted toward the nearest exit.

But through the windows she saw news vans on the street!

Pivoting, she hauled Lydia over to a door

that was closing behind a careless technician. Yanking it open, she propelled her sister through it and started to jerk it closed.

"Boyfriend, coming through." Grant muscled the door open enough to slide through, then slammed it shut.

"Grant! I'm sorry, I…"

"Forget it." He was already pushing her forward, away from the flashes of light bursting through the door's narrow, vertical windows. "This way."

"Hey! Hey, you can't be in here!"

"You're so right." Grant grinned at the irate nurse. "We're leaving as fast as we can."

"This way!" someone called. "There's an exit down this hall to the right."

"Thank *you*!" Grant hustled the girls along and out the door.

"Now where?" Harmony looked up and around at the walls surrounding them. Wait. There were only three walls.

"C'mon!" Lydia took off out of the horseshoe shaped area. "Maybe we can get a taxi and…"

"Wait!" Harmony was after her like a shot, with Grant easily keeping pace.

"It won't take them long to find a way after us," Harmony predicted as they caught up to each other. "And we can't be here when they do."

"So let's hurry!" Lydia tugged on her sister's

restraining hand.

"Hang on." Grant spoke up. "Reporters in the lobby, news vans out front, and who knows what out back?"

"Exactly." Harmony was about to suggest that Grant be the one to find out when he suddenly started walking toward the building.

"Hey, where are you going?" Lydia headed after him.

"Great question," Harmony muttered as she followed them both.

"Quick, in here." Grant showed them a rear maintenance entrance.

"How'd you get that open?" Harmony marveled as they piled inside.

"Trade secret." He winked and led them down a deserted hallway to a stairwell. "We'll go down to the parking garage and call a cab. Maybe they won't see us leave."

Harmony prayed the entire time that they waited for the cab, then hunkered down in the back seat while they left the hospital grounds.

"You okay, lady?" The driver peered at her in the rearview mirror when she sat up at Grant's signal.

"I am now." Grant's arm around her waist felt wonderful as they rode to the airport. Harmony had to admit, there were perks to not being alone.

Lydia gave the wrong terminal when the driver asked, and they decided to take two separate routes the rest of the way to the airplane.

"We'll be okay," Grant promised, holding up Lydia's hand so Harmony could see he was holding it securely.

"See you in a few." Harmony hated to split up, but she took the interterminal train so she could start the preflight.

Chapter 22

"You're pretty good at this," Lydia remarked to Grant as they 'casually' traversed the airport.

"You're not bad yourself." Grant wove through the foot traffic on the moving sidewalk with practiced ease. "I didn't realize you were a veteran traveler."

She laughed. "I'm not, but that isn't what I meant."

"I know." He winked and guided her to an escalator. "We're getting close."

Lydia voluntarily sat in the rear seat of the airplane this time, and neither she nor Harmony managed a deep breath until they were in the air.

"That was scary." Lydia brought her knees up to her chest. "And did you hear that dingdong?"

"Which one?" Harmony did her best to laugh the incident off.

"The one that asked if I was your daughter." Lydia snorted derisively. "Do I look like a toddler or something?"

"Nah." Harmony snickered. "I just look old."

Grant listened to them go back and forth until the adrenaline wore off, then engaged them in generic conversation until he thought

Harmony had settled into a comfortable rhythm with her plane.

"Sorry you had to be there for that." Harmony shot Grant an apologetic look. "I called my lawyer while I was doing the preflight, and they're going to see what they can do to minimize the damage."

"So there's a chance we won't see our faces on the tabloid covers?" he asked bravely. He'd been rehearsing a mental speech to his parents for the last hour.

"It helps that they don't really have a story to tell." Harmony shrugged as if her skin wasn't crawling at the thought of how everyone in Cadmia would change when they found out. Instead of talking to her, people would start whispering about her. Pleasant conversations would become pitches for loans or donations. And, of course, there would be those who gleefully scurried to the local press to 'tell all.'

"A few months ago, I would've turned this plane in any direction except Cadmia." Harmony couldn't laugh at that. She was too busy assessing their options. Again. "We could still do it. Vanish, I mean." Just thinking about it made her heart sink to her toes. She'd never had this much to lose.

"No." Lydia spoke up right away. "They'll find us wherever we go, right?"

"Eventually." Harmony had enjoyed her months of peace, though.

"Then we won't run. Other people live with it. So can we."

"I'd like you to stay, too." Grant touched Harmony's hand lightly. He didn't have the words to express the fear that lanced through him when she suggested they 'vanish.' As someone who hated the limelight, though, he could understand the temptation.

"That makes it unanimous." Harmony choked out the words around the emotions crowding her throat. Switching on the autopilot, she clung to Grant's hand and tried to wordlessly convey how badly she wanted to stay. It would've been a lot easier to communicate through a kiss, even if she did initiate it.

For Lydia's sake, she didn't pursue the thought.

In fact, they all lapsed into a subdued silence that lasted more or less for the rest of the flight.

Grant didn't mind at first, but he was starting to think that he had never heard such loud silence as they started the drive back from the airport. He'd persuaded the girls to ride with him that morning and now he was extremely glad they'd agreed. After their encounter with the paparazzi, Harmony had been shaking so badly he'd almost insisted on taking a commercial flight.

"Do we have to go straight to the food kitchen?" Lydia asked as Cadmia's lights came into view. It seemed strange to be in Missouri when, mentally at least, she'd never left her father's side.

"No, we have some time. What're you thinking?" Harmony, who was going through much the same thought process, twisted in her seat and reached for her sister's hand.

"Hungry, I guess." Lydia wasn't quite sure. She kind of felt like someone had siphoned off all of her energy.

"We skipped lunch, didn't we?" Grant shot her a smile via the rearview mirror. None of them had felt much like eating before taking off. Having the reporters descend like a flock of chicken hawks probably had something to do with that.

"I guess it's time to introduce you to Blinky's." Harmony injected as much enthusiasm into her voice as she could and was rewarded with a small smile from Lydia.

Lydia hung back when they arrived, her eyes racing around the room, picking out all of the things that needed to be repaired, refurbished, or replaced.

"My." She rubbed her hands on her jeans. "How…retro."

"Nothing retro about Blinky's." Harmony looped her arm through her sister's and coaxed her in far enough that she wasn't blocking the door. "It's vintage."

"Oh."

Grant gently took her hand. "Trust us. It's a nice little place."

Together, they led her to a freshly cleaned booth and Harmony showed her the menu on the wall. In the end, though, it was the cute teenage waiter that tipped the scale in Blinky's favor.

"I forgot to ask for no ice in my soda!" Lydia excused herself.

"Ah, young love." Grant let his arm drape around Harmony's shoulder and she laughed.

"So." She leaned against his side. "What did you want to discuss with my dad alone?"

"You first."

"Me?"

Chuckled, he said gently, "You just saw your father for the first time in ten years. How are you doing?"

"I... I suppose I'm fine." She suddenly became fascinated with the salt shaker. "I didn't know what to expect going in." Grant shifted an inch closer and she smiled, appreciating the supportive gesture. "He said he's going through his life, trying to find the people he's hurt so he can make it right."

"Do you believe him?" It was a hard question to ask, and her hesitation made him wonder.

"Yes." She looked up at him then, eyes wet with unshed tears. Funny, she thought she'd was all cried out for the day. "He talked about how staying in the hospital made him feel uncomfortable and out of place. That it was *too* white and *too* clean." She twiddled the salt shaker and watched it briefly rattle around in a circle. "He said he didn't want to feel that way when he got to heaven."

"I'm glad he's doing what he can to make his peace." Grant used a napkin to dab at the tears that began to slip down her cheeks. Her watery smile reassured him slightly.

"I actually told him I was sorry." She nodded at his surprised look. "Not for…ninety percent of what I did. For staying mad at him for so long. I could've sent him pictures of Lydia through Mr. Lawrence. Called him once in a while." They still had a long road ahead of them, and she hoped they'd have enough time to work through the rest of the emotional knots.

"Darling." He kissed her damp eyes and held her as best as he could on the bench. "I'm so proud of you."

She coughed, cleared her throat, and nudged him. "Your turn."

"Ah…"

"Listen, you two, if you're going to kiss every time I turn my back, I'm going to have to hire someone to help me keep track of you." Lydia's grin told a different story.

Harmony groaned and straightened away.

"Not kissing." Grant held up his hands. "Just talking."

"Uh-huh." Lydia sat down and leaned out of the way as the waiter began setting their plates on the table.

"Good timing." Grant slipped the waiter an early tip for showing up with the food right then. "We better eat and get going. Noella's expecting us to help them prepare the meal for the food kitchen."

"It's so cool that you're performing your dress rehearsal for the kitchen's volunteers and guests!"

As he listened to Lydia, who somehow managed to eat and talk almost simultaneously, Grant once again considered writing an article about her for the medical journals.

"Are all teenagers this exhausting?" he asked Harmony on their way out. Lydia wanted to pay 'this time' and, surprise, surprise, was presently engaged in conversation with a different cute boy.

"Don't be silly," Harmony answered loftily. "At eighteen, she's practically twenty."

"Give me strength." Even as he spoke, he hugged Harmony and dropped a kiss on the top of her head.

She pondered his words the rest of the way to the food kitchen, where she kissed his cheek when he opened her door for her.

"What was that for?" He would've loved to kiss her back, a real kiss this time, but a bunch of other vehicles had pulled up almost exactly as they did.

"I just like the idea of you being around for Lydia's twentieth birthday."

"Count on it." Instead of closing her car door, he reached in and got something out of the glove box. While he'd known the act of proposing was a necessity, the sheer vulnerability involved in formally offering her his heart made it hard to breathe.

"What's that?" She tried to get a peek, her curiosity spiking when he hurriedly stuffed it into his coat pocket.

"I'll show you later. C'mon."

"You're also going to tell me what you said to my dad. Later."

"Absolutely."

They had fun peeling potatoes and chopping carrots, then helped serve the food once the kitchen opened.

Noella introduced them to her friend Sterling, who told such sweet stories about his stray cat, Found, that even Lydia didn't interrupt.

Grant, concerned by some slight medical symptoms Sterling was exhibiting, made a phone call as soon as the supper was over.

"Hi, Justin? Yeah, it's Grant." Harmony joined him and he slipped an arm around her waist. "I've been thinking about that job you offered me." Harmony's eyebrows went up and he realized he hadn't said a word to her about it. Strictly an oversight on his part, given that they hadn't been dating at the time Justin tried to talk him into it. "I'm not in a position to take a full-time job right now, I'm sorry." He nodded while he listened, then interrupted, "Believe me, I've given it a lot of thought. And I'm prepared to make a counter-offer."

Harmony listened intently as he outlined his idea of volunteering at the hospital's outreach clinic. She thought it sounded great and made a point of nodding when he quirked an eyebrow at her as if asking for her approval.

"I've looked into getting my Missouri licensing," Grant explained, both to Justin and Harmony, "and I should have it out of the way before the end of the year. That's right, strictly pro bono."

"Places, everyone." Noella's calm voice cut through the chaos of trying to round up a five person cast and settle an excited audience. "Take your places, please."

"Justin, I've got to go. Yes, I can be there on Monday at two." Ending the call, he put his phone on silent and hustled Harmony onto the stage. "You'll be great!"

Harmony shifted so that she had a view of Noella, who smiled and nodded as if to echo Grant's words. Hey, compared with multiple, high-pressure shows every week on a water-borne hotel, this should be a cinch, right?

She jumped at the sound effect of a slamming

door. *Right.*

"Mom!" Sarah burst out from behind the curtains, backpack slung over one shoulder and a look on her face that said she was mad enough to spit nails. "Toby won't quit teasing me."

Josh, or rather, Toby, came in next, wearing earbuds and a bored expression.

Harmony played her part as a stressed mother of three in a severely out-of-balance family. The only time she came out of character was when Grant stepped through the 'door' for the first time, hair and eyes a little wild.

Time seemed to slow down as she stared at him, wondering if this was a preview of what life with Grant, hectic doctor extraordinaire, would be like. What if he decided to take a full-time doctoring job again someday?

"Hey, honey." He blew past her as if she wasn't there. "Sorry I'm late. Is supper ready?"

With an effort, she pulled herself together and gave her lines. There was no point borrowing trouble.

"Don't wait up for me, dear." Grant shoved his hand through his hair and tugged on his already loose tie. "The boss dumped a huge account on me at the last minute. If I stay up late, I *might* be able to get enough of a handle on this to do something useful with it tomorrow."

Harmony exited the stage and hugged Lydia, who whispered that the audience seemed to love it.

Noella played Christmas music wherever Helen Montgomery would sing during the actual performance and Harmony enjoyed humming along, laughing inside at the convincing way the younger actors complained every time she tried to get them to do anything remotely related to the real meaning of Christmas.

"This is a tough role," she complained to Lydia the next time she was off-stage. "I hope my kids aren't like this."

Lydia giggled. "Well, Grant isn't like that." She pointed at the self-absorbed character hunched over his desk.

"So?"

"So the two of you will have a gaggle of wonderful children that you could actually pick out of a lineup," she added hastily, "but will never have to because they love you as much as you love them."

Harmony chuckled. "Can I get that in writing?"

The banter with her sister helped her keep her perspective through the second half of the play, where things got worse before gradually getting better, building up to a supremely happy ending.

She started cleaning up from their 'late Christmas morning breakfast' while Grant helped the kids into their coats.

"Alright, everyone, you have an hour for sledding before we need to head over to Grandma and Grandpa's!" Grant announced as he straightened from helping with the youngest boy's scarf.

Sarah and Freddy's characters gleefully made their final exits, stage right, but Josh lingered, a worried expression on his face.

"Aren't you coming out, Dad?"

"I'll be there in a minute," Grant promised. Looking over his shoulder at Harmony, he stage-whispered, "I need to talk to your mother first."

Josh gave him an understanding smile. "Don't take too long. I want you to show us how to zigzag."

Grant nodded and patted him on the shoulder, then wiped his hands on his trousers as if nervous. His fingers bumped the pocket with the jeweler's box and it was like hitting the eject button on his heart, which got lodged in his throat for the second time that day.

He turned back to where Harmony was pretending to wash dishes. She was so beautiful.

"You should go with them, Darling." Harmony injected as much enthusiasm into the line as she could. Dutifully, she stacked clean plates and carried them over to the table they were pretending was the cardboard sink they'd use during the actual play.

"I will." Grant snagged the broom and started sweeping up imaginary crumbs. "I just didn't want to leave you with all of this mess to clean up." They worked silently for a few minutes, until Noella coughed, signaling they'd waited long enough.

"I wanted to apologize," he admitted abruptly, setting the broom aside.

"For what?" Harmony smiled up at him sincerely. "For giving me the perfect Christmas?"

He sighed softly and caught her hands in his. "For getting so caught up in trying to *buy* you the perfect Christmas gift that I nearly ruined Christmas for all of us."

Noella started playing "Merry Christmas, Darling." They had no way of knowing what Helen would choose to sing since she was bringing her own music, but the song was romantic enough for the dress rehearsal.

Lifting a hand free, Harmony touched Grant's cheek. "I will always remember what you did to make it wonderful."

He waited a beat, then cupped her face in his hands. And in front of over fifty people, pressed his lips to hers.

Fire rippled through her as she kissed him back, the roaring in her ears worthy of a space shuttle launch.

The sound of clapping and whistling brought

Grant down to earth again, where he reluctantly ended the kiss so they could bow with the other members of the cast.

As soon as he thought he could get away with it, Grant pulled her behind one of the curtains, where he hugged her tightly.

"Do you still want to know what I said to your dad?" he whispered into her hair.

"Of course I do!" Prickles raced up and down her arms as he drew away to arm's length.

"I haven't been able to think straight for the last ten days because my every thought circles back around to you. I wonder what you're doing. If you're happy." He looked down at the hands he held and prayed for the right words. "Then today I got to meet your dad. He knew right away that I loved you and wanted to marry you." Grant watched her eyes widen and hurried on. "He didn't think he deserved a say in the matter, but it was important to me to ask."

"What did he say?" Harmony didn't know whether to laugh or cry or just burst into tears. Her emotions were still reeling from everything that had happened earlier that day.

"He told me to respect you and to love you." Grant slowly dropped to one knee as he dug the box out of his pocket and opened it, revealing a diamond ring with a 'hare'-raising number of carats.

"Wait." Something about the sight of the

ring jump-started her panic drive and she pressed her free hand to her stomach. She had to be insane to interrupt the man of her dreams mid-proposal, yet how could she not? He didn't realize what he was doing. "I…I love you so much that it hurts. More than I thought I'd ever dare to love anyone. But you don't know what you're getting into." Her voice cracked and she had to force out the last few words. "Today was nothing compared to the way they'll hound us once we announce…"

"Harmony Wells." He came abruptly to his feet and crushed her in his arms, the ring temporarily forgotten. "Neither of us knows what the future holds, but I already can't imagine my life without you in it. Mansion or cardboard box or media circus, I love you. Will you marry me?"

"I…" She pressed her palms against his cheeks. "Yes. Mansion or cardboard box or," she half-laughed, half-sobbed, "media circus, you're my home now." She waited until the ring was on her finger, then kissed him with all of her heart.

Thank you for reading <u>Home Free</u>, I hope you enjoyed it!

To learn more about Grace, Noella, and Merry, read the rest of the "Gifts of the Heart" series.

Visit me at
leacarterwrites.wixsite.com/flinch-free-fiction

More titles by Lea Carter:

Contemporary Romance
"Gifts of the Heart"
Four single Latter-day Saint women find love in the tiny, fictional town of Cadmia.
A Country Mile
In Due Season
Food For Thought
Home Free

Fantasy
"Silver Sagas"
The ongoing adventures of the royal fairy families.
Silver Princess
Silver Majesty
Silver Verity
Troubled Skies
Dress Blues
The Seeker's Storm
Heartwood
Wedgewood
Fission – coming soon
Fusion (2021)

"Coddiwomple"
Three high-flying adventures in the fictional world of Jattori.
Dragon Sparks
Dragon Fugue
Dragon Thunder

www.ingramcontent.com/pod-product-compliance
Lightning Source LLC
Chambersburg PA
CBHW070826190726
48292CB00006B/2118